ON HER
WATCH

ALSO BY MELINDA LEIGH

BREE TAGGERT NOVELS

Cross Her Heart

See Her Die

Drown Her Sorrows

Right Behind Her

"Her Second Death" (A Prequel Short Story)

Dead Against Her

Lie to Her

Catch Her Death

MORGAN DANE NOVELS

Say You're Sorry

Her Last Goodbye

Bones Don't Lie

What I've Done

Secrets Never Die

Save Your Breath

SCARLET FALLS NOVELS

Hour of Need

Minutes to Kill

Seconds to Live

SHE CAN SERIES

She Can Run

She Can Tell

She Can Scream

She Can Hide

"He Can Fall" (A Short Story)

She Can Kill

MIDNIGHT NOVELS

Midnight Exposure

Midnight Sacrifice

Midnight Betrayal

Midnight Obsession

THE ROGUE SERIES NOVELLAS

Gone to Her Grave (Rogue River)

Walking on Her Grave (Rogue River)

Tracks of Her Tears (Rogue Winter)

Burned by Her Devotion (Rogue Vows)

Twisted Truth (Rogue Justice)

THE WIDOW'S ISLAND NOVELLA SERIES

A Bone to Pick

ON HER WATCH

MELINDA LEIGH

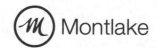

Published by Montlake, Seattle

www.apub.com

Amazon, the Amazon logo, and Montlake are trademarks of Amazon.com, Inc., or its affiliates.

ISBN-13: 9781542038713 (hardcover)
ISBN-13: 9781542038690 (paperback)
ISBN-13: 9781542038706 (digital)

Cover design by Shasti O'Leary Soudant
Cover images: © Maria Heyens / ArcAngel; © Eleanor Caputo / ArcAngel; © getgg / Shutterstock

Printed in the United States of America

First edition

For Tom:
I'm so proud of you

CHAPTER ONE

The fairy tales in Jen's imagination leaned toward the dark, Grimm variety, but in the real world, the worst monsters looked like everyone else.

Fear tasted like pennies: cold, dry, and metallic. The bitter tang hovered in the back of her throat, blocking her breath as she eased her bedroom window open. Night air wafted through the gap. She smelled the woods behind the house and the lingering smoky scent of a neighbor's barbecue. The wooden window frame of the old house groaned, and she froze. Her heart banged against her breastbone so hard it hurt.

Her sister slept like a corpse. Jen wasn't worried about waking her. But she couldn't wake her parents.

She shuddered. She couldn't even think about what her father would do if he caught her. He'd warned her—if she got into any more trouble, she'd regret it.

Sweat broke out under her arms as she strained to listen. Through the open window, she heard an owl, but inside the house, all remained quiet. She pressed a palm to her chest, where her pulse scrambled like a cornered mouse, and willed her heartbeat to slow. She swallowed, then inhaled.

Keep going.

She gave her room a final glance. Her sister snored in the second twin bed. A few dolls and toys lined the top of the bookcase. Jen hadn't played with any of them in years, but their presence gave her comfort.

The books she'd miss more, but they were too heavy to carry. She didn't know where she'd be staying. Better to pack light.

She was used to not having many possessions. She was used to being hungry. But going from poor in her family to poor and alone felt worse.

She continued slowly raising the window. When it was fully open, she leaned over the sill and lowered her backpack and duffel bag to the ground below with a rope. She hoisted one leg out, then the other, and slipped onto a branch of the tree near the window. She climbed partway down, then dropped, keeping her knees soft. Her sneakers landed on the grass with barely a thud.

It wasn't the first time she'd sneaked out, but it would be the last. She couldn't decide how that made her feel. Relief and sorrow vied for equal footing. She would miss her home, her sisters, her mom, maybe even her dad. She loved him, even if he also terrified her.

She scooped up her bags and ran toward the street. At the corner, she stopped behind a huge oak tree, turned, and looked back at the house. The windows remained dark. Gnats swarmed around her face, and she waved them away.

For one heartbeat, regret seized her. She wasn't ready to leave her childhood behind, but she didn't have a choice. She had to leave.

She clutched her backpack to her chest. From this moment forward, it contained all her possessions, including the $400 she'd saved from her summer job. She thought about going back and telling her mother, but then ruled it out. Daddy was the head of the household. Mom always did what he said. Even her sisters couldn't be trusted not to tell. Her stomach recoiled when she remembered how Daddy had reacted when she'd been caught shoplifting last month.

But she'd been hungry. Poverty was relentless, and she was tired of it.

"No excuse," he'd said. His cold calm in the police station had shifted into hot rage the second they were home. Her cheek burned with the memory of the slap that had knocked her off her feet.

No. Daddy could never find out.

She turned, jogged three blocks to the park, and looked for her ride. Would he even be there? He'd promised, but she didn't know him that well. If he didn't show, what could she do? She couldn't even call him. Her cell phone sat on her nightstand. Too risky to bring it. Her father could use it to track her down. He'd done it before when she'd missed curfew. For a few seconds, she relived the humiliation of being dragged from a friend's house, all the other kids watching. She knew she was supposed to obey her father, but she couldn't summon a scrap of guilt for wanting to have friends.

When she turned the corner and saw the car, relief made her knees wobbly. She raced to the car and got in, pulling the door closed with a slam that sounded final enough to bring hot tears to her eyes.

"You OK?" He reached across the console and patted her hand. "You're sure no one followed you?"

"If my father followed me, you'd know it. He'd probably shoot you." She was only half kidding. She leaned back against the headrest. She should feel safe, but anxiety swarmed in her belly like wasps.

It was done. She could never go back. Tonight's decision could never be changed. It was as permanent as a tattoo. She wouldn't finish high school. She wouldn't go to prom. If she ever got married, her mother wouldn't help her into her wedding dress. Her father wouldn't walk her down the aisle.

The man started the car and drove out of the lot. The dim light of the dashboard highlighted his profile, the shadows making him look harsh. At the main road, he turned onto the country road that led out of town.

"Where are we going?" She pressed a fist to her burning solar plexus. Stress seemed to be eating a hole right through her.

"I told you," he said in an irritated voice. "I have a place you can stay tonight."

She watched the miles roll by as they left Grey's Hollow behind. "How far?"

"Far enough," he snapped.

"I'm sorry." She knew too well how to placate a hot temper. "You've been great. I just worry about my dad finding me."

He glanced at her, his hand opening and closing on the wheel as if he were making a fist. "Don't worry. No one will find you."

CHAPTER TWO

Present day, March

The drunk swung a wild punch at Sheriff Bree Taggert's face. She ducked, and the fist sailed over her head. Thrown off-balance by his own unchecked momentum, the drunk staggered.

Heart hammering, Bree caught his arm by the wrist and elbow, put him in an armlock, and introduced him to the sidewalk in slow motion. Once he was down, she reached for the handcuffs on her duty belt. "Hold still, Mr. Killian."

Howard Killian was going to jail. All this flailing around was futile. But Bree saved her breath. Killian had had just enough booze to make him mean and weaken his impulse control. But he was definitely not in a mood where he would listen to reason.

Belly-down on the sidewalk, Killian turned his head sideways and squirmed, trying to get out of the hold. "Get your hands off me! You have no right . . ."

An inch or two over six feet tall, Killian outweighed Bree by a good fifty pounds. At thirty-nine, he had the broad build of an athlete going soft with age and heavy drinking, but he was still strong. Unfortunately for him, leverage was real, and Bree knew how to use it. She snapped the cuffs on his wrists. "You shouldn't have taken a swing at me."

"I want to call my lawyer," he yelled, his cheek pressed into the concrete.

"You'll get your phone call." Bree sat back on her heels to catch her breath. The altercation had been short but intense. The quick burst of adrenaline left her pulse pounding. Under her uniform, sweat trickled down her back and soaked the T-shirt she wore beneath her body armor.

One of Bree's younger deputies, Juarez, rushed from the front porch, where he'd been talking to Killian's girlfriend.

Killian grunted. The toes of his boots shuffled, as if he were trying to get some leverage but couldn't. She could feel his hostility. It radiated off his tense body like steam from a sewer grate. He turned his head to glare at her over his shoulder, his eyes white-rimmed with rage.

Not a fan of women in charge, are you, Killian? Too fucking bad.

Bree straightened. "Howard Killian, you are under arrest for assaulting a law enforcement officer."

Among other things.

"I didn't even hit you!" Killian yelled, spit flying from his mouth.

Bree ignored the drops of saliva that landed on the knee of her tactical cargoes. "You tried, and that's enough."

Tamping down her anger, she maintained her professional face and demeanor, but not without effort. This wasn't the sheriff's department's first domestic violence call this week. It wasn't even the first DV call today. Bree was damned tired of her deputies being forced into dangerous situations. Domestics were one of the riskiest types of calls for law enforcement. The earlier call hadn't involved physical contact, but this one had already escalated.

She patted him down and turned out his pockets. Satisfied, she hauled him to his feet before handing him off to her deputy.

"Come on, Killian." Deputy Juarez spun Killian around and marched him toward the car.

"Are you going to arrest him?" Grace called from her front porch.

"Yes, ma'am." Bree walked up the driveway, past a silver BMW, to the front porch, and faced the young woman. As sheriff, Bree didn't usually work patrol. Most of her time was spent behind a desk dealing with politics, the media, and never-ending mountains of paperwork. But her small force had been hit with a nasty strain of flu, and Bree was filling a shift.

Grace Abbott was five one, undernourished, *maybe* a hundred pounds. Her shoulders slumped, her spine bending to the weight of her life like a question mark. Red marks circled her throat, blood trickled from her upper lip, and the shadow splotching her cheekbone would be a nasty bruise in the morning. Though she was only twenty, she looked worn beyond her years. Her skin was dry and sallow. Lines bracketed the corners of her mouth, as if frowning were her natural state. Her eyes were on Killian's back.

Bree followed her line of sight. She couldn't hear what the man was saying, but he seemed to be mouthing off at Juarez, who was ignoring him and maintaining his calm—at least on the outside. Inside, she suspected her deputy was seething. But his self-control made her proud. She turned back to Grace.

Anxiety, fear, and pain filled the young woman's eyes. She looked like a rabbit that had spotted a threat and frozen, hoping it was invisible to a predator. Bree gave her a minute to settle.

At four o'clock, heavy cloud cover dimmed the late afternoon. Drizzle began to fall from a slate-colored sky. Despite the unseasonably warm day, the water hitting Bree's neck felt cold as it trickled under her uniform collar. She shivered hard, the adrenaline spike ebbing as she stepped farther under the porch overhang.

Bree's gaze swept down the street, over the neat row of older homes. The neighborhood wasn't anything fancy, but it looked solid, with mature trees, basketball nets, and late-model minivans. But none of those things mattered. Most people thought wife beaters all lived in trailer parks, but Bree knew the truth. Socioeconomic boundaries didn't predict domestic violence. Men who beat their wives could be plumbers, lawyers, or frigging ministers. Killian was a former college professor. Like drugs, DVs were a scourge that showed no sign of abating.

From behind a curtain of stringy blonde hair, Grace finally looked at Bree with furtive eyes that immediately darted away again.

"You know this is going to get worse," Bree said in a matter-of-fact voice.

Grace chewed a ragged thumbnail but said nothing.

Bree glanced at the curb, where Deputy Juarez opened the rear door the patrol car. Compared to his girlfriend's submissive posture, Killian's chest puffed like a prize rooster's—all cocky indignation. His red face shone with belligerence. As if he could sense Grace's focus, Killian's head swiveled, and his attention zeroed in on her.

Grace flinched, as if her boyfriend's fist—not his gaze—had landed on her. The young woman's leggings and oversize sweatshirt were inadequate for the afternoon's damp cold. She trembled and rubbed her biceps.

Even with Killian handcuffed and under arrest, she was terrified. Killian's gaze shifted to meet Bree's, and the vehemence in his glare almost unnerved *her*. She met his eyes with a direct, challenging stare—the same look that had prompted him to attempt to punch her in the face—until he looked away first. Her confidence angered him. But Bree knew that backing down to a man like Killian would embolden him. Cowards liked to pick on the weak. Once she'd established she wasn't going to put up with his nonsense, she turned back to Grace.

Bree knew the dynamic as well as her own reflection. In her mind, she saw her mother react the exact same way. Fear had been a major component of Bree's childhood. Anticipating violence—walking on broken glass instead of eggshells and wondering what act or glance or noise would set off her father's rage—had been a way of life. She'd learned to be quiet, invisible, and hide when necessary.

She wanted to get this woman away from this house. Grace would resist efforts to help her, but Bree had to try. Her best chance was to get Grace out of her abuser's line of sight and hopefully break the psychological hold he maintained over her.

"Can we talk inside?" Bree stepped sideways, between the couple, blocking Grace's view of Killian.

The young woman nodded once. Bree herded her into the foyer and closed the door. Except for a framed photo lying broken on the floor, the small place was spotless. The old wood floor gleamed. Vacuum lines scored an area rug. Not a single speck of dust marred the dark furniture.

Without the pull of her boyfriend's direct glare, Grace didn't know where to look. Her eyes roamed the space for a few seconds before settling on the broken glass shards at her feet. She went to the closet, took out a dustpan, and swept up the mess. She returned the glassless picture to a wall hook. It was a picture of Howard and Grace at some event. He had one arm around her shoulders. He wore a suit and a smug grin. She looked stiff and uncomfortable in an ill-fitting dress, like a little girl playing dress-up. Grace straightened the photo and continued to stare at it.

"Ms. Abbott," Bree began.

"Grace." Her voice shook. "Call me Grace."

"Grace," Bree said. "The neighbor said she heard you and Mr. Killian shouting. She was walking her dog past your mailbox and could see through the living room window. She said he struck you across the face." The visual turned Bree's stomach, but she suppressed her emotional response and kept her voice even. Pity or perceived judgment would not benefit Grace. She needed empathy from someone who understood her circumstances from her perspective.

And she *needed* real help. Without resources, family, and/or money, she would not be able to remove herself from the situation. Predators like Killian intentionally selected victims who didn't have a support system.

Without lifting her gaze, Grace shook her head. "No. She's mistaken."

"I know the truth, Grace."

Grace shook her head, her lips pressing together hard enough to push all the blood—and color—out of them. "I fell," she murmured.

Disappointed but not surprised, Bree breathed, then tried a softer appeal. "We can help you. You don't have to live like this."

Panic enlarged Grace's pupils. "No. I won't testify against him."

"You don't have to. I'm arresting him anyway." In fact, Bree was required by law to arrest Killian based on the domestic violence complaint called in by the neighbor and her own observation of Grace's visible injuries. But the swing Killian had taken at Bree would no doubt help convince the judge he was dangerous.

In the back of the house, a child cried softly, "Mama."

Bree lifted her brows. No one had mentioned a child. But this changed everything. Grace was no longer Bree's primary concern.

Grace turned her ear toward the hallway. Her weight shifted to the balls of her feet. "My daughter, Riley."

My, not *our*, Bree noted. "How old is she?"

"Four."

The same age Bree's little sister had been the night their father had murdered their mother. Bree blinked to eradicate the images and the emotions that accompanied them. Grace would have been sixteen when Riley was born.

"Has Killian ever struck her?" Bree asked.

"No." Grace resumed chewing on her thumbnail.

Is she lying?

Worry for the child gnawed at Bree's gut. "I need to see her. I need to make sure she's OK."

"Mama." The second cry was drawn out but still soft.

Grace led the way to a small bedroom. She turned on the light. The room didn't belong to a child. It was a guest room, decorated in unrelenting shades of gray. A little girl, petite like her mother, lay among half a dozen stuffed animals in a queen-size bed. In the corner, toys spilled from a pink backpack. Tiny clothes in brilliant shades of pink and purple filled a plastic hamper.

"Mama?" Her voice was heartbreakingly soft, as if she were trying to not be heard beyond her own doorway. She'd learned to be quiet—to not wake *him*. Bree knew this because she had lived it.

"It's OK, baby." Grace went to the bed and perched on the edge. She smoothed baby-fine blonde hair away from the child's face.

A tiny hand reached up to touch her mother's bleeding lip. The sleeve of her pajama top was neon pink decorated with sparkles. Grace wrapped her hand around her daughter's and kissed it. "Everything's OK, baby."

Riley's eyes remained sad and scared. Children were more perceptive than people realized. They hadn't learned to rationalize away the truth. Riley knew.

Bree backed out of the room. In the hall, she glanced through two additional doorways. One was a home office. The other was the main bedroom, decorated in masculine shades of maroon and navy blue. No flowers, no decorations, no knickknacks. Bree poked her head into the kitchen. It smelled like roast beef, and a pot in the sink brimmed with soapy water. The fridge held milk, cheese, the usual condiments, and beer. Bree's own kitchen was full of school papers, Kayla's drawings, et cetera. This entire house was very much a male space. Grace and her daughter had clearly not been afforded permanent status. They didn't *live* here; they were allowed to sleep here. Bree had no doubt that Killian reminded Grace of his generosity and her precarious position on a regular basis.

How could Bree get through to her? Grace's circumstances would not improve. They never did. There was only one trajectory for these situations: downhill.

Grace reappeared in the living room. She wrapped her arms around her own waist as if physically holding herself together.

"How long have you both lived here?" Bree asked.

"About eight months." A long time to be houseguests.

"Where did you live before that?"

Grace's shoulders jerked up and down once.

"You were homeless?"

"I had a friend who let us crash on her couch for a while, but then her boyfriend moved in." The rest went unsaid. Grace and her daughter had been forced to move on. Grace's body trembled with a deep sigh.

"Do you have any family that can help?"

Grace's mouth tightened.

There was a story there, but Bree let it go for the moment. "He's not going to change. You and your daughter need to get away."

Graces shook her head hard and fast. "I can't."

"It's getting worse, isn't it?" Bree asked. "He drinks. You do something he doesn't like. Dinner isn't good enough. The house isn't clean enough." She gestured around the dustless room. "You folded his shirt wrong. When he hits you, it's always your fault." Bree deepened her tone to mimic a man's. "You always make me hurt you." Her father's voice echoed in her head, and sickness rolled around her belly.

Grace flinched. Naked truth shone in her eyes.

Bree had nailed it. Too well. Swallowing, she shoved the memory back into its mental corner. *Not now. This is about Grace, not your mother.* But then, this was about a lot of women.

"It didn't start out like this, did it?" Bree didn't expect an answer.

A single tear escaped from Grace's eye.

Bree said, "It'll get worse. You need to leave him before he escalates."

Grace whispered, "That'll just make him madder." The *he'll kill me* was implied.

"I'm putting him in jail."

"His brother will bail him out."

"I'll keep him as long as I can." Despite Grace's protests, Bree sensed a crack in her resolve. "I won't lie. Leaving him will be hard. Maybe the hardest thing you've ever done. But do it for your little girl. Is this what you want for her?"

Grace didn't move. She barely breathed.

"We *can* help you," Bree said.

"You can't." Grace's words sounded flat, lifeless, as if part of her were already dead. "You don't understand."

Bree exhaled. What could she say? The most dangerous time for an abused woman was when she decided to leave. That's when their abusers lost their shit—when they lost control of the thing they felt they were entitled to. While men were largely murdered by strangers, women were most often killed by husbands and boyfriends.

No.

Women were killed sounded as if there were no one to blame. As if the abused women got themselves murdered—as if they were to blame for the violence inflicted upon them. Words mattered. They influenced how people thought. Passive language was the devil. Blame needed to rest where it was due.

Abusive men killed women.

In a very active sense.

On average, three women in the US were killed by current or former partners every day. Nothing would change if everyone danced around issues that needed to be confronted head-on.

Bree took a deep breath. She had one chance to get through to Grace. "I *do* understand. My father was a mean drunk. He abused my mother." *Be honest. You need to connect with her.* "He abused all of us." Even after all these years, admitting the truth felt shameful. *Why?* Why were victims conditioned to feel as if they were responsible for the actions of their abusers?

Grace's gaze snapped to meet Bree's. "Did she leave him?"

"No." Bree paused for two heartbeats. "He killed her."

Grace recoiled. Her lips parted but she uttered no words.

"My siblings and I were there. We're very lucky he didn't kill us too."

Domestic violence calls brought Bree back to the childhood she'd worked hard to put behind her. Her father's abuse had escalated until he'd eventually shot his wife and then himself. If eight-year-old Bree hadn't hidden herself and her two siblings under the porch, he'd have taken the entire family to hell with him. In her heart, she knew that he would have killed them all if he'd had the chance.

Instead of suppressing the memory, Bree let it play in her mind—and on her face. "So I know how this is going to turn out. He will get more and more controlling. You've probably already seen that."

Grace stared, unblinking. Her head tilted a few millimeters. She wasn't just listening now. She was hearing what Bree had to say.

Good.

Bree continued. "Soon, you won't be able to leave the house without him. You won't be able to answer a call without him listening in. He'll check your phone and monitor your internet use. He'll separate you from family. Won't allow you to have friends. But no matter how hard you try to please him, he'll still find a reason to get mad. You'll smile at the clerk in the grocery store, and that'll be enough to set him off."

"He won't let me go," Grace said without contradicting any of Bree's assumptions.

"I know." Bree would not make promises. "But there are people who specialize in helping women like you start over."

"I don't know." Grace bit off a piece of her cuticle.

"I can take you and your daughter to a shelter tonight. He won't know where you are. You never have to see him again."

Blood welled from beside Grace's thumbnail. She shook her head and whispered, "I can't. He'll find me."

Bree didn't give her any bullshit about a restraining order, though she would be advised to obtain one. Killian may or may not obey it.

"I'm going to have a counselor contact you to discuss your options. I'll need your cell number."

Grace shook her head hard. "No. I can't talk to anyone."

"So he's already monitoring your phone."

Grace looked away. Her cheeks flushed.

"A social worker will come here tomorrow." Bree held up a hand to cut off any protest. "You'll meet with them. It's not optional. Your daughter's welfare is at stake."

"He doesn't hit her." Despite her protest, Grace's voice lacked conviction.

"Maybe not. Yet. Even if he never does, she will suffer long-term effects from living with domestic abuse."

"She doesn't know."

Bree lifted her eyebrows. "Do you really think she sleeps through the fights? She's probably too afraid to get up. I lived with it for eight years. I heard every insult, every blow. Saw every black eye and swollen lip. Concealer can only do so much. Most children in homes where domestic violence occurs can describe the abuse in great detail. So, the social worker will come tomorrow, and you will talk to them or risk losing custody."

A tear leaked from Grace's swelling eye. "You can't . . ."

"My job is to serve and protect the citizens of this county. That includes your daughter." Bree felt like a bitch, but the child had to come first.

Grace touched her split lip. "I'll tell them I fell."

Bree had no doubt she would do exactly that. "And bruised your throat?"

Grace paled.

"They'll have my report detailing your injuries." Bree had taken a photo when she'd first arrived. "Your neighbor saw him strike you. Regardless, he took a swing at me. For that, he'll be charged."

Grace pressed a palm to the base of her bruised neck.

"He won't be back tonight. Get some rest. Ice your face." Bree paused, waiting for Grace's eyes to connect with hers. "You could pack your things. I could have you out of here tomorrow before he makes bail." If Killian was arraigned first thing in the morning, by the time he obtained bail and all the paperwork was processed, it would be afternoon at the earliest. "Be brave, Grace. Do it for Riley."

Grace hugged herself harder but didn't respond. If the young woman stayed, Bree knew her department would be back here, responding to another violent incident. What would they find that time?

Hoping she was wrong, hoping Grace also saw the glaring neon light, Bree went outside and pulled her phone from her duty belt. The call to social services went to voice mail. Bree left a message, but she wouldn't wait for them. She'd drive Grace and Riley to a shelter herself if necessary.

Juarez approached, gesturing to his patrol car. Killian glared at them from the back seat. "We just got a 911 call. Couple of hikers found a dead body out near the Echo Road Bridge. What do you want me to do with him?" He gestured toward Killian.

"Take him to the station and put him in holding." Bree turned toward her SUV. "Then meet me at the bridge."

"We're charging him?" Juarez asked.

"Yes, but not right now. If that call is accurate, then I'm going to need you at the scene. We might not be able to process him for a while." She gave Juarez a pointed look.

The deputy nodded. He understood. Technically, they had forty-eight hours to charge Killian. Bree didn't like to stretch that time, but there were cases where exceptions needed to be made. Bree had to convince Grace to leave. She would do everything within her power to get the woman into a DV shelter and out of Killian's reach. She refocused on her deputy. As hard as it was, she needed to switch gears and clear her head for another call. "Meet me at the scene."

Juarez gave a quick nod. Though a young deputy, he'd proved to be a fast learner with plenty of empathy, ethics, and common sense.

Bree slid into her vehicle and used her radio to call dispatch. "Sheriff Taggert en route to Echo Road Bridge."

Next, she would call criminal investigator Matt Flynn, who was also her live-in boyfriend, for lack of a better word, while simultaneously preparing herself to deal with a dead body.

CHAPTER THREE

Light rain misted Matt's face as he led his Percheron gelding out of the pasture. Beast slopped through the mud around the gate. Matt stepped over the deepest spots. It had rained every day for what seemed like the entire spring.

Sitting on top of the fence, Bree's nine-year-old niece, Kayla, laughed. "Beast rolled in the mud like a pig."

"He did." The horse was completely crusted in mud. Matt led him into the barn and put him in his stall.

After her sister had been murdered, Bree had assumed guardianship over her niece and nephew. Since Matt had moved in, they were starting to feel like a family.

Three other horses, all rescues, watched from over their own half doors. Bree's nephew, seventeen-year-old Luke, walked out of a stall, an empty feed can in his hand. "How did he get mud between his ears?"

"Practice." Matt latched Beast's door and returned to the pasture for the last horse, Kayla's sturdy little Haflinger, Pumpkin.

But Kayla had slid off the fence and already had a lead rope snapped to Pumpkin's halter. "I've got him."

"Watch the mud!" Matt called a second too late.

"I'm stuck!" Kayla giggled, wobbling back and forth, unable to extract her feet from the ankle-deep mire. Behind her, Pumpkin waited with the patience of a shaggy saint.

With a sigh, Matt waded back into the muck and lifted Kayla by the waist. Her feet came loose with a loud sucking sound. He set her on her pony's back.

She grinned and held one sock-clad foot off Pumpkin's side. "I lost a boot."

Matt glanced back at the mud. No sign of a polka-dotted rain boot. He was soaking wet. He was not digging through a foot of solid muck today. "We'll get another pair."

"OK." She hummed a Disney song.

He turned to lead Pumpkin to the barn, slipped, and fell on his ass. As he tried to rise, he slipped again, this time splashing down on one hip. Matt sat up. Cold mud soaked through his underwear. He attempted to wipe his hands on his pants but couldn't find a clean spot.

"Are you OK?" Kayla stared down at him, wide-eyed. "You're as dirty as Beast."

Pumpkin nudged Matt with his nose. He gave the pony a pat and climbed—carefully—to his feet. "I'm fine. Just dirty."

By the time they put the pony away, Luke had finished filling water buckets and distributing hay and feed. He stared at Matt, the corner of his mouth twitching.

"You can laugh," Matt said.

"Bwahahahaha." Luke doubled over.

Matt closed up the barn and herded the kids toward the house. Kayla kicked off her single boot and skipped toward the house in her socks. She did a double-footed jump in every puddle in the yard. Matt followed, scooping up the boot on his way.

They burst into the house. Kayla's wet socks slapped on the hardwood. The black tomcat, Vader, watched from the windowsill as they stripped off wet gear. His gaze of feline superiority seemed to imply he was the only one smart enough to be inside on such a miserable day.

Matt couldn't argue. "Everybody shower. Bring your muddy clothes to the laundry room." He cringed at his tone, which sounded unnecessarily harsh. They were doing well for kids whose mother had been murdered a little over a year before. He would hate for a sharp word to dim any amount of joy they found.

But Kayla shot him a teasing salute. "Yes, sir."

He grinned at her. "Go!"

With a happy squeal, she bolted for the steps, leaving Matt holding one muddy polka-dotted boot. Twenty minutes later, they were showered and dressed in dry clothes.

Matt settled on the sofa with his German shepherd and Bree's rescue dog at his feet. "Pizza?"

"Yes!" Both kids whooped.

Matt made the call while the kids argued over movies. His phone buzzed in his hand before he could put it down. "It's your aunt Bree."

Luke's smile disappeared, and he muted the TV. Bree usually texted with questions about dinner and such. Actual phone calls were typically official business.

Matt answered the call. "What's up?"

Without a greeting, Bree asked, "Am I on speaker?"

Definitely a case, thought Matt. "No."

She continued without a beat. "Hikers found a dead body."

"Where?"

Bree gave him the location.

"I'll meet you there." Matt ended the call and glanced at the kids. Their biological father had never been part of their lives. Also, he was currently in prison. Bree was raising the kids and, in Matt's opinion, doing a damned good job. Since moving in with them, Matt had new respect for all working parents. Juggling responsibilities was hard.

Before he could say a word, Luke held up a hand. "I'll look after Kayla. Go."

Matt nodded. "Pizza will be here in twenty minutes. Dana should be home from spin class soon." Bree's former homicide partner and best friend served as an unofficial nanny.

"We're cool," Luke said. "Kayla, want hot chocolate?"

"Yes!"

Matt leaned over and gave Brody a pat. He hated leaving the kids alone, even for a short time. Luke was mature and responsible, but Matt always felt better if Brody was home. The retired K-9 would protect the kids with his life, and his honed senses were superior to any electronic sensor.

"Set the alarm," Matt reminded Luke.

Luke nodded. "I've got this."

Matt smiled. "I know. But I have to say it."

Humor shone in Luke's eyes, and he jerked a thumb toward the door. "Go. She needs you to watch her back."

Matt jogged upstairs and changed. As a civilian consultant, he didn't wear a uniform or a sidearm, but dressed in a long-sleeve polo bearing the sheriff's department logo, tactical cargo pants, and boots. Matt had been a sheriff's deputy years ago, until he'd been shot in a friendly-fire incident. Nerve damage in his dominant hand prevented him from passing the handgun certification and being an official law enforcement officer. But he was glad to put his investigative skills to work on an as-needed basis.

Downstairs, Matt grabbed his jacket, locked the door behind him, and hurried toward his truck. With the flu outbreak, Bree might not have backup, and Echo Road Bridge was in the middle of nowhere. She'd be isolated with night approaching. The possibility that the call was fake and she would walk into an ambush was always in the back of Matt's mind.

At his vehicle, he donned his body-armor vest and jacket. He popped the flashing red light on the roof of his Suburban and sped along the dark country road. On the way, he sent Dana a text to let her know about the callout. When he arrived at the old covered bridge, he found Bree's SUV parked on the shoulder behind a silver Prius. As expected, hers was the only official vehicle.

A small breath of relief escaped him as he spotted her standing behind her SUV talking to two men. Slim even with the added bulk of her body armor, she was an average-size woman, but she had a commanding presence. Every movement signaled purpose. Her size was the only thing average about her.

Matt parked behind her vehicle, pulled a hat from the rear seat pocket, and joined them in the drizzle. Bree was writing notes in a small notebook.

"This is Investigator Matt Flynn." She waved between him and the hikers. "This is Doug Winner and his brother, Steve. They found the body."

Doug and Steve both exhibited a strong green-and-crunchy vibe. Heavy backpacks sat at their feet.

Doug tugged on his thick beard. He was tall and broad-shouldered, an outdoorsman judging by the quality and worn appearance of his clothes, pack, and boots. "I think it's a woman because of her long hair. I know dudes can have long hair"—he gestured toward Steve, who had long, shaggy hair under a knit cap—"but this just didn't look like a dude."

"You're positive she's dead?" Matt asked.

Steve nodded. He was smaller, more wiry, and clean-shaven. "Oh, yeah."

"Where is she?" Bree asked.

Doug gestured to the woods behind the bridge with a gloved hand. "It's about half a mile up that game trail."

Bree turned to the cargo hatch and shoved a few items into her backpack. "Can you give us directions?"

Doug and Steve exchanged a look. Steve shook his head.

"We'll take you," Doug said.

Steve nodded. "You won't find it on your own. It's off the trail."

"How did you find her?" Matt asked.

Steve pulled his hat down lower on his ears. "Like I told the sheriff, it was just luck. I stepped into the trees to take a piss. The wind shifted, and I smelled it. I thought it was an animal. Not even sure why I went looking." Regret creased his face. He clearly wished he hadn't searched for the source of the odor. "I'm going to see it every time I close my eyes."

"There are things you can't unsee." Matt empathized.

"How's the terrain?" Bree zippered her backpack. "Can we navigate it in the dark?"

"Yes." Doug waved a flashlight. "The trail is a bit overgrown, but it's relatively flat until we get almost to the body. As long as we take our time and watch our footing, we should be fine."

Matt returned to his vehicle for the backpack he kept ready. Like Bree's, it was stuffed with basic survival gear and a crime scene kit. When you worked in a rural area, finding a body in the woods wasn't a daily occurrence, but it happened. Usually, the deaths were accidental or natural. The elderly wandered. People hiked alone. They got lost. They weren't prepared for the elements and died of hypothermia or heatstroke. They fell or suffered other medical emergencies.

Now and then, they were murdered.

Matt shrugged into his pack. Bree and the two hikers donned theirs as well. Four heavy-duty flashlights switched on as they headed into the woods. They had an hour before sunset. But trees, clouds, and the steady drizzle prematurely darkened the forest. The game trail was narrow, and they walked single file. Doug and Steve took the lead. Matt brought up the rear.

"You've been on this trail before?" Bree asked.

"Yeah," Doug called out. "I have a secret fishing spot near the river not far beyond the body. Me and Steve head out here every spring for a couple of days. It's not far from civilization, so if the weather turns too nasty, we can get back pretty quick. But it's not on any real trail, so it feels more isolated."

"You consider this weather acceptable?" Matt asked. He would not choose a rainy night for camping.

Doug added, "I've had a rough week with work. Camping is the best way to disconnect."

"Always," said Steve. "You just need the right gear."

The darkness slowed their progress. The trail might have been flat, but it wasn't clear like the popular hiking spots in the area. Watching for tree roots and skirting any muddy, slick spots, they walked for about twenty minutes until Doug stopped. He pointed the beam of his flashlight upward to illuminate a tree scorched by lightning. "It's up there, about forty feet up this hill." He turned and led the way up a steep grade.

Matt caught the unmistakable scent of decay. Ahead of him, Bree hesitated. Clearly, she smelled it too.

Steve hung back. He shrugged out of his backpack and leaned it on the base of the tree. "I'm going to wait down here."

Doug also stopped. "Same." He gestured with his flashlight. "There's a small, mostly flat clearing behind that weird boulder. She's there."

Matt spotted the flattened vegetation that marked the hikers' trek through the brush.

Next to him, Bree also shined her light along the slope.

"What do you think?" he asked.

"I don't see any other trail of broken vegetation. This seems like the most logical way up. Anyone else who accessed the clearing probably went this way. Your thoughts? You've worked more remote scenes than I have."

Matt turned to the hikers. "What's above the clearing? Is there any other way to access it?"

Doug shook his head. "I doubt it. Above it, the grade is even steeper. It's rocky too."

So, Matt and Bree had two choices. They could stay in the hikers' path to minimize the impact of their total footsteps. Or they could carve out their own route to avoid destroying any evidence left behind by the deceased and/or their killer. Better safe than sorry. You couldn't decontaminate evidence. Once it was compromised, that was it.

"We do it the hard way," he said.

She sighed. "Of course."

Matt moved twenty feet to the side and started up. Underbrush pulled at his boots, and thorns snagged his pants as he plowed through it. Still, his long legs made quick work of the short climb. At the top, he reached back and hauled Bree over the edge. Bits of vegetation clung to their pants and the laces of their boots. She was breathing harder. She was fit, but her backpack was as heavy as his, a greater burden for her smaller size. Having been on patrol tonight, she was also outfitted with a fully loaded duty belt. Her armor, radio, handcuffs, sidearm, extra clips, baton, pepper spray, flashlight, and cell phone amounted to an additional twenty pounds of equipment.

"Thanks." She huffed, shining her flashlight around on the ground. They didn't walk any farther for fear of disturbing the scene.

Matt scanned the clearing with his own light. He found the body in less than a minute, curled at the base of a tree. One bare arm was flung out at an unnatural angle. The smell and the color of the skin told him the hiker had been correct. She was definitely dead and had been for several days, likely longer. A camouflage-printed tarp was wrapped around the body, only the single arm and head exposed. Her face was turned away. Leaves and dirt matted the long, wet hair that trailed out from under the tarp.

"Murder victim," Bree said.

"Yeah." He let Bree go ahead of him, then walked in her trail. They proceeded slowly, shining their lights on the ground and searching for potential evidence. Recent heavy rains had wiped out any footprints, flattened weeds, and likely washed away most evidence.

She halted a few feet away and studied the body for a few seconds. Then, with careful steps, she moved in an arc to get another view from a different angle. Matt followed. She crouched next to the head. Using one gloved fingertip, she lifted the edge of the tarp a few inches. Their beams fell upon the victim's face at the same time. They simultaneously recoiled.

The victim was a young woman. Her tongue, black and swollen, protruded from her mouth. Maggots wriggled in the light. Horror rocked him back a few inches on his heels, the wet earth squishing beneath his boots.

"I guess it hasn't been as cold as I thought." Bree's voice rasped. "The flies found her."

"They usually do."

And they always went for the eyes, nose, and mouth first. Gray and green blotches mottled the bloated skin. Equal amounts of pity and rage filled Matt.

"I never get used to it," Bree said. Before taking the job as sheriff of Randolph County, she'd been a homicide detective in Philadelphia. She'd no doubt viewed countless dead bodies, but she hadn't become hardened to the sight, something Matt appreciated. It was easy to become jaded in their profession, to forget that each set of remains had once been a family member, loved by someone.

"In fact, since I have the kids," she said, "I feel like I'm moving in the opposite direction. It's getting more difficult to compartmentalize."

"Same." Living with her niece and nephew and developing a mentor-type relationship with them had affected him as well. He was growing more sensitive to all the awful crap in the world, as if he filtered everything he encountered through new eyes. He scanned the length of the tarp. "Even bloated, she looks small."

Please, not a child.

There was nothing worse.

"Yeah." Bree cleared her throat and looked away for a few seconds, as if gathering strength. "But whoever dumped her here isn't weak." She glanced around them. "I don't see any way to get the body up here except by carrying it. That took some physical strength and size. I could barely get to the top with all my gear. A dead body would be two or three times heavier."

"Agreed, and she obviously didn't walk here." Matt gestured to the tarp.

"I have to call the ME." Bree took a step backward and pulled her phone from her pocket. "We're in luck. There's a signal."

Matt stood, eyeing the length of the tarp. They wouldn't touch anything until the medical examiner arrived, but he took in the details. The clearing was the size of a volleyball court. Tall trees surrounded the space, along with a few clumps of evergreens. The killer likely chose this spot because of its isolation. But the area felt more remote than it was. The walk to the road would take fifteen minutes in better weather.

Bree finished her call in a few minutes. "Dr. Jones is on her way. ETA to the bridge is thirty minutes." She scrolled on her phone. "Juarez texted. He's also en route. He's bringing lights. He'll need help carrying them in. The ME might also need assistance with her equipment and with removal of the remains."

"I'll hike to the road and bring them in."

"Thanks. I'll get started here." Bree nodded. "I'll call for a forensics team and a couple of deputies as well."

Everything packed in and out would have to be hauled by humans. The game trail was too narrow for any vehicle, including an ATV. Even a dirt bike would struggle with the tree roots.

As Matt started down the slope, he heard the zipper of Bree's pack open. He glanced over his shoulder. She was pulling out a roll of crime scene tape. He scrambled down. Doug and Steve waited side by side.

"Did you find her?" Doug asked.

"Yes," Matt said.

"She was murdered, wasn't she?" Steve's voice broke.

Always mindful of the media, Matt skirted the question. "It'll be up to the medical examiner to determine cause of death."

"She was wrapped in a tarp," Doug said. "Someone dumped her up there."

Matt couldn't argue. They all knew the truth, but he couldn't say anything, not officially. "I'm walking to the road to escort the medical examiner back here."

Doug frowned and looked up at the giant boulder. "Should we wait here? I know she's the sheriff and all, but I wouldn't want to leave anyone alone out here with . . ."

"It would be helpful if you waited here in case the sheriff needs any assistance." Matt reached for his phone. "I'll text her and let her know you're here."

Bree could handle herself, but it was dark, shit happened, and he wouldn't be back for at least an hour.

CHAPTER FOUR

After calling for a forensics unit, Bree spoke with dispatch. She had two additional deputies on patrol. Both were tied up with a vehicle collision involving injuries, but they would respond to the crime scene ASAP. She put out calls to the state police and small-town PDs within Randolph County for assistance, but available help was limited. Her crew wasn't the only one being slammed by the flu.

Bree was on her own for now.

She rummaged in her pack at the edge of the clearing. She kept movements and equipment within the smallest area possible.

Her phone buzzed with a call from her chief deputy, Todd Harvey. She answered. "Aren't you sick?"

"I heard about the body." He wheezed. "I could help if you need me."

"And infect the healthy deputies I have left? *No.*"

"I'm much better today." He coughed for a full thirty seconds, sounding like a barking seal, then choked out, "Sorry. It's just a residual cough."

Bree's eyes rolled all the way to the back of her head. "Stop trying to talk before you hack up a lung. Go back to sleep. You're human, and humans get sick. I appreciate the offer, but the best thing you can do is get well so that when those of us still standing finally fall, you'll be able to take over."

"I'm sure I'll be better in a day or two."

"Then I'll see you in a day or two." This flu was blazing through county employees like a wildfire. It was only a matter of time before it got everyone. "Eat soup. Feel better." She ended the call and turned back to her task, outlining the crime scene with only a flashlight to cut through the darkness.

Outdoor crime scenes could be a nightmare to process. Animals scavenged and scattered remains. Weather destroyed evidence. She eyed the steep slope on two edges of the clearing. Gravity and rain would have washed evidence down the descending slope. She'd have to include the likely path of the killer as well. In short, there was a ton of ground to cover, and all of it was wild terrain.

In Philadelphia, electricity had generally been available, and most areas were accessible to vehicles. Also, there had usually been plenty of uniforms on duty to help. Rural policing was a different animal. In Randolph County, she was learning on the job, utilizing common sense, and relying on Matt and her chief deputy for wilderness-specific knowledge.

She considered the perimeter of the scene. *Go big* was her personal motto. It was simple to reduce the size of a scene later, but it was much more difficult to extend the boundaries after responders had been crawling all over the ground, leaving their own footprints and disturbing possible evidence with every step.

Unrolling the crime scene tape, she began circling the clearing. It was slow going. Not only did she have to check the ground for potential evidence before taking a step, but tree roots and foliage threatened to trap her feet. Rain and mud made the ground slick. The last thing she needed was a twisted ankle. They already had to carry a body out of the woods. No one needed to carry the sheriff as well.

She had to work around the bear-shaped boulder at the front of the clearing. Larger rocks obstructed portions of the rear, where the ground sloped upward sharply, making the terrain impassable. Bree cordoned off the east side, tied the tape on a tree branch, then retraced her steps to mark the western perimeter. By the time she'd finished, Matt had texted to say he was on his way back with the ME, Juarez, and the lights.

After acknowledging his message, she marked the area of the downslope where runoff could have washed away evidence. When she returned to the charred tree, she found the two hikers waiting patiently at its base.

"Thanks for sticking around," she said, joining them. "Investigator Flynn will be back shortly with reinforcements." She'd already taken the brothers' contact information and statements when she'd arrived. "Someone will escort you back to the road. I'll need you to come to the sheriff's station and sign an official statement in a day or two." She tugged off a glove and withdrew a business card from her pocket. "I'll have someone call you when it's ready." She would be here all night and likely into the morning. But their statements wouldn't take long to write up. They'd found the body and returned to the road to call 911. She'd also order a background check on both of the hikers, just to cover her investigative bases.

"OK." Steve shuddered.

Doug stamped his feet. "As much as I was looking forward to our trip, I'll be glad to be home."

"It's going to be a while before I want to go camping again," Steve agreed.

Bree tugged her glove back on. In the two minutes she'd had it off, her hand had stiffened with cold. "I'm also going to ask you not to talk to anyone about the body. I won't give out your contact information, but the press has its way of discovering things. I don't want details to reach the families of any missing persons before we can identify the remains and notify the next of kin."

"We understand," Doug said. "That poor woman."

"And her poor family." Steve sniffed and swiped at his face with a glove. "We won't talk to the press or anyone else without checking with you."

"Thank you for your cooperation," Bree said.

Doug nodded. "We'll help in any way we can."

"I appreciate that." Bree pulled out a notepad and attempted to make a very rough sketch of the scene. She shielded her work with her upper body, but it was impossible to keep the pages dry.

The sound of movement in the woods caught her attention. She turned toward the noise and saw flashlights coming toward her. A few minutes later, four figures approached through the trees. In the lead, Matt hefted a fifty-pound portable light. Behind him, Dr. Serena Jones carried her med kit. The ME was a tall African American woman with a long, athletic stride. She wore full water-proof gear, including knee-high boots and a hood. The ME's assistant followed with another kit. Hunching against the weather, the young man looked miserable and cold. Juarez brought up the rear. Thankfully, the deputy was young and fit. He wore a loaded back-pack and hauled the second light.

The ME stopped in front of Bree. "We're going to need to make a second trip for a body bag and gurney."

"I'm trying to get more uniforms here," Bree said. "Everyone has the damned flu."

"We're short-staffed as well." Dr. Jones gave her a grim nod. "We might as well get started."

Bree showed Dr. Jones the sketch. The ME illuminated the note-book with her flashlight. Bree used her pen to point up the hill toward the bear-shaped rock, then tapped on the damp page. "The body is here. This is the most likely path the killer used. Matt and I made a fresh trail over here. I've cordoned off this entire area." She made a circular motion over the perimeter she'd marked on the paper.

The ME squinted at the sketch, then up the hill. "Got it."

Bree slid her notebook into her backpack. "Let's go." She instructed Juarez to take the hikers back to their vehicle, so they could leave before any reporters showed up and noted their license plate number. Then Bree led the way to the clearing.

Dr. Jones moved toward the body, then crouched and set down her kit. She donned gloves, lifted the corner of the tarp a couple of inches, then lowered it and straightened. "Let's get the lights set up." She indicated where she wanted them on each side of the body, and Matt went to work.

In twenty minutes, lights blazed on the body and ten feet of surrounding earth, brightening the area like a mini sports stadium. Bree and the ME's assistant took initial photos. Every step of the process needed to be recorded. Then Dr. Jones gently folded back the tarp, exposing the head and upper part of the torso. The underside of the camouflage tarp was a brown and shiny water-resistant material.

The girl was nude, lying on her side in a slightly curled position. Mud, dirt, and leaves streaked her skin. Bruises ringed her throat. The moving mass of maggots looked even more hideous in the glaring light.

Dr. Jones considered the corpse with a frown. "Female. I don't want to disturb the bugs until I get her on the table, so age is to be determined, but she's on the young side."

"Can you give us any indication of PMI?" Bree asked. Determining the postmortem interval would be crucial in the investigation.

"Putrefaction is well underway. Bacteria in the GI tract breaks down hemoglobin there first, resulting in this green staining." Dr. Jones waved a hand over the gut. "The marbling on the extremities indicates bacteria has spread though the venous system. We're still in the bloated stage. At warmer temperatures, gases produced by bacteria are released around day five or six. It's been warm for March, but still cool for decomposition . . ." Seemingly thinking aloud, the ME tilted her head. "For now, I will roughly"—she glanced up at Bree—"*roughly* estimate the PMI as seven to fourteen days. I'll attempt to narrow that window when I get her on the table and get detailed weather data, but I make no promises. The weather has been changeable over the past couple of weeks, and we don't know how long she's been here or where she was killed or potentially stored in the hours immediately after death."

"Stored?" Matt asked.

"Yes." The ME adjusted her angle to view the back of the corpse. She pointed to a darker area along each flank. "Livor was fixed before she was placed in this position. She likely spent the first four to twelve hours after death on her back."

After death, blood pooled in the lowest portion of the body, causing a purplish discoloration. Livor became fixed at approximately twelve hours at room temperature.

"We have at least one additional crime scene," Bree said.

The ME's brows knitted. "Lower temperatures inhibit both microbial and insect activity and keep the odor in check. Eggs and larvae can't survive cold, but maggots inside a corpse can produce their own heat. We'll consult a forensic entomologist. Aging the maggots could help narrow the PMI."

"If we can ID her, we might tighten the estimate through her movements," Bree said. Cell phone records, credit card activity, employment information, and friends and family could all provide information as to the victim's whereabouts in the days leading up to her death.

"Hopefully, someone reported her missing," Matt added.

The ME shifted position to lift the tarp covering the legs. "I don't see any obvious injuries other than around her throat. She has a tattoo on her ankle."

Bree snapped a photo of the infinity symbol, filled in with the colors of the rainbow.

After lowering the tarp, the ME moved closer to the head again. "I see a few petechiae beneath her eyes." Petechiae were pinpoint bruises. They often appeared in and around the eyes after asphyxiation.

"She was strangled," Matt said, his voice tight.

The ME nodded. "That's a strong possibility, especially given the bruising around her neck." She straightened and stretched her back. "I should be able to complete the autopsy tomorrow, barring any more callouts."

Bree scanned the body. The next important step would be to ID the victim. The ME stepped back, and her assistant moved forward with the camera. They would thoroughly document the body *in situ* from all angles and distances.

"I also want samples of soil under and around the body," Dr. Jones said.

After the body was removed, the sheriff's department and forensics unit would photograph, video, and search the entire clearing. Bree's phone buzzed. She lifted it and read a text. "Forensics will be at the bridge in forty-five minutes."

"I'll bring them in," Matt volunteered.

"Could we turn that light?" the ME assistant asked. "I'm getting too many shadows. Just a foot or so to the left."

Matt stepped over to swivel the fixture. He froze. "What's that?" He pointed toward the other side of the clearing, which the light now just barely reached.

Bree squinted. "What do you see?"

"It's brown and a little shiny," Matt said. "Tucked under those evergreens."

She shifted her gaze. The lower boughs of the small trees touched the ground, but through the needles, light glinted on something shiny. She stiffened as she recognized it. "It's the underside of another camouflage tarp."

"Which means . . ." Matt's voice trailed off. They all knew what it probably meant.

Two victims.

"A double murder wasn't on my bingo card for the night." Matt followed Bree and Dr. Jones toward the second tarp.

"Only one way to find out," Bree said.

They made their way around the clearing, twigs snapping and dead leaves crunching as they waded through the underbrush. Bree stopped near the evergreens and lifted the lowest boughs. The tarp had been moved around, presumably by rain, wind, and animals. She spotted the body tangled in the filthy folds. Leathery-looking bits of skin clung here and there. Leaves and mold matted the long hair. The body was deflated and unrecognizable, and the smell of decay was weak. Large portions of flesh were gone, with bones showing in some places. "Definitely another body."

Fuck.

"Body number two has been here longer," Dr. Jones said.

Needing to number the bodies was never a good sign.

Matt moved closer, looking over Bree's shoulder. "Any idea how long?" he asked.

The ME crouched next to the tarp. She eyeballed the remains. "It's significantly decayed. There's some flesh left, but much of the remaining tissue is cartilage. A few months?" Dr. Jones shook her head. "It'll be hard to pinpoint."

"What about maggots?" Bree asked.

"Not useful at this stage," Dr. Jones said. "But other insects—like beetles—that come to the body later might be." She sat back on her haunches. "We'll take samples."

"The long hair suggests it's female," Bree said.

"To be determined on autopsy." Dr. Jones's face remained noncommittal.

"But it was likely the same killer." Bree waved a hand. "Same tarp."
The clearing went silent as they all considered the implications.
Matt straightened. "We need to search the whole area."
Bree pulled out her cell phone. "I'm calling for the K-9 unit."
If there were two bodies in the clearing, then there could be more.

CHAPTER FIVE

Two hours later, Matt stood back as the K-9 team worked the last section of the clearing. The sleek, black German shepherd was all business. Her handler, Deputy Laurie Collins, was mostly just letting the dog do her thing. Collins and Greta had completed their training, been certified, and officially joined the sheriff's department several months before. Since then, they'd proved to be valuable additions to the team.

Forensics stood by, kits in hand, waiting to see what the dog found before beginning their search for evidence. Bree had called in two deputies on their day off. The first body had been bagged and carried out of the clearing. Dr. Jones and her assistant were working on the second body under lights.

Despite the night's gruesome discoveries, Matt watched the dog with pride. He'd found her accidentally through his sister's canine rescue. The same high drive and relentless energy that made her a difficult house pet also made her an excellent working dog. After the friendly-fire incident, Matt had planned to raise and train K-9s. He'd bought a suitable property and built kennels—which his sister had immediately filled with rescues.

Greta sniffed the ground, lifted her head, then took a deep inhale of night air. She glanced back at body number two. No doubt sorting out the competing scents of multiple bodies so close to one another. Matt had faith. She was a young dog, and new to the job, but she had great instincts. She naturally seemed to know what was needed or expected of her.

Greta returned her focus to the ground in front of her. The dog took another sniff, another step, then sat and whined. Matt had seen her bark in excitement when she found live suspects. Most K-9s loved a good chase and takedown. They were trained to think of work as a game. But her alert for the dead was more subdued, even sad. She looked over her shoulder, giving Collins a second thin, desolate whine.

The dog knew.

He didn't believe for a second that animals didn't have emotions or souls. Dogs were more honest, more loyal, and frankly, better than most people. Canines encompassed all the good qualities of humanity and none of the bad. If there was a heaven, and Matt ended up there someday, he'd be seriously upset if there were no dogs. He might not even want to stay.

Bree and Dr. Jones moved in. Bree used gloved hands to carefully shift dead leaves—one by one—piled up against a tree trunk. She uncovered a piece of fabric. Faded camouflage on one side, worn brown on the other. "Here's another tarp." It was twisted around the base of the tree. Matt's flashlight caught the dirty white of bone. He craned his head to see better. Lodged in the dirt was a human skull.

"Light, please!" Dr. Jones shouted.

At Bree's direction, a deputy shifted one of the lights.

The ME changed her gloves, then squatted next to Bree. "Victim number three. This one is mostly skeletonized."

Small and large bones were scattered. With loose bones, there was no doubt that animals had carried off some of the remains. They'd be lucky to recover a majority of the victim. Matt glanced at the downward slope. Bones could have been washed down the hill.

"Older than the first two," Bree said.

"Yes." Dr. Jones cocked her head. "It's been here longer. Probably since early fall or late summer, since it would have needed time to decompose before winter set in." The ME moved her flashlight. "The skull appears female, but I need additional bones to confirm."

All the victims would be female. Matt knew it in his gut.

Dr. Jones stood, stripped off her gloves, and turned to scan the clearing. Her gaze landed on the dog. "Do we think Greta found all the remains in this clearing?"

Collins nodded. "She seems done."

"OK, then." Dr. Jones took a deep breath. "Let's get cracking. We're going to be here all night."

The forensics team and sheriff's department would be here longer.

Chapter Six

A large wet dog nose woke Bree. A glance out the window told her it was dreary and drizzling for what seemed like the millionth consecutive day. So much for spring. The bed was empty and cold. Matt was already up. She touched the phone on her nightstand. Ten a.m.

After leaving the forensics team to do its job, Bree and Matt had come home just before dawn, had breakfast with the kids, then fallen into bed for a couple hours of sleep. Bree rubbed her forehead, where fatigue throbbed in a dull ache.

Ladybug nudged Bree's chin. She put a hand on the dog's neck and scratched. "You're right. I need to get up."

Vader gave her the stink eye from his perch on Matt's pillow. Not everyone was happy that Matt had moved in. Bree gave his head a scratch, then slipped out of bed. After taking a five-minute shower and dressing in a fresh uniform, she headed for the stairs, the dog at her heels. Bree grabbed the banister as the dog bumped her knees on the steps. "You don't have to be touching me at all times."

In response, the dog pressed against her legs even harder.

In the kitchen, Ladybug stretched out on the floor next to Brody. Matt stood at the counter, pouring coffee. He was six three with a broad, muscular body. Short reddish-brown hair and a trimmed beard gave him a Hollywood Viking vibe. If they hadn't spent the previous night at a crime scene, his low-riding sweatpants and snug T-shirt would have sparked the desire to take him back to bed. Still, she appreciated the view, the kiss . . . and the mug of coffee. "Morning."

"Morning." His grim expression matched her mood.

Neither of them was looking forward to the day. There was no denying what they were facing. Three sets of remains with varying post-mortem intervals. No clothing. All victims wrapped in camouflage tarps and abandoned in an isolated clearing in the woods. The hikers had stumbled upon a serial killer's dumping ground.

The news played on Matt's tablet, which was propped on the counter, the volume low. She focused on the weather. The miserable drizzle would continue for the rest of the week. "Glad I put on my thick socks. Don't want a repeat of my icicle toes from last night."

"I don't want any more of your icicle toes either."

Bree grinned. She'd used his calves to warm them up.

Matt took a long sip of coffee. "Dana is at spin class."

After retiring and following Bree upstate, Dana had become an honorary aunt while she figured out what she wanted to do with the rest of her life. Lately, she'd been dating Matt's older brother.

"How long have you been up?" Bree drank deeply, willing the coffee to work its magic.

"About five minutes." He lifted a glass dome on the counter.

Bree grabbed a chocolate croissant from the selection. "Calories aside, there are days I'm very glad Dana has been working on her patis-serie skills." Uniforms could be let out, right?

Not bothering with a plate either, Matt selected a pastry. "Today is definitely one of those days." He finished his croissant in three bites.

A voice from the TV shifted, taking on an urgent tone. "Multiple dead bodies were found last night in the woods near Echo Road Bridge."

Bree spun and stared at the tiny screen. Matt reached over and turned up the volume.

The reporter stood in front of the covered bridge. She wore a bright-blue rain jacket and held an umbrella to shield her sleek blonde bob from the light rain. The bridge's neglected condition was glaring. Dark-red paint peeled on the exterior walls, and graffiti and rust marred the guardrails. "Sources say a serial killer is loose in Randolph County."

"Who are her sources?" Matt stroked his beard.

Bree shrugged. "I've given up trying to locate the leak. There are too many options. Could be someone from the department, the ME's office, anyone with a police scanner . . ."

"Our luck was due to run out."

"We were fortunate the press didn't show up last night."

Matt drained his cup and set it in the sink. "I'll shower. Be ready in ten."

Bree spent those precious minutes maximizing caffeine and sugar consumption. By the time they drove to the sheriff's station, her headache had faded into the background.

The new addition to the station loomed unfinished on the opposite side of the building. The renovations were behind schedule due to nationwide shortages in building materials.

As she expected, news teams clustered around the parking lot. Reporters giving sound bites lowered their mics as Bree cruised through the gate and into the fenced rear parking lot. No doubt they'd gather their gear and storm the lobby now that they'd spotted her. Entering through the back door, Bree went directly to her office. Matt veered off to drop his jacket at a computer station in the squad room.

There were no sounds from the addition. No drilling, no hammering, no banging.

Bree switched on her computer. The machine was still booting up when her administrative assistant, Marge, appeared in the doorway. In her sixties, Marge wore comfortable slacks and a cardigan. Reading glasses hung from a chain around her neck. "The interview you had scheduled with Renata Zucco for tomorrow canceled." She looked down at a note in her hand. "She has the flu."

"Just as well. We need a new deputy, but I don't have the time to spare. Reschedule for the week after next."

Marge made a note. "Did you check your email?"

"Not yet." Bree hung up her jacket and took her place behind her desk. "What's happening with the construction?"

"Everyone is sick. They shut down the project for the week in hopes they will stop spreading the flu among each other." Marge sighed and forged into the room, her practical shoes squeaking. She handed Bree a stack of pink message slips and a cup of steaming coffee. "Phones have been ringing all morning."

"Thanks. It was a long night." Bree lifted the coffee to her mouth. A caffeine IV wouldn't be enough today. She set the slips on the desk. One sip of the station's harsh brew had her reaching for the bottle of antacids in her pencil drawer.

"Which is why I didn't bother you this morning." Marge nodded at the bottle of antacids. "It's a little early in the investigation for those."

"Again. Long night." Bree flipped through the messages.

"Some of those are from reporters looking for info. The board of supervisors is panicking."

"Always." The county administrators lived in terror of bad PR. Crime did not encourage tourism. Pretty B and Bs, fishing charters, and campgrounds depended on the short, upcoming summer season to generate income.

Marge's lips tightened. "But there were calls from people with missing relatives. A couple of parents . . ." She cleared her throat. "You'll want to handle them gently."

"Yes." Bree's monitor blinked to life. "I'll check in with the ME and give a quick statement this morning. I'll schedule a press conference after I know when I'll have details."

"Sounds like a plan."

Bree knew that if she put off the statement, the media would speculate. No good could come from that. "Tell them I'll be out shortly."

"Also, Howard Killian is still in the holding cell."

Bree had forgotten about him.

Marge said, "He's been vocal about wanting his phone call and lawyer."

Bree would make the time to stop and speak with Grace today. "Have Juarez handle it when he comes in." She'd sent her deputy home for a few hours of sleep as well.

Marge exited the office, and Bree texted the ME. Matt appeared in the doorway. Bree motioned him inside. Her phone vibrated. "Dr. Jones." She answered the call, but she didn't bother with small talk. "The press is camped in the lobby. What can you tell me?"

"I'm starting the first autopsy in a few minutes." Dr. Jones sighed. She'd left the scene earlier than Matt and Bree but probably hadn't gotten much sleep either.

"The public is scared. They need some information." Though Bree would hold back specifics to enable investigators to determine real leads from false.

"All three victims are females with approximate ages between sixteen and twenty at time of death. Come by later this afternoon," Dr. Jones said. "I'll have more for you then."

"Thank you." Bree ended the call and repeated the information for Matt. "Let's go talk to the press."

A few minutes later, Bree faced a bank of reporters in the lobby. "Last night, the remains of three females between the ages of sixteen and twenty were found in the woods near Echo Road Bridge. None of the remains have been identified at this time, and the medical examiner's office has not yet determined causes or times of death. Autopsies are scheduled shortly."

"Were the girls murdered?" someone asked.

Bree leaned closer to the mic. "All three deaths have been classified as homicides."

"Do we have a serial killer in Grey's Hollow?" another reporter called out.

Though she'd been expecting the question, Bree still winced. If the board was already in panic mode, they would lose it when they heard the words *serial killer*. She chose her next words carefully. "I can't answer that question until the medical examiner completes the autopsies. But I assure you all, these cases are our top priority."

Another reporter lifted his mic. "You're not denying the possibility that there's a serial killer in Grey's Hollow?"

"No." Bree didn't hesitate. "The truth is that we don't know what we're dealing with yet. Speculation and panic help no one. Let's stick to the facts."

Another reporter stepped forward. Nick West. He was young and sharp. He had potential star quality. But historically, he'd displayed some moral flexibility, when his integrity was occasionally overridden by his ambition. "How long have the victims been dead?"

Bree was not surprised Nick would home in on that important detail. She hedged. "The medical examiner hasn't issued times of death yet."

"But are the remains in the same state of decomposition?" Nick would not be put off that easily.

Bree hesitated. Technically, she should defer the question. She was not the medical examiner. But would she be perceived as withholding or hiding important information? She couldn't take that chance. She had vowed to be transparent with the public. She worked for them. Bree took the words *protect and serve* to heart.

She leaned close to the mic, knowing her next words would spark fury from county politicians. "While I cannot give specific times of death, the remains were in varying stages of decomposition."

Nick continued. "They were killed at different times and left in the same location in the woods?"

"Yes," Bree answered.

The room went quiet for one breath, then bedlam broke out, with all the reporters shoving themselves forward and yelling questions about a serial killer.

Bree held up her hand. The noise level dropped from a boil to a simmer. "The medical examiner's office is working hard to complete the autopsies. I'm scheduling a press conference for this evening, when I expect to have more details."

With nothing more to say, she left the room. Matt followed her to her office. He closed the door and paced the small space next to her desk. "You made the right call."

"Didn't really see an option."

"Because we both know the chances that we're dealing with a serial killer are about ninety-five percent. Evading the question today would only make you look incompetent or dishonest tomorrow. No one wants a sheriff who's hiding the truth."

"Especially when lies could get someone killed." Bree's intercom buzzed. She pressed the button. "Yes."

"Madeline Jager is here," Marge said in an annoyed tone. "Apparently, she came into the station just as the *SK* bomb dropped."

"Send her back." Bree lifted her finger off the intercom button and smoothed back her hair, as if containing her professional bun would also hold her composure in check. Jager was the county administrator. She was also one of the only people who could get under Bree's skin—like chiggers. Her head began to throb proactively. "And so it begins."

Matt snorted. "I'd ignore her."

"I can't." Bree squared her shoulders. "You know how she is."

"Like a Belgian Mal on a suspect." Matt stood and opened the office door.

Brisk footsteps approached. Jager appeared in the doorway. Her lips were freshly filled, and her forehead was frozen in a state of mild surprise. Bree instantly pictured Cruella de Vil but with red hair. The completely inappropriate vision was Matt's fault. He'd made the comparison once, and Bree's brain wouldn't let go of it. Expression might be impossible for the top third of Jager's face, but her eyes snapped with bright fury. She paused for dramatic effect, then swept into the office on a wave of indignation.

Matt closed the door and stood with his back against it, his arms folded over his chest, like a sentry.

"How could you?" Jager bit off each word.

"Excuse me?" Bree would make her spell out her complaint.

"You practically admitted we have a *serial killer*." Jager hissed out the last two key words.

Bree lifted a brow and held Jager's eye. "Because we do."

Seemingly speechless, Jager's mouth opened and closed again. A petty flash of satisfaction swept through Bree. Jager usually had plenty to say. She recovered quickly, though, clearing her throat. "You just said the medical examiner hadn't issued a cause of death for any of the victims."

"We have the remains of three women left in an isolated clearing. The women were all about the same age and have been dead for varying lengths of time. All were wrapped in identical tarps." Bree omitted the color of the tarps. She had no faith that Jager could keep the detail in confidence. "If you can think of another explanation, please go ahead." Bree leaned back in her chair and waited.

Jager froze for a few heartbeats. Then she took a step, turned, and sank into Bree's guest chair. "You're sure?"

"About those details? Yes. Matt and I were at the crime scene."

Jager shot Matt a questioning look.

He nodded. "Classic dumping ground for a serial killer. There was nothing natural or accidental about that scene. They were all murdered."

"Maybe the remains are old?" Jager's tone held a tiny spark of hope. "Maybe whoever killed them is long gone."

Bree shook her head. "The most recent remains are maybe a week or so old."

Jager rubbed her knuckles. "And the others?"

Bree shrugged. "Older. Not sure how much yet. We should have more information later this afternoon."

Jager frowned. "There's no other way to spin this?"

Bree swallowed a lump of anger at the suggestion to *spin* the news. "I'm afraid not. If we deny what is obvious, then we end up looking very bad when the facts come out in such a short time. And the facts always get out."

Jager gave a curt nod. "You're giving a press conference later today?"

"Yes. Being transparent and honest will be important in maintaining public trust." Bree shouldn't have had to point that out, but Jager was a politician at heart.

"We can't have a serial killer running around." Jager stood. "I want those details before the press conference."

Bree exhaled through her nose. She had no time to waste with politicians, but a quick phone call with Jager was much preferred to another in-person conversation. "I'll call you." The *don't call me* was implied.

Jager headed for the door. Matt reached for the knob. Jager hesitated. "What are the chances they'll kill again?"

"Speculation isn't helpful," Bree said.

"You have experience," Jager snapped, her gaze darting between Bree and Matt. "You must have an opinion."

"Off the record?" Bree didn't trust Jager.

"I'm not a reporter." Jager rolled her eyes. "I'm the last person who will tell anyone there's a killer running around the county."

Bree and Matt shared a grim look, then Bree turned back to Jager. "They don't usually stop until someone makes them."

CHAPTER SEVEN

Several hours later, Matt suited up in protective gear and followed Bree into the autopsy suite at the medical examiner's office. The smell of formalin combated the putrid scent of decay in a nauseating blend. Neither the chilly temperature nor the suite's air filtration could conceal the most recent body's stage of decomposition.

He worked not to gag. "I'm grateful we didn't take time for lunch."

Bree made an indistinct but unpleasant sound as they crossed the tile. "Same."

Across the room, Dr. Jones studied an X-ray. She turned and greeted them with a curt nod. "Let's start with the most recent body and work from there." The remains occupied three stainless-steel tables.

"I've mostly finished the autopsies." She gestured toward the first table, where the body lay on its back. A block under the corpse's neck tilted the head back. The neck was flayed open, and the mouth yawned in a silent, horrific scream. Dry, the hair was dirty blonde, long, and mostly straight. "First of all, we had luck with her fingerprints. Her name is Ally Swanson, age nineteen." Dr. Jones looked at Bree. "Do you want to do the death notification?"

"No, but yes," Bree said.

Behind her face shield, Dr. Jones's eyes softened with understanding. "It's always a difficult task."

"We need to interview the next of kin anyway," Bree said.

Delivering the news to a victim's family was one of the worst tasks, but investigators needed to see the reactions of close family members. Everyone was a potential suspect.

"Cause of death?" Matt asked.

The ME gestured toward the corpse's neck. "Superficial and deep injuries confirm she died by manual strangulation. Other elements of note: there's bruising around the wrists. Ligature marks indicate the victim had been restrained."

Matt leaned in to examine the marks. "Didn't break the skin, so probably not handcuffs or zip ties." Victims tended to resist. Metal and stiff plastic restraints often left bruising or cuts. The marks around Ally's wrists were wide and faint.

"No," Dr. Jones agreed. "We found black nylon fibers embedded in the skin. Forensics is attempting to identify the source of those fibers."

"Anything else?"

"The body was washed. We found traces of a surfactant, possibly dish soap." The ME moved to the foot of the table. "The bottoms of her feet have injuries. Some began to heal. Others have not."

"She was tortured." Bree's voice was flat. "The healing would suggest he held her for a while."

"Yes," Dr. Jones said.

"Was she sexually assaulted?" Matt asked.

Dr. Jones said, "Findings are inconclusive. There are no obvious internal or external injuries to indicate sexual assault. We found no semen in or on the body. Nor did we find any trace of lubricant or other sign that he used a condom." She shrugged. "But we all know that lack of evidence proving rape occurred doesn't mean that it did not happen."

"Any other significant findings?" Bree asked.

"Yes," Dr. Jones said. "She was approximately three months pregnant."

"At three months, that wouldn't have been obvious?" Matt asked.

"No. It's unlikely she was showing yet," Dr. Jones confirmed.

"Is there fetal DNA?" Matt thought of the baby's father, also a potential suspect.

"Yes." Dr. Jones nodded.

"Good," Bree said. "We'll be able to determine the father, if we have a sample to compare. Anything else?"

"Not on this one." Dr. Jones peeled off her gloves and tossed them in the trash. "Postmortem interval remains at seven to fourteen days. I'll let you know if the entomologist can narrow that window. Forensics is processing the tarps and other trace evidence."

"What about the other remains?" Matt glanced at the other tables.

The ME pointed to the second table. "We are not able to identify victim number two at this time. Fingerprints are obviously not possible." She moved toward a light box and gestured toward an X-ray of the victim's jaw. "Two wisdom teeth have erupted. This process typically occurs around age eighteen, so I'll age her at approximately sixteen to twenty years of age. She has several fillings and one capped tooth. So, she likely has dental records somewhere to compare. She was small, approximately sixty-one inches tall."

Small women would be easier to control.

Easier to kill.

"Could you determine cause of death?" Bree asked.

"Not at this time." Dr. Jones pointed to the victim's left eye socket on the X-ray. "She had an orbital fracture."

Bree shifted and propped a hand on her hip. "He beat her up."

"And he's right-handed," added Matt. "There's no chance this happened to the skull after death?"

"No." The ME traced the fracture line on the X-ray. "Postmortem fractures tend to be jagged because the bone becomes dry, and there's some healing, so the break definitely occurred prior to death."

A large man beating a small woman. *Coward*, Matt thought.

Matt studied the X-ray. "Can you tell how long before death it happened?"

Dr. Jones tilted her head. "Bones heal by forming callus. It begins soft, becomes hard, then remodels into true bone. Callus begins to appear at seven to ten days." She jabbed a forefinger at the X-ray. "You can see it beginning to form here. So, the break occurred a week or two prior to death."

"He could have punched her in the face when he abducted her." Anger and disgust burned in Matt's chest.

Bree jerked a thumb at the first victim. "Ally Swanson was kept long enough for injuries to her feet to have begun to heal."

"Can you tell if she was strangled?" Matt asked.

"No." The ME turned up a gloved palm. "The hyoid bone is intact, but we only see a fracture in about one-third of cases of manual strangulation. If she had bruises, we have no way of knowing. Soft tissue has mostly decomposed. Sometimes we see broken cartilage in the neck in manual strangulation, but that's not always the case. Remaining cartilage in her neck is intact. I can't say she was strangled, but I can't say she wasn't. Tox screens are pending."

Not much info.

Dr. Jones consulted a laptop mounted on a rolling cart. "After reviewing temperature fluctuations over the past several months, I estimate her PMI at six to twelve weeks. I'll let you know when the entomologist issues his report."

Which could take months. Matt wouldn't hold his breath.

"Moving on to victim three." The ME stepped to the head of the third table, where recovered bones were laid out in the shape of a skeleton. "As you can see, the remains were heavily scavenged. We only found about sixty percent of the bones. The skull indicates the remains belong to a female. Measurements of the femur suggest she was around five feet tall, give or take an inch or two either way."

"Any clues as to her identity?" Bree asked.

"Not yet," Dr. Jones said. "We recovered the skull, jawbones, and about half of the teeth, but I see no obvious dental work. In fact, several of the molars have unfilled cavities, suggesting she didn't receive the best dental care."

"Age?"

The ME sighed. "Approximately sixteen to twenty."

"Any idea how long she's been dead?" Bree asked.

The ME tilted her head. "Since late summer, at least. We'll send her to the forensic anthropologist at the university for a more specific time frame. There are some new techniques that might prove useful."

"Cause of death?" Matt asked.

"Undetermined at this time. I found no obvious injuries to the bones that would suggest specific trauma. There's no soft tissue remaining to analyze. We should be able to extract DNA for a match."

Again, experts took time. Too many deaths. Too few resources. Everyone had a backlog. By the time most of the additional reports came back, the case would either be solved or cold as an ice pack.

Fifteen minutes later, Matt stepped into the parking lot and took a deep breath of cool, damp air. "All I smell is decomp."

Bree lifted her arm and sniffed her uniform sleeve. "Same. We can't do a death notification or press conference smelling like this. We need to stop at home."

The house was empty midday, with the kids at school and Dana running errands. They left their boots on the boot tray just inside the kitchen door. The last time Matt left his boots outside, a field mouse had invaded one. The dogs greeted them with wags and snuffles. Brody gave him a suspicious sniff. Having been a police K-9, the shepherd knew the smell of decomp. Ladybug rubbed against Bree's legs. The former stray considered roadkill second breakfast. The smell didn't bother her at all.

Matt felt eyes on him and turned in a circle until he spotted Vader staring at him from the top of the refrigerator. "Your cat hates me."

"He doesn't hate you. He's just not happy to have another male living on his turf. He'll adjust." Bree reached up and scratched behind the cat's ear. Vader purred and rubbed against her hand. But he continued to glare at Matt.

They stripped in the laundry room and stuffed their clothing into the washer. Matt added generous doses of detergent and white vinegar and started the machine on the heavy cycle. He left a note for Dana, asking her to transfer everything to the dryer. As a former homicide cop, she'd know why and would probably double wash everything.

Upstairs, they showered. Matt used Bree's herbal-scented shampoo to infuse his nostrils with anything other than the smell of a rotting corpse. Dressed in clean clothes, they returned to the kitchen.

Matt sat on a chair and reached for his boots. A foul scent hit his nostrils. "What is that smell?" He lifted a boot. The smell intensified. He spotted something inside. Something wet. "Argh. Puke."

She took his boot from him, peered inside, and wrinkled her nose. "Hairball."

"You puked in my boot." Matt turned to Vader, who returned his gaze without blinking. The cat looked smug. He was definitely not sorry.

Bree's mouth twitched. "Sorry about that."

"You want to laugh."

"I'm sorry. I do." She pressed a knuckle to her mouth and cleared her throat. "I'll try to clean them."

"Hard pass. I'll order a new pair," Matt said. Vomit had soaked the insoles and the leather interior. "They're old anyway. We need a closet with a door."

Bree grabbed her jacket and stepped into her own boots. Slipping into a pair of sneakers, Matt left the house, tossed his disgusting boots in the garbage, and went to his Suburban for his spare pair. He changed shoes, then met Bree in her SUV. "Death notification?"

She nodded. "If the family is available. I'd like to talk to them before the press conference."

He used the dashboard computer to look up the victim's address. He cross-referenced real estate tax data. "Ally Swanson lived right here in Grey's Hollow. The house is owned by Heath Swanson."

"I know the neighborhood, typical suburbia. She probably lived with her parents. Criminal record?"

"Yes." Matt scrolled. "Drug possession. A prostitution charge was dropped."

"Was a missing person report filed on her?"

Matt checked. "No." He plugged the address into the GPS and braced himself to inform Ally's parents that their child was dead.

CHAPTER EIGHT

Bree looked at the GPS. "I want to make a stop on the way. Yesterday, before the 911 call about the bodies, Juarez and I handled a DV." She gave him the details on the domestic violence call while she drove.

"You could let social services handle it."

"I could."

"But you won't," Matt said quietly.

"I understand her situation." Too well.

Matt reached over the console and gave her hand a squeeze. "You also know how important—and difficult—it will be to get her out of that situation."

"Half of the staff at social services is also down with the flu." Bree paused. "Plus, Grace has a four-year-old."

Matt rubbed the bridge of his nose. "Ah, hell."

"Yep." Bree parked at the curb.

"Want me to wait outside?" Matt asked.

She glanced over. DV victims could be intimidated by men, particularly large men. Kayla had never been afraid of Matt. Kindness shone through his eyes. Children saw through physical trappings. They saw *you*. She thought Riley would be OK. And Grace? It was time she learned that not all men were like Howard Killian. There were plenty of good men in the world. She shouldn't settle for a jerk. "No."

They stepped out into the gloom and walked to the front door. Bree raised her hand to knock, but the door opened before her knuckles touched wood.

Grace started at the sight of Matt. Bree introduced him. "It's OK, Grace."

Grace held the door open, and they stepped inside. Three black lawn bags stood in the living room next to a child's car seat.

Probably all their possessions.

"Have you heard from social services?" Bree asked.

Grace shook her head.

"The zipper's stuck, Mama." Riley emerged from the hallway, dragging her bulging pink backpack. A stuffed animal paw waved from the opening. Riley was dressed in pink leggings and a white sweater with a glittery purple unicorn on the front.

"Can I help?" Matt asked before approaching the child.

She assessed him with big blue eyes, then nodded. "OK."

Matt crossed the room and sat on the floor. The little girl thrust her pack into his hands.

With the little girl occupied, Bree spoke to Grace in a low voice. "Are you going to a shelter?"

Grace frowned. "No. There's no childcare, and I have to get a job. Howard didn't want me to work. He liked me to focus on him. But I'm going to try to get my old waitressing job back."

"Where are you going?"

Grace frowned. "I called my parents last night. They agreed to let us stay there for a while."

"Howard won't look for you there?"

"No." Grace's voice went tight. "My father . . . well . . . Howard will be afraid of him."

"Are *you*?" Bree worried.

"Afraid?" Grace swallowed. "No."

"You didn't want to call them last night."

Grace's eyes went misty. "When I got pregnant, I was still in high school. I denied it for months. Wore baggy clothes, didn't look in the mirror. That sounds dumb, but you'd be surprised how long you can ignore something that terrifies you. By the time I was forced to face the fact, I was five months along, and I couldn't disguise my stomach with sweatpants and big shirts anymore. My mom guessed. They wanted me to give up the baby. I was afraid they'd make me, since I was a minor." She sniffed and swallowed. "I moved in with Riley's dad, Zach, and his mom. It was OK for a while. Not great, but OK. I had Riley. Zach finished high school. I got my GED. We fought a lot. It wasn't the best situation, but we kept moving forward for Riley's sake." Her sigh trembled through her entire body. "Then Zach died in a car accident."

"I'm sorry."

Grace shook her head. "I wasn't in love with him anymore. He wasn't in love with me either, but he was still good to us. He loved Riley and pulled his weight with the baby. He was all me and Riley had."

"What happened with his mom?"

"She couldn't live with his death. She got into drugs hard-core after he died. It wasn't safe for Riley there anymore." She paused, clearly skipping over much of her story. "When I met Howard, and he asked us to move in here, I thought we'd finally gotten a break, but that's never gonna happen to me."

"You'll *both* be safe with your parents?" Bree worried about Riley living with grandparents who didn't approve of her existence.

Grace nodded once. "It won't be fun, but we'll manage. I believe my parents will treat Riley just like my siblings. I don't think they'll hold the circumstances of her birth against her. They put a hundred percent of the blame on me." She took a quick inhale, as if to fortify herself. "Plus, I'm the oldest of nine. Finding someone to watch Riley while I go to work shouldn't be a problem."

"But?"

She shook it off. "But nothing. I just have to keep my head down and follow my parents' rules until I save up enough money for my own place." She seemed miserable, resigned, and determined all at once. Her face softened. "My brothers and sisters will love her, and she's going to love having older kids around."

Bree wanted to ask about the rules but sensed she wouldn't get any information. "And I can't talk you into filing a complaint against Killian?"

Grace's body tensed. "No." Her tone did not waver.

Bree didn't push the issue. She'd rather maintain open communication with Grace than alienate her by being a hard-ass. If Grace ran into trouble, Bree wanted her to feel comfortable reaching out for help. "Do you have a ride?"

"My father is coming for me." She brought her fist to her mouth and gnawed on her thumbnail. "I haven't seen him since before I had Riley."

"Your family is aware of the whole situation with Killian?" Bree asked.

"They are." Grace chewed her lip.

A vehicle door slammed outside. A minute later, footsteps sounded on the porch. Grace opened the door, her posture stiff. The man who stepped into the house was six and a half feet tall with the shoulder span of a refrigerator. In his late forties and balding, he had the musculature of a man who'd performed physical labor every day of his life. Everything about him seemed hard: his expression, his stature, the look in his eyes. His brows were a stern line across his forehead. He did not smile at the daughter he hadn't laid eyes on in years or the granddaughter he was seeing for the first time. His entire countenance was locked in disapproval.

Kneeling on the floor, her knees bent at an angle possible only for yogis and children under ten, Riley looked up at him. There was none of the near-instant trust she'd shown with Matt. Instead, wariness shuttered her eyes as she assessed her grandfather. Even at her young age, she'd learned to take stock of a person. Bree understood. So had she. Survival instincts kicked in early when kids lived with violence.

Grace clasped her hands in front of her and bowed her head. "Hello, Daddy."

Frowning, he tipped his head a mere inch toward Riley. "Is that her?"

"Yes, sir," Grace answered, her eyes still downcast in submission.

He acknowledged the child with a jerk of his chin, then turned toward Bree.

She offered a hand. "I'm Sheriff Taggert, and this is Investigator Flynn."

Mr. Abbott's hands were work-roughened and thick with calluses. "Elijah Abbott. Do you need anything from us?"

"No," Bree said.

Grace moved to the trash bags and hefted two. Her father immediately took them from her, then picked up the third as if they weighed nothing. He headed for the door. "I need to get back to work."

"Yes, sir." Grace held out her hand toward Riley. The little girl leaped to her feet and obediently went to her mother's side, dragging the backpack. Grace slung the strap over one shoulder and met Bree's gaze. "Thank you."

Bree followed them toward the door. "Call me if you need anything."

Matt got to his feet, picked up the car seat, and carried it to the porch.

Outside, Grace locked the door. "What do I do with the key?"

"I'll take it and see that it gets returned to Killian." Bree pocketed the key. She didn't want him to have any excuse to contact Grace.

"Thank you for everything," Grace said.

"You're very welcome. You and Riley stay safe."

Mr. Abbott opened the rear door of an extended-cab pickup and placed the trash bags inside. He squinted at Bree over his shoulder. "They'll be safe in my home." Without waiting for a response, he climbed behind the wheel.

Matt secured the car seat. Riley held her arms up to him as if she'd been doing it since birth. He plucked her off the ground, swung her into the truck, and buckled her in place.

He stepped to Bree's side, and they watched the big truck drive away.

"I don't think Howard Killian will mess with Mr. Abbott," he said.

"Me neither," Bree agreed. Grace and Riley should be safe from Killian at the Abbott house. Hopefully, Grace would have the opportunity to save some money and get back on her feet.

"Not sure they'll be happy, though." Matt headed for the vehicle.

Bree slid into the driver's seat. "Apparently, today is not a day for happiness."

CHAPTER NINE

The rain picked up, drumming a steady beat on the vehicle. Bree drove to Ally Swanson's address, parked, and braced herself.

Exhaling long and hard, Matt reached for the door handle. "I hate this."

"Me too." Bree stepped out into the rain. The house was a neat rancher. The shutters could use fresh paint, but purple and white pansies had been planted in the front flower beds.

"Seems early for flowers. Won't they die in the cold?" Matt asked.

"Pansies are very resilient." After a deep breath, Bree knocked. Heavy footsteps approached.

The tall man who opened the door staggered when he saw Bree. She introduced herself and Matt. "You're Ally Swanson's father?"

He nodded. "I'm Tony Swanson."

Like middle-of-the-night phone calls, a uniformed officer on your doorstep never brought good news.

"Can we come inside, Mr. Swanson?" Bree asked gently.

He nodded and stepped backward. Bree and Matt entered a worn but tidy living room. They steered Mr. Swanson to a couch. His knees gave out and he sat down hard.

Bree sat in a chair across from him. "Mr. Swanson, we're here about Ally."

His eyes went lifeless. "She's dead."

Bree nodded. "Yes. We're very sorry for your loss. Mr. Flynn and I are investigating Ally's case."

Mr. Swanson's head snapped up. Something dawned in his eyes. "She was one of the girls found in the woods? I saw it on the news."

There was no way to soften the blow. Bree said, "Yes."

"Someone killed her." The disbelief in his voice broke Bree's heart. Her throat closed with grief for a few seconds.

"We're going to find out what happened," Matt said.

But Mr. Swanson didn't seem to be listening. "Three girls. He killed three girls. He killed my Ally." His voice broke. "Who would do such a thing? She never hurt anyone except herself."

Matt got up and disappeared through a doorway. Bree heard a cabinet door bang and a faucet run. Matt returned with a glass of water that he pressed into the man's hands. Mr. Swanson drank like a robot. Then he dangled the glass between his knees and slumped forward over it.

Bree recovered. "Is Mrs. Swanson home?"

Mr. Swanson's eyes closed for a breath. When he opened them, they were full of tears. "My wife died two years ago. Cancer." His gaze shifted to a photo on the end table. A high school–age Mr. Swanson wore a football uniform. A tiny teenage girl stood next to him. She was dressed in a red-and-white cheerleading uniform. Their arms were slung around each other's shoulders, their eyes bright with promise.

"We weren't the whole cliché. I was no quarterback. Barely made second-string running back. But Angela, she was a star. The flier—the girl that got tossed way up in the air. Every time I watched her twist and flip, I'd have to hold my breath until her team caught her. People don't know how dangerous cheerleading is—especially back then." He paused for a trembling breath. His gaze shifted to another photo. The happy little family hugged and smiled behind a birthday cake sporting ten candles. "Ally looked so much like her mother."

"When was the last time you saw your daughter?" Bree asked.

"A little more than two weeks ago. We had a fight. This is all my fault. I was a shitty father." His next breath sounded painful. "After my wife died, I lost hope. I lost me. She'd fought cancer for years. The end was brutal. Cancer is a thief. It robs you of your life long before it kills you. It's a soul-sucking disease that drains the happiness from your entire family and leaves them nothing more than empty shells. After Angela died, I started drinking. I went through her prescriptions one by one. Anything to dull the pain of losing her, of living without her. She was my light, and my future looked like a grave-deep hole." He paused, shame shining through his pain. "I was so selfish in my grief. I couldn't even help my daughter with her own. I was here, but she was still alone. What kind of father checks out when their child needs them?"

Bree and Matt shared a sad look.

Mr. Swanson continued. "Six months ago, I mixed the wrong pills with too much booze. Almost died. Kind of wanted to. But my brother, Heath, he wasn't having any of it. He took me straight from the hospital and put me into rehab. Once I detoxed, I realized what I'd done to Ally. I'd failed her when she'd needed me the most." He stared down at the water glass. "But I'd been buried so deep in my own depression, I couldn't see anything else." He set the glass on the coffee table. "I've been sober since I got out of rehab. But the damage was done. I was home all of ten minutes to learn that Ally was using drugs and alcohol too. Maybe she was more like me than her mother. That's what we fought about a couple of weeks ago. I joined a grief support group, in addition to AA. I tried to take her to meetings with me. I told her she needed to get clean, to heal from her grief." He flushed. "She told me to go fuck myself. Actually, she yelled it. Then she packed her bags and walked out the door." He shuddered. "I wasn't surprised that she chose addiction over me. Until I was sober, I did the same thing."

"You don't know where she went?" Matt asked.

Mr. Swanson shook his head. "I tried to call her. She blocked me. I prayed she'd come back. But she's an adult. I can't make her." He also couldn't stop using present tense.

He'd have no grounds to report her missing either. She'd left willingly. An adult was free to come and go as they pleased.

Bree took out her notepad and pen. "Did Ally have friends?"

"She had some in high school. Lately?" He shrugged. "The only friend I know she kept in contact with is Jana Rynski. I don't know her number, but she lives in an apartment on Greenwood Avenue. I assumed that's where Ally went when she moved out."

"Did Ally have a boyfriend?" Bree asked.

"She liked girls, not boys," Mr. Swanson said. "But she and Jana had been best friends since grade school. I don't think there was anything romantic between them."

"How about a girlfriend then?" Matt asked.

Mr. Swanson shook his head. "Not that I'm aware of."

"Did Ally have a job?" Bree asked.

Mr. Swanson's voice sounded robotic. "She wasn't very reliable. She worked on and off as a maid at the Shady Acres Motel. They're desperate for help and tolerated her spotty attendance."

Shady Acres was known for the nefarious activities of its clientele.

"What do you do?" Matt asked.

"Nothing. I had to quit my job to care for my wife."

"May we see Ally's room?" Bree stood.

He didn't lift his head. "Top of the steps. First door on the right. But she took most of her stuff with her."

Matt and Bree left the man to grieve alone. Viewing a dead child's room always felt like an intrusion into parents' grief. But it couldn't be helped.

They stopped in the doorway. The room was both empty and messy. Dirty glasses and plates crowded the dresser, along with white cup rings, crumbs, and mysterious sticky patches. A bottle of black nail polish spilled across the beige carpet. Makeup covered the nightstand.

"Are all teenagers this sloppy?" Matt asked.

"Luke isn't, but I don't think he's typical." Bree suspected Kayla would be messier.

Technically, Ally was an adult, but her bedroom held on to her childhood. Teen vampire books and Stephen King novels shared space with *Charlotte's Web*. A row of Breyer horses topped the shelving unit. Posters of K-pop girl bands covered the wall. A string of lights had been mounted to the headboard. Polaroid photos hung from the wire by clips. A girl with dirty-blonde hair was in most of the pictures with Ally. *Jana?*

"Would you video the room?" she asked.

"Yes." Matt used his cell phone to take several videos. Then he donned gloves, and they began opening drawers.

"Looks like she took most of her clothes," he said.

Bree pulled gloves and an evidence bag from her pocket. She took her own pictures of the light string and Polaroids before unclipping the photos and sliding them into the bag. She went to the small closet, which stood open and empty, except for hangers and a few discarded shirts on the floor. A doll stared at Bree with blank eyes from the top shelf.

Matt dropped to his knees, opened the flashlight app on his phone, and looked under the bed.

"Anything?" Bree asked.

"Just dust." He sneezed, then stood and wiped at his face.

Bree moved to the opposite side of the bed. Together, they lifted the mattress. But it didn't seem as if Ally had left much behind. Matt removed the drawers to check behind and under them. Bree pulled down a few books to look for hiding places. Ironically, it was the Bible that had been hollowed out. "Whatever she hid in here is gone." She sniffed. "But it smells like weed." She methodically looked inside every remaining book but found nothing.

Matt sat down at the small white desk. "Two empty prescription bottles." He tilted his head. "Both opioids prescribed to her mother."

"She was definitely hitting up Mom's leftovers." Bree turned in a circle.

A footstep caught her attention. She spun around. Mr. Swanson stood in the hall.

His gaze swept around the room. "I haven't even opened her door since she left. I couldn't face my failure. I abandoned her without ever leaving the house."

"Is this Jana?" Bree showed Mr. Swanson a picture.

"Yes," he confirmed, then asked in a whisper, "How did Ally die?"

Bree debated how much to tell him and decided he needed to know anything she was willing to tell the media that evening. "She was strangled."

He made a keening sound, then pressed a knuckle to his lips.

She had no words to soothe him. "Can we call someone for you? A friend or family?"

He blinked hard, as if holding back tears. "I alienated most of those. I was a selfish bastard."

"Your brother?" Matt asked.

Mr. Swanson sighed. "He's done enough for me, and he's had enough *of* me."

He didn't ask for more details about Ally's death, and Bree didn't offer any. More details would come out over time—it couldn't be helped—but there was only so much a person could take at once.

Bree hated to ask the last question, but she had to. "Did you know Ally was pregnant?"

Mr. Swanson's head snapped up. "That can't be. Like I said, Ally liked girls, not boys. She *never* showed any interest in boys."

Bree shot a glance at Matt, who lifted one eyebrow.

"She was pregnant?" Mr. Swanson leaned on the doorframe, confusion blurring his grief.

Bree nodded. "About three months."

He bowed his head into one hand. "I didn't know."

There were no words of comfort.

"Where is Ally now?" Mr. Swanson's voice was a hoarse rasp.

"She's with the medical examiner," Bree said, her voice as rough as sandpaper in her throat. "She took care of my sister. I know she's taking care of Ally just as well."

Mr. Swanson looked up. The bleakness in his eyes was achingly familiar. "How do I get her . . . back?"

"Call the medical examiner's office." Bree took her notepad from her pocket, wrote down the number, and handed it to him.

"Do you have a sponsor?" Matt asked. He'd dealt with a close friend who struggled with addiction.

Mr. Swanson nodded.

"Call him now," Matt said, his voice firm.

Mr. Swanson stepped away, pulling his phone from his pocket. A minute later, the sound of his sobbing cracked Bree's heart wide open. But she put the echo of her own grief aside and turned back to the job. She couldn't save Ally. Maybe she could save someone else.

They finished their search, left the bedroom, and found Mr. Swanson in the living room, sitting in the same place as when they'd delivered the terrible news. He stared straight ahead, his face swollen, his shoulders stooped. He looked as if he'd aged twenty years since they arrived. Bree followed his gaze to the wall, where school photos displayed Ally's progression from kindergarten to high school. From pigtails and freckles to braces and acne. In the third-from-the-last picture, Bree thought it would have been sophomore or junior year, Ally had turned from awkward adolescent to pretty teenager. But the shine disappeared in the next one. Had her mother's health declined that year? In the final photo, Ally looked brittle and bitter. Her mother had died.

Mr. Swanson swiped a hand under his nose. "I got sober too late. I failed her. It's my fault. Her death is on my hands."

Bree touched his arm. "No, sir. Her killer is responsible for her death, and we will do everything possible to find him and get justice for Ally."

"What good is justice? It won't bring Ally back." Mr. Swanson's voice was disturbingly devoid of emotion.

Someone knocked on the door. Matt rose to open it for a man of about sixty. The sponsor, Bree assumed.

Mr. Swanson grabbed Bree's forearm. "Stop him before he takes someone else's baby."

"I promise you I will do everything in my power to find him." Bree's years in homicide had taught her not to make promises to victims' families. Some cases were never solved. Others took decades. But she made a vow in her own heart.

She would find this killer.

But would he murder again before she could?

He'd already killed three women on her watch.

CHAPTER TEN

Matt called forensics for an update from the passenger seat of Bree's vehicle. "They're still logging evidence." Forensics had worked in the cold rain for nearly twenty-four hours. "Outdoor scenes are a bitch to process, but they didn't find much other than the bones. The clearing is isolated. They didn't find a single water bottle or protein bar wrapper."

"They're shorthanded too." Bree turned toward the sheriff's station, slowing the SUV.

"I'm almost glad I was sick last week." Matt hoped he was now immune. "The press is here."

Ahead, news vans clogged the street and filled the station parking lot. Crews clustered in groups, no doubt giving sound bites.

Matt spotted a major network. "They're not all local. I see two national stations."

"Serial killers are major news." Bree grimaced, then sighed. "People are scared. The public *does* have a right to know."

"But using that fear to drive clicks, amplify panic, and then profit from that escalation is wrong."

"I agree, but I can't control that." She drove into the rear lot. Cameras pointed at them as they went in the back door. Inside, the squad room was empty. But Matt could hear what sounded like chaos in the front of the building.

Marge appeared in the hall. "I'm glad you're here."

"What's happening?" Matt draped his jacket over the back of a chair.

Bree dropped her things in her office. She flipped through reports on her desk. Two more deputies had the flu, but two who were sick the previous week were back. No net loss at least. Howard Killian had been released on bail that afternoon. "The press conference isn't for another thirty minutes."

"Reporters started showing up an hour ago. Also some parents of missing girls have arrived." Marge gestured toward the lobby. "Juarez is out there, doing his best to keep the reporters outside and reserving the lobby for families. But he's alone, so you can imagine how that's going."

Bree reappeared in her doorway. "Assuming not well. How many deputies are out on patrol?"

"Four," Marge answered.

"Let's call two back here," Bree said.

"Already done." Marge really could run the office.

Matt started toward the lobby. "I'll give Juarez a hand. I wish Collins and Greta weren't off duty. The K-9 unit would keep those reporters in line."

But the dog needed downtime after the long night.

"It's funny." Bree fell into step beside him. "I'll call in a human to work overtime, but I'm more considerate of the dog."

"That's a good practice." Matt nodded. "Dogs will work themselves into the ground. They don't know when to stop. *You* have to provide the pacing for them."

The lobby was swarming with people. Spotting Bree and Matt, a reporter with a microphone tried to shove his way to the front of the crowd. A tall, gray-haired man turned and pushed him back. Juarez was on the other side of the room, speaking with a couple in their sixties. He started toward the altercation. People moved out of the way for him, but Matt and Bree were closer. Matt, being larger and taller, cut more easily through the fray.

"Sheriff!" The reporter surged forward again.

What did that dumbass think he was doing? Did he think Bree would give him an exclusive when she was already giving a statement shortly? Matt knew most of the local media. With a few exceptions, they were generally respectful. This guy wasn't one of them.

The tall man grabbed the reporter by the shoulder and yanked him backward. "Wait your turn! You think you have more rights than people with missing kids?" His face flushed.

The reporter, younger and stronger, shook off the hand. "Get your hands off me. This is my job, man. Back the fuck off."

"Your job?" the man shouted. "You think that's more important than my daughter?"

"Fuck you, man," the reporter yelled back.

Someone grabbed the tall man's arm, but he would not be held back. He gripped the reporter's jacket, spun him around, and punched him squarely in the face.

Honestly, even as Matt trudged toward the pair to stop the fight, he couldn't blame the man.

Blood spurted from the reporter's nose. He dropped his mic, his hands automatically covering his face. The crowd shifted away, leaving an empty circle around the two men. The reporter lowered his hand, looked at the blood on his fingers, then drew back an arm, ready to strike.

Matt stepped between the two men, catching the reporter's fist with his much-larger hand. He towered over both of them. But the desperation that shone from the tall man's face put him on warning. This was the one to watch. This was the man with nothing to lose. Matt turned his back on the reporter, barking a single order over his shoulder. "Stand down."

In his peripheral vision, Matt saw the reporter take a step backward. One hand returned to his nose as he stooped to recover his dropped mic. "I want to press charges," he said in a nasally voice.

Ignoring the reporter's statement, Matt faced the tall man. "Come with me." He took the man's arm to steer him through the throng.

Bree positioned herself on the man's other side and raised her voice. "If you're with the media, you'll wait in the parking lot. If you're a family member, you may stay in the lobby." Grumbles sounded, but her tone allowed for no argument. "Except for you."

Without looking, Matt knew she was talking to the bloody reporter.

Matt led the tall man behind the counter and through the locked door that separated the lobby from the rest of the station. Before taking him any farther, Matt halted. "Raise your hands."

The man obeyed, and Matt patted him down. Desperate people did desperate things. While he sensed the man was grieving, he could take no safety risks. When he was satisfied the man had nothing but keys, a wallet, and a cell phone in his pockets, Matt ushered him into the first conference room.

A few minutes later, Bree entered the room and closed the door behind her.

"Where's the reporter?" Matt asked.

Bree jerked her head sideways. "Next room."

"Does he still want to file a complaint?" Matt asked.

Bree shrugged.

The tall man's body sagged, as if the anger had bled from him—and taken all his energy with it. Having just dealt with Mr. Swanson, Matt recognized the man's anguish. He pulled a wheeled chair closer and guided the man into it.

Bree sat in a chair facing him. She leaned forward, her hands on her knees, giving him her full attention. "What's your name?"

"Joel Hopkins." He swiped at his face again.

"Why are you here, Joel?" Bree asked.

"My daughter, Sabrina—" His voice broke, and he began to sob.

They gave him a minute to vent his frustration.

He drew a shaky breath. "I'm sorry. My wife told me not to come. She refused. She said we'd know if one of the bodies was Sabrina soon enough. We've been through this before."

"When did she go missing?" Matt asked.

Raising his head, Mr. Hopkins wiped his face with his sleeve. "She disappeared last August. I reported her missing to the Redhaven police. They barely looked for her."

"How old is she?" Matt asked. He and Bree had dealt with the Redhaven police chief recently. Matt wasn't a fan.

"Seventeen then, but she turned eighteen in February. They said she was almost an adult, but she was still in high school. She's just a kid, really. No sign of foul play, they said." He stared at his hands. "We'd had an argument. They said she probably ran away. Who hasn't had an argument with their teenager? She didn't pack anything. Nothing. She went to work and never came home."

Matt pictured Mr. Swanson and his brutal grief. Would Mr. Hopkins be getting similar news soon?

"What does she look like?" Bree asked.

Mr. Swanson brushed a fingertip under his eyes. "Five two, one oh five, blonde hair, brown eyes." He recited her description as if he'd done so a hundred times.

Dread sank through Matt's gut. Sabrina fit their rough assumption of the killer's type. He couldn't imagine his child going missing. Every discovery of remains would send him into panic mode. Like Mr. Hopkins, Matt would never give up looking.

Bree made a few notes. "Are Sabrina's dental records on file?"

He nodded. "And recent X-rays, her DNA."

"I'll call the medical examiner." Bree touched Mr. Hopkins's arm. "She can pull the report. We'll find out if Sabrina is there as soon as possible." Bree ducked out into the hallway, returning in a few minutes. "The ME's office is on it."

Mr. Hopkins's head jerked, and his shoulders trembled. "I want to know. I have to know. But I also don't."

"I understand," Matt said. "You don't have to explain. What did you and Sabrina argue about?"

Regret tightened Mr. Hopkins's face. "She'd missed curfew the night before. She's supposed to be home by ten on school nights. I grounded her for the next weekend. She was mad. She was turning eighteen in February. Soon I wouldn't be able to tell her what to do." He paused, staring at the wall as if he were replaying the argument in his mind. "Sometimes, you don't know how to control them, and you hear your own parents' words coming out of your mouth. I told her as long as she lived under my roof, she'd have to follow my rules." He closed his eyes for a few seconds. When he opened them, utter desolation filled them. "Can you believe I actually said that? The rational response would have been to tell her we'd discuss it when she got home from work and to spend the day considering options. But I lost my temper. Damn it. I know better. She's the teenager. I'm supposed to be the mature adult."

Matt didn't say anything. He sensed Mr. Hopkins wasn't finished. Plus, words would not comfort him.

"I called her friends. I called the school. I called her boss. No one had seen her. That's not like Sabrina. Sure, she's gotten a little mouthy in the past year or so, but I hardly think that's unusual. Our older kids did the same, though I think we spoiled Sabrina a bit. She's the youngest. She tested our boundaries more than the others."

"How many other kids do you have?"

"Two. A son and a daughter. Both in college." He inhaled deeply. "They both tested limits their last year of high school. Kids that age are impatient to grow up. It's natural."

They sat in silence for a few seconds. Matt had no doubt Mr. Hopkins was thinking the same thing as him: Would Sabrina get to grow up? Or was she one of the bodies from the clearing?

"I looked for her everywhere." Mr. Hopkins looked confused. "Drove all over town for weeks. But she was gone. Vanished. How does that happen in the modern world?"

"Did she have a credit card?" Matt asked.

"Yes," he said. "It's tied to my account, so I can see that it hasn't been used. She worked at a clothing shop in the mall. She finished her shift at nine p.m. The parking lot surveillance camera showed her getting into her car and driving away, alone. She never came home. I drove every possible route to the mall and back. There was no sign of her car."

Bree pushed to her feet. "OK, Mr. Hopkins. You need to wait here while I talk to the reporter."

Mr. Hopkins nodded but didn't look concerned about facing charges. Probably didn't care at all.

On her way out, she gave Matt a look. He understood the silent request to babysit.

She returned in less than five minutes. "He isn't filing a complaint."

Mr. Hopkins stared at her with no reaction.

Bree gestured toward the door. "You're free to go."

"What about Sabrina?" he asked.

"I'll call you when I hear from the—" Bree's phone buzzed, cutting her off. She read the screen. "She isn't one of the victims. Her dental records aren't even close."

Mr. Hopkins's shoulders slumped. "I don't know how to feel." When he raised his head, his eyes were lost, the anger evaporated. "I should be relieved. Instead, I'm . . . I don't even know."

Bree touched his forearm. "Go home, Mr. Hopkins. Tell your wife."

Shaky, he got to his feet. "Thank you."

"I hope you find Sabrina," Bree said. "I'll see you out."

Matt followed them from the room, watched her escort him to the lobby door.

A minute later, she returned. "I wish I could have actually helped him."

"You listened," Matt said. "And you got the answer to his question."

"Doesn't feel like enough." Bree turned back toward the lobby. "Let's get this press conference out of the way."

Matt thought of the sea of desperate faces he'd seen in the lobby. "All of the parents out there want—need—to be heard."

She stopped. "How many people in the lobby didn't look like press?"

"Twenty?"

Bree sighed. "Let's offer to meet with them privately. We can give each family an interview."

"If we split up, we can manage it this evening," Matt said. "We might end up ID'ing another victim."

Bree whipped out her phone. "I'll let the kids and Dana know we won't be home for dinner."

The families they'd been meeting with sat down to dinner every night not knowing if their missing member was alive or dead. Would that change tonight?

Matt wanted answers. Identifying the victims was essential to finding the killer. But each victim had a family who would be devastated to learn their child was dead, tortured and left to rot in that clearing. In the third victim's case, the family wouldn't even be able to bring home a complete set of remains.

He followed Bree outside. There were too many reporters to hold the press con in the lobby. Under the roof's overhang, she gave a brief statement on the facts of the case. "One of the victims has been identified as Ally Swanson, age nineteen. Ally was a resident of Grey's Hollow. The other two victims' identities are still pending."

"The women were definitely murdered?" a reporter yelled.

"Yes," Bree said, with more patience than Matt could have summoned.

More reporters clamored for attention, yelling questions.

"Is it a serial killer?"

"That is a definite possibility," Bree answered without hesitation. "But it's early days in this investigation, and I don't want to make any premature proclamations." She pointed to another reporter.

"Will you call in the FBI?"

"If I feel it's warranted, definitely," Bree said. "The only things that matter to me are finding this killer and keeping people safe. I'll use whatever tools I have to do my job."

"Should the residents of Randolph County be worried?"

Bree nodded. "I don't want anyone to panic, but everyone should be extra careful and use commonsense precautions. Stay in groups. Lock your doors. Make sure people know where you are and when you're expected to be home."

After a few minutes, the questions became repetitive, and Bree raised a hand. "We don't have any more information at this time. I will update you when we do." She took a moment to stare directly into several cameras, as if making direct contact with viewers. Her hazel eyes narrowed with determination. "This killer thinks they're smart, but they're not. I *will* find whoever is responsible for these depraved acts."

Her tone sounded almost menacing, and the crowd quieted, leaving Matt with an uncomfortable sensation that she had been talking not to the county residents but to the killer.

The move didn't surprise him. Bree would do anything to save girls, even direct the killer's attention toward herself.

Was the killer watching, and how would he react to a direct challenge?

CHAPTER ELEVEN

In the conference room, Bree waited for the last parent in tonight's queue. Over the past few hours, she'd met with the families of five missing girls. So far, she had two additional names to send to the ME's office, girls who had been missing for the right approximate time. In the next room, Matt was finishing up with another couple. At nearly nine o'clock, the lobby was finally empty.

A deputy ushered a man and woman in their forties to the open doorway. Bree's belly knotted, her gaze riveted on the woman, small, slender, and blonde.

Just like Ally Swanson.

The man was tall and broad-shouldered with thick, jet-black hair. "I'm Ronald Bitten, and this is my wife, Miranda." Mr. Bitten herded his wife with one hand on her back.

Bree stood and gestured toward the empty chairs facing her desk. "How can I help you?"

Mrs. Bitten eased into a chair as if her entire body hurt. She sat stiffly, clutching her purse on her lap like a life ring.

Her husband waited for her to be seated before taking the chair next to her. He leaned forward, his hands clasped between his knees. "Our daughter, Trish, went missing the first week of January after attending a special winter college class."

"How old is Trish?" Bree asked.

"Eighteen." Mrs. Bitten pulled a photo from her purse. With shaking hands, she held it across the desk.

Bree stood to retrieve it. She schooled her face to show nothing, even though her stomach went hollow as she took in the picture. The tiny blonde girl bore a startling resemblance to Ally Swanson.

"When was the last time you saw her?" Bree set the photo on her desk.

Mrs. Bitten's mouth opened, but no words came out.

With a quick frown, her husband spoke for her. "Trish attended class from about eight in the morning until noon. No one has seen her since."

"Have you reported her missing?" Bree asked.

Anger flashed in Mr. Bitten's eyes. "Of course we did!" He stopped, raised a hand, then took a breath. "I'm sorry." He composed himself. "We filled out a report with the Scarlet Falls police. They've found no sign of foul play, whatever that means, but they haven't found our daughter either. They say they're still investigating, but we haven't had an update from them in weeks."

Mrs. Bitten began to cry. Her husband's face reddened. Was he embarrassed that his wife was breaking down?

"Calm down, Miranda," her husband chastised.

His wife didn't object, but Bree resented his commanding and condescending tone for her.

Mrs. Bitten's breaths came faster until she was nearly wheezing. Bree left the office to grab a paper bag and a bottle of water from the break room. Returning, she opened the bag and handed it to Mrs. Bitten. "Breathe into this."

Her husband held the bag for her. "I told you to stay home tonight," he said in a sharp tone.

Bree bristled. He sounded angry his wife hadn't obeyed.

Mrs. Bitten shot her husband a resentful look. She snatched the bag out of his hand and leaned back out of his reach. She breathed into the bag. After her breaths smoothed out, she lowered the bag to her lap. "Thank you," she said to Bree.

"It's been a long night." Bree handed her the bottle of water. The woman twisted off the cap and took a small sip.

"Miranda isn't strong." Her husband crossed his arms over his chest. "She should be resting."

"I'm sorry." Mrs. Bitten hiccuped. "I'll be all right in a moment. I can't just sit home—and wait. I need to *do* something."

"There's no reason to be sorry." Bree returned to her seat. "You're not the only parent to break down this evening. It's perfectly understandable." She shifted her gaze to the husband. "And perfectly normal."

Mr. Bitten's mouth flattened into a solid, disapproving line. Had he caught the implication that his overly controlled manner was less than normal? Bree didn't care. Her heart broke for his poor wife.

Mrs. Bitten lowered the water bottle. "The police never even found Trish's car. How can a girl and a car just disappear?"

Bree could think of twenty ways, but she didn't list them. "How was the weather the day Trish went missing?"

Mr. Bitten answered before his wife could speak. "Cold. It was January."

Bree bit back a retort. For all she knew, Mr. Bitten's overbearing behavior was his coping mechanism for a situation that was out of his control. She would reserve judgment, even if his manner was abrasive. In a controlled tone, she asked, "Was it icy? Raining? Snowing?"

He shook his head. "Cold and clear."

An accident was still possible. Even when the streets were relatively clear in town, rural roads could have icy patches. Snow melted, ran onto roadways, and refroze into black ice. Cars went off roads into ditches, down slopes, and into lakes. Sometimes they didn't show up until spring. They could stay underwater or in ravines—undetected—for years.

Bree would get all the investigative details from the original police report. "I will pull the report and send it to the medical examiner. She has dental and medical records on file?"

"Yes." Mr. Bitten nodded sharply.

Bree folded her hands on her desk. "Then the ME should be able to tell if Trish is one of the victims."

Mr. Bitten gave her a cell phone number. "How long? How long do we have to wait?"

Bree couldn't make promises, but these people had been waiting for months. "I'll contact you tomorrow whether or not I have an answer."

"Thank you." Mr. Bitten's tone softened. "We haven't had many of those recently." He rose to his feet and offered his wife his hand. After a brief pause, she took it, leaning into him. The tension between them eased.

Bree reminded herself that this couple had been under enormous stress for months. They were bound to have conflicts.

"I'm sorry this happened to you." Bree stood.

"I know you are, but it doesn't change anything." He wrapped an arm around his wife and led her out.

They were going to have another long night and, Bree feared, an even worse tomorrow.

Weary, she gathered her files and stuffed them into her messenger bag. Matt met her at the exit, looking as troubled as she felt. He carried an accordion folder under his arm. In the SUV, he said, "Well, that was heart-crushing."

"Completely." She turned toward home. "I wanted to stay late, but I also really need to see the kids. And not on a screen." She had missed Kayla's bedtime for the second night in a row.

"Same." He patted his folder. "We can work from home later."

What would it be like to have a normal job and leave work at the office?

They arrived home to find Dana in the kitchen, making tea. "I saw you on TV and assumed neither of you ate dinner."

"That would be correct." Bree shed her jacket and boots at the back door. Brody greeted them politely. Ladybug slammed Bree in the knees. The rescue loved hard. After giving the dog some scratches, Bree stopped to rub the cat's head. Purring, Vader watched with smug amusement as Matt carried his boots into the laundry room and set them on a high shelf.

"What's up with your boots?" Dana retrieved leftovers from the fridge.

Bree turned on the faucet and lathered up her hands. "Vader left Matt a message in the form of a hairball."

"Ah. Cats." Dana took two bowls out of the cabinet and spooned pasta into them. She stopped and studied the cat for a few seconds. "Sorry, Matt, but the cat is projecting *challenge accepted.*"

Matt sighed. "Let's hope not. My new boots won't get here until tomorrow."

"You should have ordered extras." Dana nuked a bowl and gestured toward the laundry room with a wooden spoon. "Did you cover them?"

Matt's brown knitted. "No."

Dana pulled a chunk of fresh parmesan from the fridge. "You should."

Matt gave the cat a look, then backtracked to the laundry room for a minute. When he returned, he washed his hands in the sink. "Anyone else want coffee?"

"Yes, please." Bree dried her hands. "I'm going to go up to check in on the kids." She took the steps two at a time, her sock-clad feet silent on the hardwood. Ladybug followed, practically Velcroed to Bree's legs. Kayla's room was dark, the door pulled almost closed. Bree touched the wood, opening it a few more inches.

Sheets rustled. "Aunt Bree?"

Bree stepped into the room. "I'm sorry if I woke you."

"You didn't." Kayla sat up and turned on the light on her nightstand. Ladybug jumped up and stretched out, her big head in the little girl's lap.

Bree sat on the edge of the bed and hugged Kayla. Her hair smelled like detangling spray. "How was your day?"

"Good. I want to ride Pumpkin in the 4-H show. Can I?"

"Sure. When is it?"

"In two weeks."

"I'll mark the calendar, but you have some work to do. The pasture is muddy, and your pony loves to roll."

Kayla giggled. "Not as much as Beast, but I still make a dust cloud when I pat him. Will you help?"

"Of course," Bree said, but guilt nagged at her. Would she have time? The murder investigation would consume her days and nights until she caught the killer.

Hopefully, she'd solve the case before two weeks was up. If not, she'd make time.

You cannot work 24/7.

Kayla yawned.

Bree glanced at the bedside clock. "You'd better get to sleep. Love you."

"Love you too." Kayla snuggled into her covers. "I'm glad you came home in time to say good night. I don't like going to bed without seeing you."

"Me neither." Bree tucked the comforter around the little girl. "Good night."

When Bree left the room, the dog stayed behind. She went to Luke's room next. His door was open. He sprawled on the bed, dozing over a book.

Bree knocked on his door. "Hey."

His head jerked up. Rubbing his eyes, he said, "Hey."

Bree leaned on the doorframe. "Whatcha reading?"

He lifted the book. "*Hamlet*."

Bree grimaced. "That's tough reading when you're tired."

"Yeah." He blinked hard, as if to clear his vision. "Glad you stopped by. I was almost asleep."

"I'll let you finish." She straightened. "Want hot chocolate or something?"

"Nah. I'm almost done." Luke yawned. "I still have to do barn check."

"I'll do it."

"Thanks."

She shrugged. "I don't mind. The horses settle me."

"I get that." Luke met her gaze.

Bree wondered if their connection to the animals was genetic, or because they both felt close to Erin in the barn. Whatever it was, they shared it. "Good night."

"Night." Luke stretched his long arms and broad shoulders. He'd grown several inches in the past year. He'd matured too. His mother's death had thrust him into adulthood. He was more man now than boy.

And her sister was missing it all. Just like she'd miss taking him to his first play. Sadness flooded Bree, but it didn't last. Erin would be happy that Bree was stepping into her boots. Before Erin's death, Bree had never imagined a domestic life. She'd assumed she'd investigate murders until she retired. Like Dana, Bree had never had a plan for afterward.

"Night. Love you." Bree had made it a habit to say she loved them every single day, and the kids had picked it up. They all knew that tomorrow was not guaranteed.

"Love you too." Luke turned his attention back to his book.

She changed into sweats and returned to the kitchen. Matt was already digging into a bowl of pasta. Bree sat next to him. Dana carried a cup of tea to the table. Bree wasn't hungry but ate anyway. Afterward, she and Matt went down to the barn. Large bodies shifted. Big heads popped over half doors. The biggest horse in the barn—the biggest horse Bree had ever seen—Beast—nickered. Steam plumbed from his nostrils.

"I'm coming, you big baby. Move over." Giving the horse a nudge, Matt slipped into the stall.

After she'd finished checking hay and water, Bree ducked into her paint gelding's stall. Cowboy had been Erin's horse, and being with him gave Bree peace. She absorbed his calm for ten minutes before returning to the house and the murder investigation.

Matt carried mugs of coffee into the home office, where they typed and compared the statements from the evening's parental interviews. An hour later, Matt scrubbed a hand down his face. "I've worked on missing kid cases in the past. I always felt horrible for the parents, but now just the thought of either Luke or Kayla not coming home from work or school . . ." He paused, staring out the window. "Makes me feel physically sick."

"Me too." Bree didn't think she could survive it—and she was the ultimate survivor. "Raising them has made me a different person."

"Living with them has changed me too, for the better. I have more . . ." He snapped his fingers. "I want to say *sympathy*, but that isn't the right word."

Bree knew exactly what he meant. "Empathy."

"That's it. I could always feel awful for people who suffered violence and tragedy, but now I *understand* how they feel so much more deeply. The kids have made me a better person."

"Enough to endure having a cat puke in your boots?"

"Even that." He laughed. "Though I intend to find a safer place for my footwear until Vader works through his issues."

Bree didn't tell him cats didn't work through the issues. Humans did. She tucked her reports and laptop back into her bag. "Let's get some sleep. Tomorrow is going to be rough."

They'd sent four names to the medical examiner's office. Would any of them match the remains?

Matt packed up his paperwork. "It's ironic. We don't want any of those girls to be dead. We don't want to have to notify any of the parents. But we still need the names of the victims to go after their killer."

Each of the victims was someone's child, wife, daughter, and every notification would shatter hearts.

CHAPTER TWELVE

Matt held the station's back door open for Bree. The damp wind smacked him in the face, and he was glad he hadn't taken time to shave. The beard was as good as a scarf. He'd spotted a couple of news vans doing updates from the parking lot. Nothing compared to the previous day's chaos, but the media focus would continue until they caught the killer, people got bored, or another juicy story took over the headlines.

In the squad room, Chief Deputy Todd Harvey sat at a desk, reviewing a stack of paperwork.

Bree stopped in front of him. "You're better?"

"Yep." He frowned. "Unfortunately, Cady has it now."

Matt wasn't surprised. Todd and Cady had been a couple since the previous fall. Matt made a note to call his sister and check on her.

Bree assessed her chief deputy with a squint. "Are you sure you're ready for work?"

"Definitely," Todd said. "I'm bored out of my mind."

"In that case, we're very happy to have you back," Bree said. "We need to bring you up to speed on the murders."

"Give me ten minutes to finish signing these." Todd gestured to the forms in front of him.

"Make it fifteen. I need to check messages." Bree headed for her office.

Matt commandeered a desk and deposited his jacket on the back of the chair. Then he carried his files to the conference room. He worked on the murder board, adding pictures of the clearing and a photo of Ally Swanson. He wrote the word *Suspects* in dry-erase marker, but he didn't have a single name to add. He turned to the county map on the wall and inserted three yellow pushpins over the crime scene near Echo Road Bridge.

Bree walked into the room, a folder in her hand. She stopped just inside the door and leaned back against the wall, holding her files close to her chest. "I heard from Dr. Jones. The second victim is Trish Bitten. Not sure how, but I knew it when I talked to her parents last night."

"I'm sorry." Matt wanted to hug her.

Bree pushed off the wall and joined him to stare at the board. "Best thing we can do is stop him."

Todd came in, carrying a laptop and a cup of coffee.

Bree gestured. "Doug and Steve Winner found a body hidden in a clearing while headed into the woods to camp. The most recent victim has been identified as Ally Swanson, age nineteen. She was killed by manual strangulation one to two weeks ago. Ally was approximately three months pregnant."

"Her killer used restraints, probably black nylon rope. He kept her somewhere and tortured her." Matt described the injuries to Ally's feet. "Maybe he didn't want her to run away or was punishing her for attempting to run away."

"Do we have any suspects?" Todd opened his computer.

"Maybe." Bree shook her folder. "I had a background check run on the two hikers. Doug has no criminal record, but Steve was arrested four years ago for stalking his ex-girlfriend."

Matt's head snapped up. "He's fit. He knows the trails. Let's get more details."

"Why would a killer show us the bodies he took care to hide?" Todd asked.

"Boredom?" Matt suggested. "Or Doug insisted on using the Echo Road trail, and Steve hoped they'd pass the clearing without incident. Who knows? Serial killers don't always make sense." He noted the charge on the board and circled Steve's name. "We'll have to ask him about it."

"He and his brother are supposed to come in to sign their official statements," Bree said. "I'll print them, and we'll take them out to their homes instead. We can ask them some questions while we're there."

Matt started a new list with their names. "They wouldn't be the first killers to pretend to discover bodies."

"No," Bree agreed.

"What about Ally's family?" Todd asked.

Matt added Mr. Swanson's name. "The father of Ally's baby should go on the list too."

"According to Mr. Swanson, Ally was gay," Bree said. "So the pregnancy is especially meaningful."

Todd's fingers paused over his keyboard. "Or Mr. Swanson has it wrong. Parents are sometimes the least informed."

Bree tapped her chin. "He seemed pretty sure, but we need to talk to her best friend, Jana Rynski. Girls of that age tell their besties everything."

Matt started a column for interviews with Jana's name.

"Is there a missing person report on Ally?" asked Todd.

"No." Bree shook her head. "She left home on her own. The second victim, Trish Bitten, was eighteen, also petite and blonde." She pulled a photo from a file and added it to the board. "We know she went missing January fourth."

Matt moved their photos to hang side by side. "Both girls looked young for their ages."

Bree nodded. "Trish's cause of death is undetermined due to decomposition. She's been dead six to twelve weeks." She opened her phone. "She's been gone for just over eleven weeks. He kept Ally long enough for wounds on her feet to heal. Trish suffered a fractured eye socket a week or two before she died." Bree lifted her phone. "Assuming she didn't have a broken eye socket before her abduction—and I think we can assume her parents would notice an injury that serious—he killed her somewhere between mid-January and the first week in February."

Todd tapped on his keyboard. "I'm printing a calendar." The machine in the corner chugged, then spit out a piece of paper. Todd rose and grabbed it. Back at the table, he circled January fourth. Then he picked up a highlighter and skipped a week and colored January eleventh through the first week in February in yellow. He grabbed an orange highlighter. "Ally has been dead for a week or two?"

"Yes," Bree confirmed.

Todd marked the weeks in orange. "The third girl—young woman—was killed last summer at the latest. So, he went from more than six months between kills to less than six weeks. He could be escalating."

The room went quiet for thirty seconds.

Matt picked up the calendar and affixed it to the whiteboard with a magnet. He looked at Todd and Bree. "Will he kill again soon? And how will we know?" He turned back to the map. "He won't use the same dumping ground now that we've found it."

Bree sighed. "We can't predict him. But we can investigate the murders he's already committed. Let's get background checks and financial statements for Trish and her parents."

"Cause of death for the third victim is undetermined. Identity unknown," Todd said. "Much of her skeleton was not recovered, so identifying her will be difficult. We'll pull local missing person reports for females who fit her description. We could get lucky."

"What do we know about the killer?" Matt moved to a clean area of the board.

"He's most likely male and strong," Bree said. "Those bodies were carried well into the woods."

"He must have an isolated spot to keep a woman tied up. Somewhere no one will hear her scream when he tortures her." Todd glanced at the map.

So much green, Matt thought. Much of the county was rural and wooded. "We don't know if the girls were raped, but we should check the sex offender registry anyway."

Todd coughed. "We don't know that these are his only victims. I'll check ViCAP for similar crimes." The FBI's Violent Criminal Apprehension Program was a database of violent and sexual crimes.

"Matt and I will interview the Bittens and Jana Rynski."

So much work for just the three of them.

Matt moved back to Ally's photo. In it, her eyes were so full of sadness that he felt her pain. "We should also interview Ally's coworkers at the motel, and we still don't know where she was living after she left home." He glanced at the board. The images of the dead girls were hard to look at, but he felt better having a plan. They gathered up their papers and headed for the door to perform yet another death notification.

CHAPTER THIRTEEN

Grace straightened to stretch her back. A little girl's squeal drew her gaze to the old tire swing. The twins were pushing Riley. Her daughter leaned back, her hair streaming in the wind. The kids had run outside to enjoy the short break between rain showers. Their cheeks were ruddy with cold. Riley wiped her nose on her sleeve. Grace's heartbeat stuttered, then she remembered she wasn't with Howard anymore. She didn't have to worry about him getting angry if Riley did any of the normal—sometimes gross—things all kids did.

A mother with nine children didn't have time to micromanage anyone. This was not a fussy house. Kids were allowed to get dirty. As much as Grace didn't love being back in her parents' home, there were benefits.

Grace bent and scraped the hoe through the muddy earth. She'd volunteered to prep the vegetable garden. Her mother wanted to plant the peas and broccoli this week. Weeding the garden had been a dreaded chore for all the Abbott children, but today, Grace turned her face to the damp wind, leaned on her hoe, and enjoyed being outside. The air tasted free.

The house was always crowded. But Grace's mom had surprised her by giving her and Riley the den. Grace had thought they would insist Riley bunk with the other kids, and that Grace would be sleeping on a couch. The privacy was unexpected and appreciated.

Grace turned more soil. She was trying hard to show her gratitude. She would get through this if she helped with chores and avoided her father as much as possible. Her entire plan rested on her making herself useful, so she and Riley weren't a burden on her parents. They still had eight children at home. Grace's oldest brother was a senior in high school, and the youngest—the twins currently playing with Riley— were only six years old.

A weird feeling stirred inside her, a tingling in her bones, like someone was watching her. Grace stopped working and turned in a circle, scanning the yard and empty lot. Other than the three children, no one was in sight. She faced the house but saw no one in the windows.

A flash of movement drew her to the street behind the house. She caught the tail end of a gray BMW disappearing. She froze, her fingers tightening around the handle of the hoe.

Howard drove a gray BMW.

The judge had told him to stay away from her, but Howard wasn't the kind to obey orders. He thought he was entitled to do whatever he liked. Was he scoping the place out? Learning when Grace's father was at work?

"Girls?" Grace strode toward the children. She carried the hoe across her body, gripping it tightly with both hands, as if it were a weapon, which it could be. Grace was done being a victim. "Wanna bake some cookies?"

The girls stampeded to the back door. "Yay!"

Once inside, Grace locked the back door.

Her mother was folding a mountain of laundry piled on the table. She frowned and lifted a questioning eyebrow.

Grace just smiled and began gathering ingredients. She'd keep Riley inside during the day. Once her father came home, she would relax. Howard would not mess with him.

Like every coward, Howard only bullied the smaller and weaker.

Riley knelt on a bench and rested her elbows on the table. Grace inhaled to the count of four and exhaled even more slowly. Her hope for a better future felt as brittle as her forced smile.

It could have been someone else driving on the next block in a gray BMW. She hadn't even seen Howard. But she knew—just knew—that it had been him.

He'd be angry—so angry. She shuddered. Didn't matter that Grace wasn't the one who'd filed a complaint against him. Didn't matter that Grace hadn't been the one who'd called the sheriff. In Howard's mind, his arrest was all her fault.

CHAPTER FOURTEEN

On the way to the Bitten house, Bree drove to Steve Winner's place. He lived in a small cabin at the end of a long dirt lane. Dead leaves piled up against the front porch. Cobwebs clustered in the rafters. She parked in the empty spot in front of the cabin, and they went to the door.

Standing aside, Bree knocked. "Sounds empty." All she could hear was raindrops pattering through the canopy.

"Looks creepy." Matt cupped a hand over his eyes and tried to peer through the dirty front window. "I'm getting a strong *Deliverance* vibe."

"He's not home." She jogged down the porch steps and pivoted in a circle. Several outbuildings lined the rear yard. Even from a distance, she could see padlocks on all the doors, even a small shed. She cupped her hands around her mouth and called his name. No one answered.

Matt said, "You could scream your head off and no one would hear."

Bree shuddered.

Matt scanned the clearing. "If only we could look around."

"We can't." Any evidence they could potentially discover during an unauthorized search would be inadmissible. It would all be thrown out of court. "Let's go. Having a creepy house does not make him a killer."

They both jumped at a loud bang. An engine approached. The vehicle wasn't the silver Prius from the original forest crime scene, but an ancient Ford pickup, swiss-cheesed with rust spots.

Steve Winner stepped out, his long hair down, his head tilted with suspicion. "Can I help you, Sheriff?"

Bree said, "I was passing by and thought I'd bring that statement for your signature."

"Oh. OK." He shrugged, but he didn't invite them inside.

Bree handed him the paper. He read it quickly and signed his name at the bottom.

She took back the sheet. "I need to ask you about that stalking charge on your record."

Anger sharpened his gaze. "I didn't do anything. She made it up to get even with me for breaking up with her."

"*You* broke up with *her*?" Bree asked.

"Yes." His lips flattened. "It was her word against mine, though, and she had a better attorney, and her daddy was politically connected. I was screwed."

Bree nodded. "Thanks for the clarification."

She and Matt climbed back into the SUV. As soon as the doors were closed, Matt asked, "Believe him?"

Bree started the engine. "I don't know. Regardless, he stays on the suspect list."

Fifteen minutes later, the sun peeked through a break in the clouds as Bree parked in front of the Bitten house. Her head ached from lack of sleep. She'd considered calling Mr. Bitten before driving over, but notification should be done in person when possible. Phone calls were too impersonal for such an intimate task.

Matt squinted through the windshield. "Haven't seen the sun for a while."

"Feels wrong for it to come out at this moment." Bree braced herself to see the Bittens again. "Mrs. Bitten barely got through our discussion last night. This is going to be rough."

Next to her, Matt said, "Is it ever easy?"

The Bittens lived in an upscale neighborhood. A three-car garage concealed any vehicles, so there was no way to know if anyone was home. Motor vehicle records showed they leased two luxury rides: a late-model Mercedes and an Audi SUV.

A paver path lined with black solar lights meandered from the driveway to the front stoop. A six-foot arched window topped the glossy black door. Through it, Bree could see a crystal chandelier. Sunlight streamed through the window and reflected off the crystals in a kaleidoscope of rainbow prisms that felt obscenely cheerful given their news.

She pressed the doorbell. The elegant chime echoed inside the house. Footsteps approached, quick and light. Not Mr. Bitten.

Bree braced herself. The door opened. Mrs. Bitten froze at the sight of them. Then her knees folded. Matt leaped forward and caught her before she hit the floor.

She recovered in a few seconds, getting her feet under her body. "I'm sorry."

"I've got you." Matt steadied her.

Bree glanced up and down the street. The neighbor next door was standing at her mailbox, staring at them. Bree stepped into the foyer and closed the door. She noticed that the furnishings were sparse. The people in this neighborhood generally had money. They hired professional decorators, and they didn't leave rooms bare. Did the Bittens live above their means?

Matt helped Mrs. Bitten into the living room and lowered her onto a white sofa.

"Is your husband home?" Bree asked.

She nodded just as Mr. Bitten strode into the room. He stopped short. "Sheriff." His tone was punctuated with finality. He knew why they were there. He went to the sofa and sat next to his wife, taking her hand between both of his, before looking up at Bree. "It's Trish?"

"Yes, sir. I'm sorry." Bree choked on *for your loss*. The words felt hollow, and so did she.

Mrs. Bitten didn't react. She just stared straight ahead, not focusing on any of them, or anything.

Bree hated the words she needed to say next. "I need to ask you a few questions."

Anger flickered in Mr. Bitten's eyes. "My wife is in no condition."

But his wife straightened her shoulders. "I want—need to help." She pulled her hand out of his.

Her husband tried to capture her hand. "You should rest. You're not strong."

Mrs. Bitten's eyes were dry. Red blotches bloomed on her cheeks. "I've been resting since January. What did that get me? A dead daughter. I should have been looking for her." Her voice dropped to a whisper. "What if I could have saved her?"

"No, ma'am," Bree said in a firm voice. "You couldn't have."

Mrs. Bitten's head turned. Slowly, she met Bree's gaze. "How long has she been . . ."

"Six to twelve weeks." Bree did not say that Trish was likely beaten and held prisoner for at least a week or two before being murdered. It was always hard to decide how much information to give the family. Bree wouldn't lie to the Bittens if they asked her a direct question, nor would she omit information she expected the media to cover. No one wanted to learn horrible things about their loved one's murder on social media. But she wouldn't volunteer gory details either. Later, Bree knew, they would probably come to her with more questions. But people could absorb only so much horror at one time. Today, the Bittens had heard enough.

"All this time . . ." Mrs. Bitten pressed a fist to her mouth.

"All this time, we were looking for her," her husband continued. "And she was already dead."

"Already discarded." Mrs. Bitten's voice went flat, as if she simply couldn't understand—couldn't process—what had happened. "She was out there in the cold, all alone."

Mr. Bitten's jaw slacked, then tightened again. His hands rested on his knees, the fists opening and closing. As if, unless he was providing support to his wife, he didn't know what to do.

They sat, side by side, not touching, not connecting. How had their marriage fared before Trish's disappearance? It was broken now.

They were broken.

Finally, Mr. Bitten exhaled hard, as if he'd been holding his breath for minutes. "How did she die?"

"We don't know," Bree said.

"You don't know!" His face flushed an unhealthy shade of red.

"No, sir." Bree didn't want to tell them why. But they needed to know. "She was in the clearing too long for a cause of death to be evident . . ." She avoided the word *decomposition* but her meaning was still clear, another detail a family should never have to hear.

Mrs. Bitten keened and swayed. Her husband didn't move. But Bree could see him processing the information, unlike his wife, who was clearly in shock.

"Can you make a list of her friends?"

Mr. Bitten nodded. "Of course."

"Did she have a boyfriend?" Matt asked.

"Yes. His name is Jacob Gatt. I have his number." Mr. Bitten pulled out his cell and read off the digits.

"How long did they date?"

"About a year. He's been devastated by her disappearance. Now—" Mr. Bitten's fingers curled around his phone. Bree thought he was going to throw it, but he relaxed in a few breaths.

"Was he ever a suspect?" Matt asked.

"What? No." Mr. Bitten looked confused. "Why?" His eyes saucered with realization and surprise. "Do you know something?"

"No." Matt held out both hands, palms forward. "Police always start with the people closest to the victim, then work outward. It's standard procedure."

"Jacob is a nice kid. The first month, he texted me every day for updates." Mr. Bitten frowned. "He still contacts me every couple of days." He paused. "He's going to be devastated to learn . . ." Mr. Bitten covered his eyes with one hand. His shoulders shook for a few breaths. Then he exhaled hard and raised his head. He swiped a hand across his bloodshot eyes.

"Did Trish have a job?" Matt asked.

"Not a formal one. She was taking extra classes, trying to finish two years' worth of credits early and transfer to a state school. Sometimes, she babysat for the next-door neighbor for extra cash." He jerked a thumb at the wall, indicating which neighbor. "Their names are Kier and Marion Reich."

Bree wrote the names in her notepad. "Did Trish ever complain of issues with the Reichs?"

"No. She loved the kids. They have four between the ages of six and twelve. Whenever she babysat, Trish planned fun activities. Really creative stuff. They wrote plays and acted them out. Once she helped them direct their own short movie. She wanted to be a teacher." Mr. Bitten choked on the word *teacher*. With his elbows propped on his thighs, he leaned forward and rested his forehead in his hands for a minute. With a great sigh, he lifted his head. "She would have been a good one."

Bree gave him a minute to compose himself.

He made a fist and pounded it on his own thigh. "I wish we'd have been able to send her to a big school, but we just couldn't afford it."

"You're a lawyer?" Bree asked.

He sniffed. "I know what you're thinking. Lawyers are rich. One of our partner's has been ill. It's put a strain on the firm's cash flow." The bitterness in his voice told Bree there was more to the story. They'd dig into the family's finances.

"Do you know if Trish kept a calendar?" She cast a worried look at Trish's mother. Her eyes had not regained their focus on the present.

"On her phone," Mr. Bitten said. "It never turned up, but the police accessed the data on her cloud account."

"Thank you." Bree stood. "I'll contact them, but I'll probably have more questions for you later."

"Is there someone we can call for you?" Matt's gaze flickered to Mrs. Bitten.

Her husband turned to look at his wife. "I'll call our older daughter, Diane. She's going to be heartbroken. She and Trish were only two years apart."

"They were close?"

Mr. Bitten nodded. "Best friends."

Bree drew an asterisk next to Diane's name.

"Could you direct us to Trish's room?" Bree asked.

"Top of the stairs. Second door on the left, but I don't know what you're going to find. The police already searched it. They took some photos and papers with them." Mr. Bitten's voice cracked. "Plus her toothbrush."

The toothbrush would have been used to collect Trish's DNA.

He stared at his phone. He didn't want to make his call.

Bree didn't blame him. "I assume they took her laptop too?"

Mr. Bitten shook his head. "No. She had it with her, but she backed up her schoolwork on the cloud as well."

She and Matt took the stairs and entered Trish's room.

Trish had redecorated since childhood, and the room reflected a young adult's taste with pale lavender walls, modern white furniture, and a pale gray carpet. Framed photos of her family and friends hung in artful groupings on the walls. Some of the frames were empty. Bree assumed the Scarlet Falls PD had taken the missing pictures. Bree pulled out her cell and took photos and video of the room.

With heavy steps, Matt went to the closet and began digging through jacket pockets. Bree took the nightstand and bed. She found nothing unusual. She moved to the desk, but anything obvious and interesting would have been collected by the SFPD.

"We'll need to find out what the SFPD collected as evidence." Bree pulled off her gloves.

"I hope they cooperate," Matt said.

"The detective on the case is Stella Dane." They'd worked with Dane in the past. "She's a good cop."

They went back downstairs to find Mrs. Bitten still staring into space. Mr. Bitten had poured them each a short tumbler of amber-colored liquid. He clutched his between both hands. His wife's was untouched. He drained his glass, rose, and went to a bar cart in the corner to refill. "You'll keep us informed?"

"Yes," Bree said.

His head inclined and stayed bowed as they saw themselves out. Outside, Matt stood on the front stoop, sucking air in and out of his lungs like a bellows.

Bree touched his arm. "You OK?"

"Yeah. These cases always get to me."

She gave his forearm a small squeeze. "The day they don't is the day you have to worry."

"I know, but it sure doesn't feel that way."

"No, it doesn't." Bree felt the sadness and frustration, the crushing grief, hovering in the air. The house didn't need to be shrouded in black.

It had its own aura of darkness and despair that clung to it like ash. This would never be a happy home again.

Matt strode down the stoop. "Think they'll recover?"

Bree followed him down the driveway. "No. No one recovers from losing a child. Some do learn to move forward, but any happiness they achieve is never the same happy they had before."

Time did not heal all wounds. Sometimes they developed thick scars. Other times, they festered.

Bree left a message for Stella Dane. Then she drove in silence toward Jana Rynski's apartment, with only radio chatter filling the background. She now understood that the ultimate level of comfort in a relationship was the ability to be silent together.

Finally, Matt asked, "How many murder cases can a person work before losing perspective?"

Bree thought about her very first homicide investigation. "None?"

He snorted. "You're probably right. My first homicide investigation was a convenience store clerk who took a gunshot to the face in a robbery. Guy stole thirty-seven dollars from the register. Thirty-seven dollars. When I notified the family, when I viewed the surveillance video, when I interviewed witnesses, that number kept screaming through my head. I couldn't understand how a person can have so little empathy, so little humanity, that they can put a gun to an unarmed man's face and pull the trigger with no hesitation. Like swatting a fly."

"You grew up with a nice, normal family. Nothing I encountered on the job was a surprise for me."

"I guess it wasn't." Matt reached across the console and covered her hand with his. "I'm sorry you grew up with that."

Bree had no response. The violence in her childhood had been thrust upon her, but she'd volunteered for the rest. "A day might come when one or both of us has simply had enough. We should probably be ready for that."

Matt nodded. "Before I met you, I didn't know what to do with my life. The years stretched out in an endless timeline of uselessness. Now, I know we'll figure it out together."

"We will." Comforted, she squeezed his fingers. They would be a team no matter what the future held. A beat passed before she asked, "What do we know about Jana?"

Matt accessed the vehicle computer. "No criminal record. No moving violations. She's lived at her current address for several years."

The GPS announced their arrival, and Bree turned into the entrance. Jana lived in an older apartment complex. Three two-story brick buildings squatted in a U formation around the parking area. Units were built back-to-back, with a walkway around the building to access the units on the opposite side. Because of the design, there were no back doors, no patios, no balconies. Bree slid the SUV into a space and reported their location to dispatch.

"She's on the first floor. The end unit." Matt pointed to the building straight ahead.

They stepped out of the vehicle. Weeds grew through cracks in the asphalt. The smell of rotting garbage wafted from a dumpster at the back of the lot. A ring of broken glass surrounded the dumpster and community recycling bin.

The buildings were old and dated. Rust edged the kickplates of the white storm doors. AC units hung crookedly in windows. Black mold splotched the walkway where oak trees blocked the sunlight. This was a no-frills complex.

Two steps led to Jana's front door. A long crack bisected the concrete stoop. Bree and Matt flanked the door, as always staying away from the dead center. Bree knocked. No one answered. She knocked again.

"She could be at work."

"Bree." Matt frowned at the window next to the door. He pointed to gouges in the paint next to the window lock. He moved to the window and rose onto his toes to examine the hardware more closely. "Someone forced the lock. It's broken."

Goose bumps rose on Bree's forearms. She used her sleeve to jiggle the doorknob. It turned and the door swung open a few inches. The hairs on the back of her neck quivered. Something was not right. "It's unlocked."

CHAPTER FIFTEEN

"Who leaves their door unlocked these days?" Matt whispered as his heart rate kicked up a notch.

Bree said, "No one."

"Let's call her."

Matt pulled out his phone and punched in the digits. The line rang three times and then went to voice mail. He left a message asking for her to call him back.

Bree gave the door a one-finger push. "Hello? This is Sheriff Taggert. We are coming inside."

Matt would have preferred they sneak in, but procedure was procedure. They didn't have a warrant. They were accessing Jana's apartment out of concern for her safety and well-being.

After waiting a heartbeat, Bree drew her weapon and pushed the door all the way open to reveal a small living room. Instead of traditional furniture, the living room held an easel and painting supplies. Bree's brother was an artist, and the apartment smelled like his place. "Hello?"

Silence greeted them. Bree lifted a foot to step over the threshold, but Matt tugged her back. He pointed to the cream-colored carpet.

A trail of dark-red drops connected the back of the apartment to the door.

"Paint?" Bree asked.

Matt scanned the painting. A forested landscape. "I don't know anything about color mixing, but I don't see any red paint on this canvas."

They shared a glance.

Blood?

Bree froze and backed up a step. "I'll call for backup."

Considering how many of her department were out sick, Matt wouldn't hold his breath. Luck would determine whether a patrol unit was nearby. He jogged back to the SUV for an AR-15. He and Bree would likely be on their own. Nerve damage to his hand prevented him from qualifying with a handgun, but his marksmanship with a rifle was excellent. He would take no chances following a blood trail in the residence of someone involved in a serial murder case.

"Backup is en route," Bree said when he returned. "ETA fifteen minutes."

"Better than I expected."

Something thudded at the back of the apartment. Bree drew her weapon and entered, with Matt at her flank. Avoiding the red trail, she spun left, while Matt went right, sweeping his rifle from corner to corner. The kitchen held a small table and two chairs. No pantry. Matt opened a closet. Empty.

They didn't rush but proceeded carefully. With no back door, there was no avenue for an intruder to escape. On the other hand, maybe there was no intruder. Maybe Jana had a cat that had knocked something over.

But the hairs on the back of Matt's neck didn't like that explanation. He could *feel* someone in the apartment.

The red trail led to a narrow hallway that ended in a T. Bree went right. Matt followed the blood into the bedroom. He paused in the doorway. The droplet trail ended in a basketball-size stain in the center of the room. Several competing, sharp odors hit his nostrils. A queen-size bed occupied the far wall. The comforter had been dragged onto the floor. A wet spot stained the center of the pink sheet–covered mattress. The stain wasn't red, but clear or light-colored.

Matt noted signs of a struggle. A bedside lamp lay on the carpet next to the single nightstand. Pieces of lightbulb were scattered around it. The nightstand drawer lay on the carpet, broken. Dresser drawers hung open, their contents spilling out onto the carpet.

Matt's gaze zeroed in on an empty can of turpentine discarded in the corner. The stain on the bed wasn't blood. His veins chilled. *Turpentine?*

Matt ducked to check under the bed. The closet door burst open, and a tall man in jeans and a black hooded jacket jumped out. He swiped his hand downward at Matt's head.

At close quarters, the rifle was too long to swing into position. Matt blocked the blow with the barrel, then spun the butt of the weapon toward his assailant's face.

The man jumped backward. He reached into his pocket and drew out a matchbook. With a quick flick, he lit a match and tossed it onto the center of the bed. The covers ignited with a *whoosh.*

"Police!" Matt yelled as he lunged for him. The man turned, grabbed the TV from its stand, and threw it at Matt before bolting for the door.

Matt jumped backward, and the TV crashed to the floor.

Bree rushed through the doorway. "I smell smoke!"

The running man knocked her into the wall and raced out of the bedroom.

Regaining her balance, Bree gestured. "Go after him. I'll take care of this and be right behind you."

She ran for the door, using her radio to call for the fire department.

The smoke alarm began to blare as Matt sprinted in pursuit of the suspect. "Stop!"

He ran through the living room, reaching the doorway in time to see the suspect race across the grass. Bree was pulling a fire extinguisher from her vehicle.

Matt surged forward, gaining on him instantly. The guy glanced over his shoulder. Matt caught a glimpse of a pale face beneath the dark hood before the head whipped around again. Matt turned up his speed. The guy crossed the street and clambered over a six-foot wooden fence behind a house.

Barely breaking stride, Matt vaulted the fence. He spotted his quarry halfway over the fence on the opposite side of the narrow yard. Frenzied barking and growling sounded from the left. Matt froze. A huge white pit bull cannonballed toward him. Matt would never get across the yard before the dog reached him. He backtracked two steps and made it back over the fence just as the big dog hit the wood, shaking it.

Bree was running parallel to his path. He waved toward the street and yelled, "He went over the other side of the fence."

Matt turned, racing around the house. The intruder was a hundred feet ahead, but his endurance was clearly flagging, his strides slowing and becoming uneven. He tripped, a sure sign he was running out of gas. A much-fitter Matt stretched his stride and began to catch up. They approached another house and another fence. Hooded Guy grabbed for the top board, but Matt was on him. He reached for his shoulders, pulling backward. They both went down on the grass. Matt blocked a sneaker aimed at his face. Grabbing the foot, Matt cupped one hand under the heel and used the other to crank his toes. The motion flipped the man onto his belly. Matt had his hands behind his back before the man could catch his breath.

Bree raced up and handed Matt a pair of handcuffs. Matt secured his prisoner's wrists and left him face down on the grass.

"Thanks." Matt climbed to his feet and brushed dirt from his knees.

"You're welcome." Bree patted down the prisoner. She pulled a wallet out of his front pocket. "His name is Chevy Calhoun."

Matt got in his face. "Where's Jana, Chevy?"

"I don't know." Chevy pulled his head back. "Probably work."

"Probably?" Matt asked. "What did you do with her?"

"What? Nothing." Chevy lifted a shoulder. "She usually works until two or three—"

"Where does she work?" Bree interrupted.

"The Sunrise Café," Chevy said.

Bree stepped away to make a call. She lowered the phone a few seconds later. "No one is picking up." She turned back to Chevy. "Why were you in Jana's apartment, Chevy? Besides setting her bed on fire."

Chevy wheezed and coughed. "Getting . . . my . . . stuff."

"Your stuff?" Matt asked.

Chevy squirmed, and Matt helped him sit up. Chevy was in his early twenties, tall and lean, with scraggly, dirty-blond hair that fell across his forehead. Despite his beer breath and bloodshot eyes, he wasn't sloppy drunk. He'd been able to run and climb fences. He'd had just enough alcohol to make him stupid but still functional.

"The bitch wouldn't return my AirPods." He spit a little blood onto the grass. "You split my lip."

"Why did you light a match and run?" Matt crouched in front of him to look him in the eye.

Chevy blinked away and shifted his position on the grass. "You startled me."

Liar. The butt scoot was a classic tell.

"You'd already doused the bed in turpentine," Matt said.

Chevy glared back but said nothing.

"Get up." Bree hauled Chevy to his feet. "Let's go back to the car."

By the time they walked back to Jana's apartment, a patrol unit and fire engine had arrived. The apartment building's smoke alarm had been silenced. Two firemen walked out of the apartment, carrying an extinguisher. One jerked a thumb over his shoulder. "Fire's out."

"Thanks." Bree raised a hand in appreciation. She was 98 percent sure she'd already put out the fire, but firemen believed in being thorough, which was why cops sometimes jokingly referred to them as the EDU, or Evidence Destruction Unit.

Bree stood Chevy next to the patrol vehicle. She propped a hand on her duty belt.

"How did you get into Jana's apartment?"

"I have a key." Chevy met her gaze. "I lived there until the bitch kicked me out two weeks ago."

Bree continued. "Did you have her permission to enter her apartment today?"

Regret crossed Chevy's face. "I have a key," he repeated, raising his chin.

Bree leaned closer. "When is the last time you talked to Jana?"

"I don't know. I tried to call her a bunch of times, but she blocked me."

Wonder why?

Bree motioned for her deputy. "Put him in the back."

Bree went to her vehicle and opened the rear hatch. She retrieved a Rapid Stain Identification test kit for human blood. "Let's get back inside."

They put on booties before entering. Bree tugged on a blue glove, then touched the edge of a red stain. "It's dry. I'll confirm it's blood before we raise the alarm." She opened her RSID kit.

While she performed the test, Matt donned gloves and studied the forested landscape Jana had been working on. Up close, he could see cuts in the canvas, as if someone—presumably Chevy—had slashed it with a knife or razor blade. A small table stood next to the easel. On it, next to tubes of oil paint and brushes, lay a box cutter.

Matt followed the red trail back to the bedroom. He stood in the doorway, scanning the room. Had Chevy caused all the damage? Had he and Jana fought?

The room stank of wet ash and something else. Matt walked toward the dresser. He leaned forward and sniffed.

"Positive for human blood," Bree said behind him. "What do you smell? Turpentine?"

Had he planned to burn the whole apartment down?

"And urine." Matt straightened.

"Ew."

"Yeah."

"So, did he break in here, shred her painting, pee on her clothes, and decide to set the bed on fire in retaliation for her dumping him?"

Matt considered the state of the room and Chevy's attitude. "That feels about right."

"She's a painter, so the turpentine was probably already here," Bree pointed out. "Most people who want to start a fire use gasoline."

"Maybe the fire was an afterthought. Chevy seems like a *hold my beer* kind of guy rather than a planner."

"Maybe." Bree cocked her head. "But our killer got away with three murders."

"Killing girls and dumping them in an isolated spot in the woods doesn't take a genius."

"I suppose not," Bree said. They walked around the apartment. Matt took video of every room. Bree snapped pictures. "The problem is, if Chevy is telling the truth and he doesn't know what happened to Jana, then someone else was here."

Matt glanced at the bed. "And Chevy destroyed evidence that might tell us who."

"What the fire didn't burn, the firemen likely trashed." Bree exhaled hard. "I'm going to request a forensics unit."

Matt followed her outside. She moved to her SUV to make her call. Matt spotted an older woman of at least seventy-five standing on the stoop of the next apartment. She zipped up a black jacket against the wind. Despite her clear senior citizen status, there was no slouch to her posture. Broad-shouldered, she stood almost six feet tall. Two long white braids trailed out from under a purple Minnesota Vikings hat.

Matt walked over and introduced himself. They shook hands.

"I'm Noreen Hamlin." Noreen had the grip of a lumberjack.

"I see you have a doorbell camera." Matt pointed. "Any chance it shows who approached your neighbor's apartment?"

"No, sorry. The way the doorway is set in, the edge of the building blocks the view to that side. I told Jana she needed to get one. Packages go missing so often here, they should be on milk cartons." She jerked a thumb at the patrol vehicle. "I assume you caught that asshat ex breaking into Jana's place?"

Matt made a noncommittal noise. "Do you know where she is?"

"She's probably at work." Noreen lifted a cell phone. "I just texted her." She glanced at the screen. "She hasn't responded. She'll check her messages on her break."

"How well do you know Jana?"

Noreen waved toward the building. "I live in the next unit. Me and Jana have been neighbors for a few years. She's a sweetheart. Most of the residents here are seniors. Jana and I are always helping the old folks with their walkers and groceries."

Matt suppressed a smile. Noreen was one of the old folks, but there was nothing remotely frail about her.

Noreen continued. "Jana and I check on the other residents if we don't see them for a few days. That sort of thing. When she kicked out the dumbass loser over there"—she gestured toward the patrol car where Chevy sulked in the back seat—"I brought over a box of tissues and some homemade fudge."

"How long ago was this?" Matt asked.

Noreen tapped her chin. "A couple of weeks. I told her to change her locks. She took her key back, but I told her not to trust that bastard." Her expression went fierce.

If she took her key back, why did Chevy still have it?

"When was the last time you saw Jana?" Matt asked.

"Two days ago, so that would be Tuesday. We met at the mailbox and chatted for a couple of minutes." Noreen pointed to a communal mailbox fifty feet away. "I'd already had my dinner, so it was about five or six in the evening."

"Did she mention anything about Chevy or anyone else giving her a hard time?"

"She had to block his number. He'd been leaving nasty messages on her voice mail. Sent her a dick pic too, with a text of something like *this is what you're missing*. Like she ever wants to see *that* again." Noreen rolled her eyes, then grew solemn. "She joked about it, but I know it bothered her."

"Do you know why she broke up with him?" Matt asked.

"Oh, yeah. The walls are thin. There were so many reasons." Noreen lifted her hand and began counting them with her fingers. "Laziness, drunkenness, general inconsideration, lack of ambition. Jana would go to work—she's a waitress—and he'd lay around drinking beer all day. He contributed nothing for food or rent, nor did he cook or clean. He had a job when he moved in, but they fired him, and he hasn't managed to find another one." Noreen paused. "But something else happened. She wouldn't tell me what, but it must be pretty bad because she tells me everything else."

"Has she mentioned any other threats recently? Men following her? Harassing her?" Matt asked.

Noreen shook her head. "No. She's mostly concerned about Chevy. He's upset that his free ride is over. He had a good gig going there for a while."

Matt asked, "Do you know Jana's friend, Ally?"

"I do."

"Was Ally living here with Jana?"

"No." Noreen's lips flattened. "But Jana's been so worried about her. Ally stopped answering her calls. Ally's dad came by looking for her. Jana was really conflicted. She wanted to help Ally, but she didn't know if involving her father was the right move. There was a lot of friction between Ally and her dad." Noreen paled. "I can't believe she was murdered."

"Would Jana get upset enough about Ally's murder to have a breakdown?"

Noreen lifted a helpless shoulder. "Jana's pretty levelheaded—except for her choices in men—but finding out your best friend was murdered . . . That could mess anyone up."

"Did Jana use drugs?"

"Definitely not," Noreen said. "She works too much, and she saw the damage drugs did to Ally's life."

"Does Jana have family?"

"She's an only child. She hasn't seen her dad in years, but her mom is local. Her name is Crystal. I have her number for emergencies." Noreen pulled out her phone.

"Is she close to her mom?" Matt asked.

Noreen nodded. "Crystal was in a bad car accident six or seven years ago. She's been disabled since. She's in constant pain. I don't know how she functions." Respect deepened her voice. "There's a charity nursing service that visits a few times a week, Care something or other, but most of the work is on Jana's shoulders."

Matt took Crystal's number, then collected Noreen's contact information and thanked her.

Stepping aside, he used his phone to try a second call to the Sunrise Café. When a woman picked up, he asked for Jana. The woman said, "She's not here. She didn't show up for her shift today."

"Thank you." Matt ended the call and went looking for Bree. He found her standing behind her vehicle.

"A blue Ford Escape is registered to Jana," she said. "It's parked at the back of the lot. The doors are locked, and the engine is cold."

"Forensics needs to look at her vehicle and the outdoor area between her apartment door and the parking lot." Matt scanned the wide-open area. "If someone broke in and attacked Jana, that's ballsy. The possibility that it wasn't Chevy worries me."

"Same. Because the perpetrator would still be out there." Bree pointed to a security camera mounted on a light pole. "The apartment complex manager accessed the camera footage. Jana parked the car Tuesday after work. It hasn't moved since."

"The neighbor has a doorbell camera, but it only shows her doorway, not Jana's." Matt summed up his conversation with Noreen. "The Sunrise Café picked up their phone. Jana didn't show up for work today. I didn't want to call her mother."

"No," Bree agreed. "We'll talk to Jana's mother in person."

Matt thought about the blood in the apartment. "What are the chances Jana cut herself and went somewhere to get stitches?"

"Her vehicle is still here, but she could have called a Lyft or an Uber. Let's call around to the local ERs and urgent care centers." But Bree's tone was doubtful. She opened the rear hatch and pulled out a roll of crime scene tape. "Considering her relationship with a likely serial killer victim, we'll treat this as a crime. If we're wrong, no big deal."

But the consequences of not investigating could be deadly. They returned to the apartment, donned fresh gloves and booties, and went inside. The living room looked the same as when they'd left. They skirted the blood stains and made their way to the bedroom. Fire-extinguishing foam soaked the bed and surrounding carpet.

Bree stopped a few feet shy of the wet area. "I doubt there's any usable evidence there."

"Probably not." Matt moved to the nightstand and began to search.

Bree went to the dresser. She turned away, gasping. Her face scrunched in disgust. "I think he peed on her clothes in here too."

"What an asshole." Matt found nothing interesting in Jana's nightstand except two how-to books. *How to End a Psychologically Abusive Relationship* and *Setting Personal Boundaries*. He turned to the closet, where Chevy had been hiding.

Bree joined him. They checked coat pockets and searched between clothing items. Bree led the way back out to the main rooms and motioned toward a laptop charging on the kitchen counter. "We'll have forensics take her laptop."

Matt went to a small chest near the door and opened a drawer. "Here's her purse!"

He unzipped the top. Unfortunately, Jana didn't carry much beyond a wallet, lip balm, and sunglasses. Matt opened the wallet and found a small stack of receipts for gas and grocery purchases. "Jana actually used cash." Which would make it harder to track her movements.

"No phone?" Bree asked.

"Not in her purse." Matt unzipped a small compartment, which held a travel-size bottle of ibuprofen and a roll of antacids.

"I usually keep my phone in my pocket and carry it around the house."

Matt zipped the purse and returned it to the drawer. "Let's hope the laptop is useful." But he gave the old machine a doubtful look as they wrapped up and headed for the door.

Outside, Matt glanced at the ex in the patrol car. "It's usually the ex."

Chevy had broken into Jana's home, set her bed on fire, and tossed a TV at Matt. They had multiple options for charging him: B and E, arson, assault. He was definitely going to jail.

"I'll call in a BOLO alert for Jana. Let's take Chevy to the station and question him there. Maybe being in custody will shake him up."

"Based on his body language, I think he's lying about something," Matt said. But was he lying about Jana's disappearance or something else?

CHAPTER SIXTEEN

Bree entered the interview room. Chevy sat at the table, his handcuffs fastened to a metal ring in front of him. She faced him. "If I take off the cuffs, will you behave?"

"Yeah," he said, as if he hadn't just committed multiple acts of violence to escape police.

Matt came into the room just as Bree was unlocking the cuffs.

Chevy rubbed his wrists and glanced at Matt with respect. They were about the same height, but Matt had the physique of an action hero.

"This interview is being recorded." Bree read the Miranda warning, slid an acknowledgment across the table, and handed Chevy a pen. He signed without reading. This was not the first time he'd been arrested, but his previous transgressions had been low-level infractions: disturbing the peace, vandalism, and trespassing. He'd been fired from a job at a warehouse. In retaliation, he had climbed the fence and spray-painted profanity on the building. He paid fines and did community service.

Bree leaned her forearms on the table. "So, where's Jana?"

Chevy crossed his arms. "Already told you. I don't fucking know."

"Why were you in her apartment?" Bree asked.

Chevy emitted a disgusted sigh. "We already covered this."

"We need to get your official answer," Bree said.

"Jana"—Chevy drew out her name with the same inflection he'd used with *the bitch* earlier—"wouldn't give my AirPods back."

"How long did you live with her?" Bree asked.

"A few months." He lifted a careless shoulder.

"Until . . ." Bree waved a hand.

"Until she threw me out because I lost my job and couldn't find another one fast enough." A waft of beer breath accompanied his bitter tone.

Matt shifted forward. "When did you lose your job?"

"January."

"Where did you work?" Matt asked.

"Electronics Depot." Chevy stretched a shoulder. "I stocked shelves and shit."

"Why did they fire you?" Matt asked.

Chevy shook his bangs out of his eyes. "I didn't do anything. It was total bullshit. The manager was a bitch. I hate working for a woman. Put a woman in charge, and she becomes a man-hating dyke," he said to Matt, with Bree—his female boss—who also held power over Chevy—sitting at that very table. This fact didn't seem to occur to Chevy.

Oh, the irony.

"And you couldn't find another job?" Matt confirmed.

Chevy blinked. "Well, I was trying to find a better one."

Bree did not roll her eyes, but it took effort.

"But Jana tossed you out anyway?" Matt crossed his arms. "That doesn't sound very supportive."

"Right?" Chevy threw up both hands.

Matt played the sympathetic man's man very well. He could tap into a suspect's assholery and use it against him. The goal of an interview wasn't to win or to obtain a confession; it was information. Sometimes, achieving that end was easier through commiseration rather than animosity, even if the process felt slimy. Bree pictured the three sets of remains on the ME's tables. They needed to find Jana. She let Matt run with the rapport he was developing between him and the suspect.

"Women . . ." Matt sounded disgusted. "I can never figure out what they want. Can you imagine what people would have called you if you dumped her because she lost her job? Total double standard."

"You said it." Chevy huffed. "I tell you, man. It ain't fair."

"You must have felt like she betrayed you," Matt said.

"It hurt." Chevy went full-on indignant. "I went out for a couple of beers one night. When I came back, all my shit was outside." His face reddened.

Matt made a disgusted noise. "And she made you give back her key?"

Chevy nodded like a dashboard dog. "She wouldn't give me my laptop until I handed it over. Didn't even give me a day to find a place to stay. I had to crash on a friend's couch."

"And she didn't give you any reason?" Matt shook his head.

Chevy looked away. "Not really."

Liar.

"Where are you staying now?" Matt asked.

"Same place. Can't rent a place until I get a job." The thought of a job appeared to displease him.

Matt leaned back, giving Chevy some personal space, as if there were no pressure. "If you gave the key back, how did you get into her place today?"

Chevy smirked. "I had a copy made a while ago." He admitted this without blinking an eye. "Dumb bitch never suspected a thing."

Interviewing suspects was an art. Matt was a master.

Matt slipped in a pointed question with a neutral, nonjudgmental voice. "But you still entered her apartment without her permission?"

"Just to get my AirPods," Chevy answered, as if the *why* made a difference. "They're my property. I have rights."

Bree said nothing. Neither did Matt. Most people couldn't stand silence and needed to fill it. They let the quiet spin out until Chevy started talking again. "But when I got there, I just, I don't know, lost my shit. I miss her so much, and she won't even talk to me. It feels real unfair, you know? I want her back, and she won't even talk to me."

Matt nodded with enthusiasm. "Was she there when you got inside?"

Chevy's brows dropped. "No. She usually works until two."

Bree asked, "Does she always work the same days?"

"Usually."

"What about the red stains on the carpet?" Matt asked.

Chevy shrugged. "I didn't think much about them. Assumed that was paint."

Matt tilted his head, the first sign of doubting Chevy's story. "Which she dripped all the way to the bedroom? Is she usually that messy?" They'd seen no paint anywhere else in the apartment, and Jana had used a drop cloth under her easel.

"What else would it be?" Chevy asked.

Bree thought the answer was fairly obvious. *Blood.* But she didn't want him to stop talking yet. "What time did you get to Jana's place?"

He shrugged. "I dunno. Maybe ten."

"Did you go for a couple of beers first?" Matt asked.

Chevy shook his head. "I drank the ones in Jana's fridge. They were mine anyway."

"What happened when you got there?" Matt kept his tone neutral, but Bree could see his gaze sharpening. His questions were circling like a great white, and Chevy was a seal stuck on a rock.

"I drank my beer." Chevy emphasized *my*. "Then I started to think about how she wouldn't even talk to me. Like I had no rights after living together for months."

"That would have made me pretty mad," Matt commiserated.

"Thank you." Chevy slapped his palms on the table. Then he lowered his head. "All I want is for her to talk to me, but she just shut me out." His color rose with his temper.

"Sounds cold to me," Matt said. "When did you pour the turpentine on the bed? Before or after you pissed in it? Did you go into the apartment intending to set the fire?"

Chevy mashed his lips. "I was looking for my AirPods, and I probably shouldn't have drunk the whole six-pack." He flushed. "I ain't proud of it now, but yeah, I pissed in her bedroom. Then I started to think about her being with another dude in our bed. It made me crazy. I wasn't thinking straight. I grabbed the turpentine and poured it out. Then I heard you guys come in, and I just, I dunno, reacted."

"You never saw Jana today?" Matt asked.

"I haven't seen her in weeks." Chevy bowed his head.

Bree guessed he had. "You didn't, say, follow her?"

His eyes went furtive. *Bingo.* "Once, but she wouldn't talk to me. A couple of days after she threw me out. I waited for her by her car. Jana yelled at me to go away." Chevy frowned. "That old bitch next door came out and threatened to call the cops."

"You don't know where Jana is now?" Bree asked.

"No." Chevy glared at her.

Matt leaned forward. "And you haven't seen her in the past couple of days?"

"No," Chevy said.

"Do you know Ally Swanson?"

Chevy paused and looked at the ceiling for a few seconds. "The name sounds familiar." He shrugged. "I dunno."

"She was a friend of Jana's."

Chevy snapped his fingers. "That's it. I remember Jana talking about her. She's a junkie, right?"

Bree didn't answer. "She's dead."

"What?" Chevy's posture snapped straight.

"Likely murdered by a serial killer," Matt added.

"Oh." Chevy nodded. "She was one of those girls found in the woods?"

"Yes," Bree said.

"I dunno anything about that. I never met her." Chevy shifted his gaze. "Can I go?"

"No." Bree tapped a forefinger on the table. "We have you cold on multiple felonies."

He sobered. "Felonies?"

"Arson, breaking and entering, vandalism, assault." Bree enumerated the charges with her fingers.

Chevy's jaw dropped. "You can't . . . I was just messin' around."

Bree didn't answer except to lift one eyebrow.

"You could have burned that whole apartment building down." Matt sounded incredulous.

Chevy's gaze went cloudy, as if he were thinking and it took work. His gaze shifted to Matt, whose buddy-buddy face had gone serious. Chevy swallowed. "I want a lawyer."

With those words, the interview was over.

Bree summoned a deputy to process Chevy. Back in her office, she closed the door.

Matt asked, "Is he really that stupid? Or is it an act?"

"I don't think it was an act."

Matt stroked his beard. "He wanted to move back in and didn't think he should have to take no for an answer. He accosted her in the parking lot of her apartment complex. When she wouldn't talk to him, he broke into her apartment and trashed the place. *He set her bed on fire.*"

Bree flipped through her messages. Nothing she wanted to respond to at the moment. "Is that the behavior of a serial killer?"

"We can't prove he killed anyone. Her neighbor saw her Tuesday evening between five and six. So Jana was taken after then."

"The blood on the carpet was dry. How long would that have taken?"

"At least an hour or two," Matt said.

Todd knocked on the doorframe and stepped in. "I called the local ERs and urgent cares. No one has a record of Jana coming in."

"Thanks, Todd," Bree said.

"Do we have a decent suspect?" Todd asked. "What about Chevy?"

"We don't know yet. The good thing is that he's definitely going to jail for other crimes."

"But will he make bail?"

Bree set the message slips on her desk. "I'd like him in custody until we solve this, but we all know that's not likely to happen."

"Do you think he has the physical strength to carry a body into the woods?" Todd asked.

"He was strong enough to toss a TV at me," Matt said. "And he's clearly fit enough to run and climb a fence, even after drinking."

"Keep pulling background data," Bree said to Todd. "Matt and I are going to talk to Jana's mother and boss and determine if Jana is actually missing."

CHAPTER SEVENTEEN

Matt read from the mobile laptop in the sheriff's SUV. "Crystal Rynski is fifty-five years old. She rents her property and has lived there for at least five years. She has two old speeding tickets. Her criminal history is clean."

"No drug arrests?"

Matt scrolled. "Not that I can find."

"There it is." Bree pointed to a gravel access road.

He read the small sign. "Holiday Estates, an active adult community."

"Doesn't look very active to me." She turned the wheel. Gravel crunched under the tires as they rolled into the development. Narrow lanes meandered among tiny, nearly identical manufactured houses. The SUV bounced though unavoidable muddy ruts.

Matt read numbers on mailboxes until they reached unit 42, which was barely bigger than a single-wide trailer. Bree parked next to a rust-bitten Buick with a handicap parking placard hanging from the rearview mirror.

Drizzle pattered on the windshield, and solid cloud cover cast a gloomy gray light on the green house. Plastic flowers filled the window boxes, their unnatural pinks and blues shiny and wet. The bright colors emphasized the utter grayness of the rest of the surroundings. The roof was missing shingles, and mold crawled up the siding like a swarm of insects.

Matt took in the overall neglect and poverty. "This is depressing."

Bree sighed. "Yes, it is."

They stepped out of the vehicle and approached the house. The wooden stoop squeaked and shuddered under their weight. Light rain misted Matt's face as they knocked on the front door. Shuffling footsteps approached. The woman who opened the door looked twenty years older than her actual age. Time had been brutal to her. Deep lines fanned out from her eyes and puckered around her mouth. Wrinkles etched her sun-damaged skin like brush marks. A cigarette dangled from the corner of her mouth, quivering as she addressed them in a suspicious and unwelcoming tone. "What do you want?"

"Crystal Rynski?" Bree asked.

"Yeah." Crystal's eyes narrowed as she took in Bree's uniform.

Bree touched her own chest. "I'm Sheriff Taggert—"

"I can see that." Crystal dragged on her cigarette. With angry eyes, she plucked it from her mouth with two fingers and blew a plume of smoke at Bree's face. "What do you want? I didn't do anything." Her gaze landed on Matt with less hostility.

He said, "We're here about your daughter, Jana."

"Jana?" Crystal shook her head in disbelief. "I *know* my daughter didn't do anything wrong. She's as good as they come." Her voice rang with pride as she jabbed her cigarette toward Bree's nose. "I won't help you pin something on her she didn't do."

"No, ma'am," Bree said. "We don't think she did anything wrong. We're concerned about Jana."

Crystal coughed. "What's wrong? I just talked to her the other day. She was fine."

A sound caught Matt's attention. He glanced sideways. On the porch of the house next door, an old man leaned on his walker and blatantly eavesdropped.

"Can we go inside?" Matt nodded toward the neighbor.

With a dismissive wave at the old man, Crystal backed up a few steps, turned, and shuffled toward a living room barely bigger than a parking space. A recliner and an upholstered chair faced a flat-screen TV. She eased into a recliner.

Bree took the second chair, sinking into a clear depression in the cushion. Matt perched on the ottoman. Cigarette smoke hung in a thick haze, burning his eyes and lungs.

"Now tell me what happened," Crystal demanded.

Bree began. "Jana's friend, Ally, was identified as a murder victim. We went to Jana's apartment to ask her some questions about Ally. We found the door unlocked and blood stains on the carpet. Jana wasn't there."

Matt added, "She didn't show up for work today either."

With distrustful eyes, Crystal set her cigarette in the ashtray on the end table. "Jana always shows up for work. Always." She pulled her phone out of her pocket and stabbed the screen. "Hello? Sandy? This is Crystal. I'm looking for Jana." Her lips mashed as she listened. "You'll call me if you hear from her? Thanks." She lowered the phone. Her gaze held less suspicion now that she'd confirmed Bree and Matt weren't lying. "Jana would never be that irresponsible. Everyone knows that."

"When was the last time you saw or spoke with Jana?"

Crystal tapped on her phone screen. "She called me Tuesday night at eight thirty-five. The last time I saw her was when she came by after work on Monday. The café had a fried chicken special, and she brought me some. Sandy—Jana's boss—is real nice about sending home leftovers."

"Jana calls you regularly?" Bree asked.

"A few times a week." Crystal's gaze sharpened. "You need to find her ex-boyfriend?" She pronounced *boyfriend* like it was profanity. "His name is Chevy."

"Chevy was in Jana's apartment." Bree hesitated.

"She kicked him out!" Crystal exclaimed, then coughed at the exertion.

Bree nodded. "He was destroying property, and we arrested him."

"That son of a . . ." Crystal scrubbed both hands down her face.

"Do you know why Jana kicked him out?" Matt asked.

Crystal didn't hesitate. "He hit her."

Bree's eyebrows rose. "You know that for sure?"

Crystal grabbed her cigarette, took a last puff, and stubbed it out. "Yep. Couple of weeks ago."

"She told you?" Bree asked.

Crystal nodded hard. "We talked about it. She knew I'd understand. Jana's father left us when she was just a baby. I remarried a few years later. My new husband hit me a couple of times. Each time, he'd swear that was the last time. One day, I burned his steak. He was mad as a yellow jacket. Slapped me across the face. Crystal—she was only eleven at the time—tried to get between us, and he raised his hand to hit her." Crystal's tone rose, suggesting his decision hadn't been wise. "I grabbed his steak knife right off the table and buried it in his thigh. Nobody touches my girl."

"He moved out?" Bree asked.

"I dropped him at the ER, went home, and tossed all his shit outside. Couple of hours later, his buddy brought him back. He banged on the door and demanded that I let him in. I greeted him with a butcher knife. Asked him if he wanted more stitches. Told him if he forced his way inside, I'd stab him in his sleep. He backed right the fuck down. Never had another bit of trouble from him."

She picked up her cigarettes, tapped one out of the pack, and lit it. "When Jana came to me and said Chevy had slapped her, I told her what to do. If he hit her once, he will do it again. I waited too long with my ex. I didn't want her to make the same mistake."

"How did Jana feel about the breakup?" Matt asked.

Crystal squinted. "She was upset but she knew it was something she had to do. No woman wants to be in that situation. She'd let him move in with her, so she had feelings for him. Jana doesn't make that kind of decision lightly."

"Did she talk about it Monday?" Bree asked.

Crystal shook her head. "No. But she was definitely distracted."

A daughter wouldn't necessarily confide everything to her mother, especially when her mother had very strong opinions on a subject. Women confided in friends.

"Does Jana have any other friends we can contact?" Matt coughed.

"Other than Ally, Noreen, and me? Let me think." Crystal put her cigarette to her lips and sucked on it. "There are a couple of girls she might see a movie with once in a while. But not since she hooked up with the loser. He didn't like her to have friends."

"Does Jana have hobbies?" Bree asked. "Places she frequents?"

"Not really." Crystal blew smoke at the ceiling. "She's saving her money to finish school. She took a couple of classes at the community college, but she ran out of money and had to take this school year off. Are you going to find my daughter?" Her tone went soft, and Matt's heart broke. This woman had had a hard life. Now the one good thing she had left in the world—her daughter—was in jeopardy.

"I'd like you to fill out a missing person report," Bree said. "And get me the names of Jana's friends."

Crystal's eyes misted. "I'll do whatever you want. Just find my girl. Please."

The Sunrise Café was closed when Matt and Bree drove by, so they went out to the address listed on the owners' driver's licenses. Sandy and Eric Zolek lived on a hundred acres. There were no flowers or ornamental shrubs. Everything in sight seemed productive. A greenhouse stretched long and low. Next to it, the soil in a fenced garden had been tilled. Chickens pecked around a fully enclosed chicken coop. There were two barns, a garage, and even an old silo. The place wasn't in the best shape. Paint peeled, and fences sagged. But the chickens looked healthy, and the coop was clean.

After Bree parked, they knocked on the front door. No one answered.

Matt heard an engine. "Let's walk around back. Most farmers are usually working somewhere on their property."

They rounded the side of the house to see a man on a tractor trying to pull a tree stump out of a field. The tractor tires spun, sending chunks of mud twenty feet behind the machine.

"Can I help you?" someone called.

Matt spun. A bone-thin woman in her midfifties walked out of the large barn, pitchfork in hand. She wore jeans, a fleece zip-up with the Sunrise Café logo on the chest, and knee-high rubber boots. A metal bar as thick as his arm was dropped across the double doors of the small barn. Through the open door of the larger barn, Matt could see penned cows chewing hay. Matt and Bree joined the woman under the overhang of the barn roof.

The woman propped her free hand on her hip. "Is this about Jana?"

"Yes, ma'am." Bree introduced herself and Matt. "Are you Sandy Zolek?"

"I am," she said.

Matt waved a hand. "Is it just the two of you to farm all of this?"

"Eric does most of the farming." She gestured toward the man on the tractor. "I help him some, but mostly I run the restaurant."

"Seems like a lot of work," Matt said.

"Sunrise Café is farm to table." She lifted a shoulder. "The farm part is essential."

A bellow sounded from inside the small barn. Something large struck the wall, seemingly shaking the structure.

"What was that?" Matt asked.

"My husband's bull." Sandy rolled her eyes. "I told Eric we should turn him into a freezer full of meat before he kills somebody. Nasty animal. Eric says we can't afford another bull, so we're stuck with him."

The tractor rumbled toward them, towing the stump.

"Have you heard from Jana in the past two days?" Bree asked.

Sandy shook her head. "I knew something was wrong when she didn't show up for work today."

"What about yesterday?" Matt shoved his hands into his jacket pockets. The scar tissue on his palm ached with the cold.

"She was off, so I don't know where she was," Sandy said. "The last day she worked was Tuesday."

"Was she worried about anything?" Bree gave a small shiver.

"Yes." Sandy zipped her fleece all the way to her chin. "That jerk, Chevy, showed up about a week ago and harassed her behind the restaurant. She came inside to get away from him. Eric was there. He went out and chased him off."

The tractor rumbled into the yard. The man climbed off and removed a chain from the stump. Then he remounted the tractor and drove it into the garage.

Sandy made a thoughtful face. "I'm not sure of the exact day."

"Do you have surveillance video?" Bree asked.

"Only on the doors," Sandy said. "Our system needs upgrading, but all that technology costs money."

Her husband left the garage and approached. Sandy introduced them. "This is my husband, Eric."

Eric didn't offer a hand. But then, his hands, and most of the rest of him, were splattered with mud.

"Stump clearing is hard work," Matt said.

Eric gave him a curt nod. "My granddaddy blew off his fingers using dynamite, so I'm grateful for the tractor."

Sandy said, "I was telling them about Jana's ex following her to the restaurant."

Eric snorted his annoyance.

Sandy continued. "Anyway, Chevy was a good hundred feet away. Had his truck half behind a delivery truck, just waiting for Jana to come out."

"Thought he was being sneaky," Eric added. "I showed him." His hand flexed into a fist.

"I spotted him." Sandy rolled her lips. "We've never really had any trouble before, but we're going to add more cameras."

Eric grunted his agreement.

"Did you hear Chevy directly threaten Jana?" Bree asked.

Eric shook his head.

Sandy said, "Kind of. They were arguing. She told him he couldn't stalk her. He said it was a free country. Soon as Eric went out, Chevy ran off."

"It sounds like Jana has been having a rough time of it lately," Matt said. "Does she have hobbies? Friends? Did she talk about anything that might indicate a person she might call if she was in trouble or a place she might go if she needed some space?"

Sandy tapped a finger on the handle of her pitchfork. "She talks to her mom and her neighbor, Noreen. Her best friend wasn't returning her calls, and that worried her."

"Ally Swanson?" Matt asked.

"That sounds right," Sandy confirmed.

Bree said, "Ally's dead."

Sandy covered her mouth with her hand. "Oh, no."

Eric folded his arms, and his posture went rigid.

Bree nodded. "She was one of the bodies found in the woods the other day."

"If Jana found out . . ." Sandy looked away, as if thinking, for a minute. Then she lowered her hand. "She would have been very upset."

"There was blood on Jana's carpet," Matt said.

Sandy's gaze moved from his to Bree's. "Did something violent happen to her?"

"That's what we're trying to find out," Bree said.

"Is Jana close to any of the other employees?" Matt asked.

"I've never heard of them going out for drinks or anything like that." Twisting her mouth, Sandy mulled over the question for a few seconds. "Most of the waitresses are older, like me. Jana's the youngest by far. Jana's friendly, but not familiar, if you know what I mean."

Matt nodded. "I do."

Sandy scraped the tines of the pitchfork. "Do you think that serial killer got her?"

"We don't know," Bree said.

"My money would be on that ass Chevy," Sandy said.

Eric shifted his feet, as if impatient. "I have to get back to work. I hope you find her." He turned and walked into the barn with the cows.

Sandy watched her husband disappear. Then she turned back to Bree and Matt. "Follow me up to the house. I have to start dinner, though I don't know what else I can tell you anyway."

"Does Jana keep any personal possessions at the restaurant?" Matt asked as he and Bree fell into step beside her.

"No. We don't have lockers or anything. Everyone just throws their purses in the back cabinet. We're like family." Sandy sniffed, her efficient demeanor faltering.

"She didn't mention anyone following her or threatening her, besides Chevy?" Bree asked. "No additional worries?"

"No. Just him." Sandy froze. "Wait. That's not exactly true. One day a couple of weeks ago, she said there was a black car following her. Chevy drives a truck—a Ford, which I find ironic. Jana thought he might have borrowed a car so she wouldn't know it was him. She *assumed* it was him, but she didn't actually *know*."

"Did she say what kind of car?" Matt asked.

Sandy shook her head. "No. Sorry."

Matt nodded. "But she did say *car*, not *SUV* or *truck*?"

"She definitely said *car*, and he drives a pickup. She was making the distinction." Sandy's eyes went misty. "Jana is a sweet girl. You'll find her, right?"

"We'll work this case until we solve it," Bree said.

Sandy's stride faltered, then smoothed out again. "I guess in your line of work, you learn not to make promises."

Neither Bree nor Matt responded. Sandy walked onto the porch and toed off her rubber boots. "I'll be glad when this rain ends. Never seen this much mud. You hold on a second." She went inside, returning in less than a minute with a cardboard box, which she handed to Matt. "I'm sure you'll be working late tonight."

"Yes, ma'am." Matt took the box and opened the lid to view a homemade pie. "Apple?"

"Yup," Sandy said.

"We're not supposed to accept gifts," Bree protested.

Sandy raised a hand. "You can't find Jana without sustenance, and I'm sure you're going to have a long night. It's the least I can do. I feel useless to help that poor girl."

Back in the SUV, Bree frowned at the pie box. "We really aren't supposed to accept gifts."

"It's pie," Matt huffed. "Sometimes people want to help, but they're limited in what they can do. Besides, we will be working late, and we will be missing dinner. The sugar will help."

Bree surrendered. "Let's call home and let them know we won't be joining them for dinner."

Matt opened the box and inhaled. The scent of cinnamon flooded his nose. "At least we won't starve."

Sandy was right about one thing. It was going to be a late night.

CHAPTER EIGHTEEN

Bree carried her leftovers into the break room. She and Matt had stopped for sandwiches on the way back. Right behind her, Matt set the bakery box on the counter.

Todd was pouring coffee into a mug. He sniffed. "What's that?"

"Apple pie." Matt opened the box. "Help yourself."

Todd started toward the pie.

"Did you eat dinner?" Bree asked.

Todd shook his head.

Bree handed him her massive leftover half sandwich. "There's a quarter pound of roast turkey on this half alone."

"Impressive." Todd unwrapped one end of the sandwich and took a huge bite. "We need to review the case. Cases?"

Bree eyed her chief deputy. His triathlete body always ran lean, but he'd definitely lost weight with the flu. "I need to check my messages. You take the time to eat. Get some of that pie too."

He grinned. "Will do."

"Conference room in ten." She headed for her office to check her inbox. Then she gathered her files and headed for the murder board. Matt was already there, studying the whiteboard and adding notes and images.

Bree stopped in front of the board. A photo of Trish had been added. Matt used a magnet to secure a photo of Jana. He had used an

X to mark a place for the skeletal victim. When she was identified, her photo would join the others.

Todd walked in, carrying his laptop, a manila folder, and a piece of pie. "I never thought I'd be able to eat while working a murder."

"Starving yourself will not help you solve the case." Bree sat at the head of the table. "The sleep deprivation is unavoidable. You need to practice self-care if you want to be useful. That means prioritizing nutrition, even if you're not hungry." She wasn't sure apple pie rated very high on the nutritional scale, but you worked with what you had.

"I've been asked to do worse things than eat." Todd dug into his pie.

Bree opened Ally's murder book, a thick binder where all information pertaining to the investigation would be kept, including interview summaries, photographs, lab reports, and witness statements. "We have three murders and one disappearance. The missing girl, Jana Rynski, was friends with one of our murder victims, Ally Swanson. But we don't know if Jana's disappearance is related to Ally's murder."

"It is." Matt pointed to the board with his dry-erase marker. "I have no definitive proof, but I don't like coincidences. Jana disappears just as we wanted to question her about Ally's murder? As Ally's best friend, Jana could have known something. Or the killer might have assumed she knew something."

"The timing is suspect," Bree agreed. "My gut says the same, but our educated theories don't mean anything. We have to follow the evidence."

"Of which we have damned little," Matt said.

Todd held up a hand. "Let me start with the hikers who found the remains. We know Steve has a record for stalking his ex. He says she filed the complaint as revenge. I checked the arrest records. There was no physical evidence to support the girl's case, but the prosecutor went after him hard. The story *could* fit his narrative, but we don't have any hard evidence either way. I'd like to keep him on the suspect list."

"Yes. He stays on the list." Bree pressed her fingertips to her temples, willing her brain cells to work harder. "Do we have any links between Ally and Trish?"

"None that I can find." Todd wiped his mouth with a napkin. "I did find a potential connection between Trish and Jana. Trish attended community college. So did Jana, but not at the same time. Trish Bitten just started this past fall, and Jana attended the previous school year. Their paths would not have crossed in classes."

"Let's get their records from the college and see if there's any other connection between them," Bree said.

Todd pushed his empty plate to the center of the table and opened his laptop. "I'll work on a warrant."

"Did you make any progress with background checks?" Bree asked.

Todd woke up his laptop. "Ally is the only one who's been arrested, and all I found was the recent drug possession arrest and the dropped prostitution charge. Jana has never even had a ticket. Trish has had a couple of parking tickets, mostly near the college campus, but that's it for her." He scrolled, focused on his screen. "None of the girls have much money. Ally had no credit cards. Her bank account balance is under five dollars. Trish's father is on all of her accounts, savings and checking. He regularly deposited small sums, but she didn't have much of her own, and honestly neither do her parents. Their house is mortgaged from attic to basement, and they've been shuffling money to pay bills."

Todd paused to scroll, then continued. "Jana has the most money, with nearly a thousand dollars in savings and a few hundred in checking. She has one credit card, which she uses minimally and pays off in full each month. Her account history shows regular deposits and a frugal lifestyle."

"She's saving to take more college classes," Bree said. "What about Chevy?"

"I found nothing other than the misdemeanor charges we already knew about," Todd said. "Chevy is broke, and his three credit cards are maxed out. He's behind on his vehicle loan payments. I would predict his F-150 will be repossessed in the near future."

"Shocking," Matt said. "With him not having a job."

Bree relayed the information Sandy had given them about Jana possibly being followed by a black car. "It's vague, but we should keep it in mind."

Todd wrote *black car* on the board with a question mark. "I confirmed Ally's father suffered a huge financial setback two years ago and declared bankruptcy."

Bree checked her notes. "That's about when his wife died of cancer."

"Yes, most of the debts appear to have been medical in nature," Todd said. "His recent statements look more stable. Not much money coming in or going out. The house he rents is owned by Heath Swanson."

"That's his brother," Bree said.

Todd nodded. "Which might explain why the payments coming out of his checking account seem ridiculously low. His brother is subsidizing his housing."

Bree's phone vibrated. "This is Stella Dane." She pressed "Answer" and put the phone to her ear.

"Sheriff, what can I do for you?" Stella asked.

"You handled Trish Bitten's missing persons case?"

"Yes." Stella's response sounded curt.

"I'd like to put you on speaker," Bree said. "Matt Flynn and Chief Deputy Todd Harvey are also present."

"Fine," Stella agreed.

Bree set her phone on the table. "One of the victims found in the woods was ID'd today as Trish Bitten."

A few beats of silence passed before Stella said, "I'm very sorry to hear that, but it doesn't completely surprise me that she was a serial killer's victim."

"Why do you say that?" Bree asked.

Stella sighed. "Because she was plucked off the face of the earth with no clues as to what happened to her. We never made any headway with the case. We investigated everyone in her life and got nowhere. After weeks with no progress, the chief pulled us off. We still worked it when we had time, but no real leads ever turned up."

"What can you tell us about the family?" Bree asked.

"Hold on. Let me grab the file." Over the line, a drawer opened and closed. Papers rustled. "The Bittens have quite a bit of debt," Stella began. "Mr. Bitten is a lawyer, a partner at Grady, Howell, and Bitten. One of the partners, George Howell, suffered a massive heart attack last year. It's forcing him to retire very early. He's only forty-five. The other partners, Grady and Bitten, were required to buy out his equity. With all of the partners being relatively young, the situation wasn't expected. Partners Grady and Bitten were forced to acquire debt to cover the buy-out. The financial drain did mean that Trish couldn't go to the college of her dreams, but her parents said she handled the disappointment well." Stella took a breath. "The transaction seemed unfortunate but aboveboard. Frankly, if Grady and Bitten were inclined to kill anyone, they would have taken out Howell. If he'd died, his life insurance would have covered his equity. We couldn't find any connection between the debt and Trish's disappearance."

"Noted. The family debt could be a rabbit hole." Which didn't mean Bree would ignore it.

"What about the boyfriend, Jacob Gatt?" Matt asked.

"Of course he was the first person we looked at. He was ice fishing with his father the day Trish disappeared," Stella said. "Jacob and his father's stories matched. He seemed distraught when Trish went missing. Given that his only alibi was his father, we kept him on our suspect list, but we didn't have any evidence that tied him to the crime."

"Is there anything else that might help us?" Bree asked.

"Not that I can think of," Stella said. "I'll call you if I do. Meanwhile, I'll make a copy of my files."

"I'll send someone to pick them up," Bree said.

"Let me know if you need any assistance, but it might be better to look at the case with fresh eyes. God knows I never got anywhere." Stella sounded a little bitter. Bree understood. Some cases stuck with you, and some cases were never solved, no matter how many hours you worked.

Bree ended the call with a thanks and turned back to the board. They were organizing their case, but the investigation still felt chaotic. She needed more deputies to cover all the investigative angles for three murders and a potentially related missing person.

She turned to Todd. "Are you up to conducting interviews?"

"Yes," he said.

"Good. Matt and I can't possibly do it all. Grab a deputy and work on Trish's case. Talk to the people at the law firm. You can also take on interviewing the neighbors Trish babysat for, Kier and Marion Reich. Talk to the boyfriend and Trish's sister, Diane. Make sure you talk to Diane away from her parents. If Trish was doing anything the parents wouldn't have approved of, Diane might hold back in their presence."

"Will do." Todd took notes. "I'll pick up the files at the SFPD on my way home, read through Detective Dane's reports tonight, and jump on these interviews first thing tomorrow."

Matt added the names to the whiteboard and marked them with a capital *T* for Todd.

"Let's update our ViCAP query," Bree added.

Matt added, "The body dumping seems very organized for a first-time serial killer. I wouldn't be surprised if he's killed before."

Todd said, "I'll call over to the community college too, and confirm there's no overlap between Jana and Trish."

"Matt and I will stop at the Shady Acres Motel in the morning." Bree checked the time on her phone. She'd already missed Kayla's bedtime, but she couldn't help it. An active killer demanded her time.

Matt said, "We need to find out who got Ally pregnant. Someone must know."

CHAPTER NINETEEN

Matt stepped out of the shower, dried off, and dressed in sweatpants and a T-shirt. Outside the small bathroom window, another rainstorm brewed. Tree branches swayed in the wind. A gust sent light rain pattering on the glass. Bree had already showered and headed downstairs, where they would grab leftovers and eat in the home office. As he walked out into the bedroom, a light knock sounded on the door. He crossed the room and opened it.

Kayla stood in the hall, shivering in blue pony pajamas with attached feet. She clutched her stuffed pig close to her face. "Is Aunt Bree here?"

Matt crouched in front of her. "She's downstairs. What's wrong?"

"I don't feel good." Her lower lip quivered, and her voice carried an uncharacteristic whine. Her cheeks were oddly flushed.

She looked feverish, but what did he know?

"Let's go find Aunt Bree." He held out a hand, and she took it with a sniff.

He led the way down to the kitchen, where Bree sat at the table with a cup of tea and a bowl. Ladybug and Brody flanked her chair. Brody's eyes were closed. Begging was beneath him, but Ladybug's attention followed the path of Bree's spoon from her bowl to her mouth like she was watching a tennis match.

"Kayla?" Bree set down her spoon.

"My head hurts," Kayla mumbled.

Matt opened the fridge and took out a container of risotto. He brought it to the table cold.

"I'll get the thermometer." Bree retrieved a fancy infrared model from the cabinet and turned it on.

"Mommy could tell by touching my forehead." Kayla sniffed, a tear sliding down her cheek.

Matt's heart cracked like an egg. Kayla hadn't cried in a while. For the first few months after her mother died, she cried every day. She'd made incredible progress since then. But what sick kid didn't want their mother?

"Where's Dana?" Kayla swiped a sleeve under her red nose and coughed, the sound wet and, honestly, gross.

"Dana went to bed," Bree said.

Kayla crawled into Matt's lap. Surprised, he leaned back and wrapped his arms around her. She pressed into him, hugging her pig. Her whole body felt hot. She wasn't usually clingy, and she hadn't initiated more than a hug with him before. He felt sad and honored at the same time.

Bree pointed the thermometer at Kayla's forehead and frowned. "You have a fever."

Kayla nodded, then rested her head against Matt's chest. "My ear hurts."

Matt rubbed her back, and Bree dosed her with children's fever reducer.

She caught Matt's eye. "Want me to take her so you can eat?"

Dark circles underscored her eyes, and she looked almost as pale as her niece. Matt shook his head. "I'm fine. You finish your dinner."

She settled back in her chair, ate a few spoonfuls of risotto, then pushed the bowl away. "It's been a long day."

Matt ate his risotto one-handed, with Kayla tucked into the crook of his other arm. By the time he'd finished, Kayla felt cooler.

"Can you go back to bed?" Bree asked her.

Kayla nodded.

"Want me to carry you?" Matt asked.

Kayla gave him a sleepy grin and nodded.

"I'll bring you some water." Bree pulled a refillable bottle from the cabinet.

Matt stood with Kayla in his arms. She weighed nothing. She burrowed into him as he carried her up the steps, into her room, and slid her into bed.

"I don't want to go to school tomorrow," Kayla whined.

"You have a fever, so you can stay home," Matt said.

He tucked her stuffed pig under the covers with her, and Kayla snuggled under the comforter with it. At nine, she usually acted much older than she was. Grief aged a child. Since Matt had moved in, it had seemed as if she'd been on her best behavior all the time, not relaxed, not 100 percent natural. Tonight was the first time he felt like Kayla truly accepted him enough to not be perfect, to act like a regular kid, to be sick, grumpy, even a little needy.

"Would you read me a story?" Kayla asked.

"Sure." Flattered, Matt perched on the edge of the bed. She'd never asked him to read to her before. Usually, she curled up with a book by herself. "Which one?"

"*The Black Stallion*." She pointed to her bookshelf, which overflowed with books about horses, including the entire Black Stallion series.

Matt opened the well-worn paperback. "I read this when I was a boy."

"You did?" Kayla nestled deeper into her pillow. "It's one of my favorites."

"A classic." He knew from the parenting book he'd been reading that familiar stories were a source of comfort. Sometimes children wanted—needed—to already know how the story ended. He started with chapter one. The story was familiar and soothing to him too. In a few minutes, Kayla's eyes closed, and her breaths grew deep and regular.

Bree walked into the room and set a water bottle on the nightstand. She raised her brows at the book in his hand.

He lifted a shoulder. Sliding a bookmark between the pages, he closed it and left it on the nightstand. Then he and Bree slunk out of the room.

In the hallway, Bree glanced back. "I hope she's OK. It's not like her to be so clingy."

He slung an arm over her shoulder. "Kids get sick, and this is her first major illness without her mother."

"I know." But she sounded uncertain. "Thanks for helping. It's hard to reconcile my life before with my life now. It's been a learning curve that I'm still steadily climbing, like Mount Everest."

"Thanks for sharing your life with me."

"You're thanking me for allowing you to take on a portion of my workload?" Bree snorted.

"Yes." In the bedroom, Matt turned her to face him. He rested his hands on her shoulders. The fact that Bree trusted him with the kids meant everything. "I'm here to stay, sick kids, demanding horses, a cat who pukes in my shoes, all of it."

She looked up at him, her eyes bright. "How did I get so lucky?"

"I like to think it's fate, not luck." The answer was simple to him. "I love you. The kids are a huge part of your life."

"The most important part," she said.

He didn't take offense. His parents had always put their children first. "So, now those kids are a huge part of my life too. Then the only way this"—he gestured between them—"will work is if we function as a team. Otherwise, we're living together but still have separate lives. That's not what I want." He wanted it all, every part of her. He wanted what his parents had. Though he couldn't define it, he knew by instinct what it should feel like.

This.

Exactly this.

Bree smiled. "I love you too."

"Love you more." He pressed a kiss to her lips. "Speaking of team-work, I'll call my dad first thing in the morning, and he'll be over here with his medical bag to check on her." Matt's father was a retired family doctor. He and Kayla had bonded over the past few months. She'd asked to call him Grandpa, and his heart had melted.

Bree smiled. "Your dad is the best."

"He loves you and the kids too." Matt had always been close to his parents, but he'd never appreciated them more than during the past few years. They'd gotten him through the shooting and loss of his career in law enforcement. Now, they'd absorbed Bree and her entire household into the family.

Matt and Bree brushed their teeth side by side and climbed into bed. It felt as if Matt had barely closed his eyes when a little voice said, "I threw up."

CHAPTER TWENTY

Bree woke with gritty eyes to predawn light. Achy and fuzzy-headed from lack of sleep, she stretched a shoulder. Her neck popped and crackled when she circled her head. Next to her, Kayla snored softly. Her mouth hung open to compensate for her stuffy nose. Feverish, she'd been up most of the night.

Bree slid out of bed and tiptoed downstairs. Matt was stretched out on the couch, one arm and both feet hanging over the edges of the cushions.

"Morning." He sat up and stretched. He looked as tired as Bree felt.

"I owe you," she said.

He rubbed an eye. "You do not. Teamwork, remember?"

"Cleaning up vomit seems over and beyond."

"There's no such thing," he said.

This man was a treasure. What had she done to deserve him?

Bree leaned over and kissed him. "How's your back? You don't really fit on the couch."

"I'm fine." But his grimace as he cracked his neck said otherwise. "How's Kayla?"

"Seems OK for now. She's finally sleeping."

"Good." He stretched both hands overhead.

Bree headed for the kitchen. Dana was already up, sitting at the table with a cup of something that smelled heavily caffeinated. Through the window, clouds shifted across the brightening sky, and the tall blades of grass near the pasture fence arced in the wind. "Looks like the storm is clearing."

"I hope so." Dana set down her cup. "We have more than enough mud out there. What happened last night that sent Hottie to the couch?"

Bree gave her the rundown.

"Ugh. Poor kid." Dana rose and crossed the kitchen. "Do I need to take her to the pediatrician?"

"Not yet. It's probably that flu that's making the rounds. Matt's dad will probably stop by."

"OK. Good." Dana pushed buttons on her fancy coffee maker. "I assume you want the deepest and darkest sludge possible."

"You assume correctly. I want one step away from chewing the beans myself. Barely a step."

"Got it." Dana worked levers, and the machine whirred.

"I don't remember ever being this tired. I'm old." Bree opened the fridge and surveyed the full shelves. Nothing appealed. She closed it. "Matt and I were supposed to work last night, but that plan was derailed."

"It happens."

Bree reached for a coffee cup.

But Dana stopped her with one raised finger. "Patience. I'm foaming milk so you don't burn off your stomach lining." She poured the foam into a small cup and topped it with the sludge. The smell of very strong coffee filled the kitchen. Matt appeared in the doorway, as if called by the scent. He inhaled audibly, a wolf scenting prey.

Dana glanced at him as she handed Bree her cappuccino. "Yours is next."

"You're the best," he said.

"I know." Dana worked her espresso maker like a veteran barista. The machine hissed as if the levers were hydraulic.

Leaning back against the counter, Bree sipped. She willed the bitter brew to jump-start her brain cells.

Feet shuffled, and Luke appeared in the doorway. His eyes were bloodshot, his face as pale as the milk Dana was currently foaming. He coughed, sounding like a distressed harbor seal.

"Uh-oh." Bree walked closer and put a hand on his forehead. "You're hot." Maybe she was developing the magic palm after all.

"I can't be sick." He coughed again. "I have a big English test today."

"Sorry," Bree said. "Your sister also has a fever. You're both out for the day. I'll call both schools."

"Do you want to eat or go back to bed?" Dana asked him.

"Eat, then go back to bed." He walked toward the back door, his shoulders slumped, his steps slow.

"Hold on." Bree stood. She did not want Luke out in the cold, damp barn. "I'll feed the horses this morning, and I'll call Adam to pitch in later."

"OK. Thanks. I have to email my teacher." Luke sank into a chair at the table, but instead of reaching for his laptop, he rested his head on his folded arms.

"You need to rest. You'll make up the test when you're better." Bree donned her coat.

"I can't miss more than six days," he said into the crook of his elbow.

"Six *unexcused* days," Bree corrected. "And you've only missed three so far this year." At the moment, there wasn't much she detested more than the school's attendance policy.

Without picking up his head, he sighed.

"Stop worrying." Bree stepped into her barn boots. "I'll tell you the same thing I told my deputies. Everyone gets sick. If you focus on getting better, then you'll get back to work faster."

"I'll take care of the horses," Matt said. "You make your phone calls."

Bree called her younger brother on speakerphone while she worked. "Both kids are sick. Can you help with the horses this afternoon?"

"Sure." Adam sounded pleased to be asked. "Are the kids OK?"

"Probably that flu that's going around. If you want to remain flu-free, stay out of the house."

"Just tell me what needs to be done." Adam had come a long way over the past year, overcoming his introverted nature to be a true uncle to the kids. "I'm here for you all."

Loner tendencies ran in the family, Bree thought. *We've all come a long way.*

She gave him a list of instructions. "There's a feeding chart posted in the barn too, in case you forget."

"Got it," Adam said.

"You don't mind mucking stalls?" Bree asked. She'd lived on a farm until the age of eight. Manure didn't bother her. Adam had spent only his first year there. He lacked the olfactory desensitization.

He snorted. "I won't love it, but I'll get it done."

Bree laughed. "Yeah. No one loves it, but you won't need to hit the gym today."

"I'll text Dana and see if she needs anything from the store too."

"Thanks, Adam."

"This is what families do, right?" Adam chuckled. "As if we'd know. We're just becoming a real family."

"That's not true," Bree said. "You always supported Erin and the kids." Bree, however, had been less than attentive, something she now regretted with her whole, broken heart.

"That was just money." Adam's artwork was a hot commodity. "This is harder. This takes effort and conscious thought, at least for me. I don't always know what to do for the kids."

"Me either, but we're learning, and we're trying. I think the trying is the important thing. Being there and making sure they know that's always going to be the case."

"I can do that. Tell Dana to call me if she needs anything before this afternoon."

"Will do." Bree ended the call.

Kayla appeared in the doorway. "Aunt Bree? I feel bad again."

"Oh, honey." Bree turned to the little girl and touched her forehead. "You're burning up." She had little experience with sick kids. For the first year, their difficulties had been more emotional than physical. But somewhere in the depths of her brain, a voice said, *Eat some toast, sweetheart. You can't take medicine on an empty stomach.*

Bree paused. She knew—*knew*—it was her mother's voice. She didn't have many good memories of her childhood. The memories she did have, she didn't want. She'd been eight when her father had shot her mother while Bree hid her siblings under the back porch. Bree had blocked some memories of that time—including those of her mother— in self-defense. A child could handle only so much trauma before shutting down. But now, the voice sounded so clear.

Why? Why could this memory suddenly bob to the surface like a buoy on a lake? She closed her eyes and tried to conjure an image, but nothing appeared, leaving her feeling empty, grief welling inside her like unshed tears. How could she miss a thirty-year-old memory she hadn't known she had?

She'd always excelled at compartmentalizing, but lately that particular superpower was failing her. Getting in touch with her own emotions gave her the tools she needed to be a better guardian, but it had its downside. She had never fully worked through her own childhood grief. Did she need to do that to help the kids handle theirs? Because she didn't feel like she had the time for both of those things.

Her head bowed. She pressed a hand to her forehead, where exhaustion and sorrow knitted into a tight ache.

A hand on her shoulder broke the moment. Bree's head jerked up. Dana stood beside her, looking worried.

Dana's fingers tightened. "Are you OK?"

"Yeah. Just a headache. I could use another espresso."

Dana lifted a doubtful brow but didn't argue.

Bree halted her trip down nightmare lane and focused on Kayla. "Can you eat something?" Bree didn't even know if the advice was true, but repeating it was comforting in a weird way, as if some small part of her mother had survived inside her.

"I think so." Kayla's voice was small and heartbreaking.

Dana steered her to a chair. "I'll make you some breakfast."

"OK." Kayla sniffed.

Bree kissed the top of her head. "I'm sorry I have to go to work today."

"It's OK." But Kayla sounded so sad Bree wanted to send in her letter of resignation that very moment. Then she remembered a killer was targeting young women in her county, and Bree had to stop him. The weight of responsibility felt crushing.

How could she leave? She pictured the three bodies in the clearing and the blood stains on Jana's carpet. How could she not?

Someday, Kayla would be a young woman, like those discarded in that clearing.

She hugged her niece. "I'll call you later."

Kayla nodded.

Dana motioned toward the door. "I've got this, and I have plenty of help. Go."

Bree nodded, her voice failing her as she put on her work boots and uniform jacket. She didn't look back, and she and Matt went out the back door. The damp air smacked her in the face like a wet towel. She walked to her vehicle and slid behind the wheel.

"The kids will be fine." Matt fastened his seat belt.

"I know." Bree started the engine. "But I still feel guilty for leaving them."

"That's probably never going to change."

"I know that too." The windshield fogged, and Bree turned on the defroster and windshield wipers, which just smeared the condensation in an icy, wet arc. "I can't articulate how awful this feels. They need me, and I'm choosing not to be there."

"There's a serial killer on the loose. The kids have a virus, and my dad—the doctor—will look after them. This isn't much of a choice."

"My brain knows that, but my heart doesn't care." Bree extended her hands toward the heater vents. "I never thought I'd be in this situation. I'd planned to be alone and miserable, focused on chasing killers for the rest of my life in a hazy, neon, noir existence."

"I can't help you with your existential crisis, but if there's more vomit to clean up, I'm your man."

Bree smiled, her face softening. She reached over and took his hand, which felt twenty degrees warmer than her own freezing one. "I hope you know how much I appreciate you."

"I do." Matt squeezed her hand between his palms, warming it. "The little things matter."

"I hear that." Bree watched the windshield clear like magic as the air blowing from the vents warmed.

She shifted into reverse. Bree turned to look out the rear window. The backup camera provided a better view, but old habits were hardwired. Her tires spun in the slippery earth. Mud flew, and Bree eased off the accelerator. She worked the gear shift and gas pedal to rock the vehicle back and forth until the tires caught.

The SUV eased backward. Something creaked, then snapped. Water and leaves fell from above. A large bundle dropped from the tree branches onto the vehicle with a rattling thud that buckled the hood. The end of the bundle struck the glass in front of Bree's face with a sickening smack that sounded like a watermelon had been tossed from a second-story window. A crack shot across the windshield and spiderwebbed outward. More leaves, small branches, and water droplets rained down.

Bree's heart rate bolted, and she jerked backward, the back of her skull striking the headrest. The bundle was torpedo shaped, but the shape of the end portion embedded in Bree's windshield was the size of a bowling ball.

Or a human skull.

Next to her, Matt gasped. His hands shot out to brace on the dashboard. "What the—"

Bree couldn't respond. Her throat constricted. She felt as if she were breathing through a cocktail straw. Her eyes locked on the bundle. Like a witness to a terrible auto accident, even though she didn't want to see what was happening, she still couldn't look away.

In her peripheral vision, she saw Matt was also frozen, his gaze similarly riveted. The sun slid out from behind a cloud, the brightness of it almost blinding. It shone down like a spotlight. Bree wanted to close her eyes against the forced clarity. Her brain didn't want to recognize the camouflage tarp, but she couldn't deny what she was seeing. She knew what it was wrapped around—another body.

Matt exhaled. "Fuck."

"Yeah."

Without another word, she opened the car door. Matt did the same. They moved in a strange synchronicity, each stepping onto the soaked ground and turning to face the other over the hood of the SUV, their motions mirroring each other. Bree met his equally grim gaze. Then, as a unit, their eyes drifted upward, to the broken, dripping branches of the tree above the vehicle, and back down. Matt broke the spell, turning away to study the setup.

A surreal feeling passed over Bree, as if she were watching this scene in a movie instead of living it. She stared at the body, still mesmerized by disbelief. A rope trailed limply across the body like a dead snake. Not just rope, she noted. Black Paracord. It draped over the top of the SUV and disappeared behind the vehicle.

"The rain last night washed away any footprints that might have been here." Matt circled the vehicle, studying the ground. He stopped behind the SUV. "Simple setup. He put the body in the tree, tied the rope to your bumper. When you backed out, the rope pulled the body out of the tree and it fell on your vehicle."

"How did he get the body into the tree?"

"We already know he's strong."

Bree reached into her pocket and fumbled for a glove. She tugged it onto her hand. Her fingers shook as she reached forward, her arm stretching out toward the end of the tarp. With two fingers she grasped the edge and gently lifted the fabric, exposing a mass of blonde hair. Blood matted the hair on the side of the head. Longer strands covered the face like a curtain. A sudden gust of wind surged across the yard, a violent current of air that stirred dead leaves and sent them scurrying across the muddy ground at Bree's feet. The wind caught and lifted the hair away from the victim's face.

Staring back at her were Jana Rynski's cold, dead eyes.

CHAPTER TWENTY-ONE

Settled in the back of her Uber, Grace leaned on the headrest. Exhaustion weighted her entire body, and she hadn't even worked her shift yet. How was she going to manage? Neither she nor Riley had slept well, and Grace had risen before dawn to help with breakfast and morning chores.

And now she was pregnant. But how? She had never had unprotected sex with Howard. She'd made him wear a condom every time. That had been the one thing she'd refused to compromise on—not even when Howard had punched her.

But she'd ended up pregnant again anyway.

The phone she was clutching in her hand rang. She read the unfamiliar phone number on her screen. Normally, she didn't answer calls if she couldn't identify the caller, but she was scheduled to start her job today. The possibility that her new manager or someone from HR was calling prompted her to press "Answer." She needed this job. It wasn't easy to find work when you didn't have a high school diploma. She wanted to go back to school, but she didn't think it was possible, not on her own.

"You need me." Howard's voice slid through her like used fryer grease.

Her insides curled up like a frightened armadillo.

She'd blocked his number, so he was either using a borrowed phone or spoofing his number. Either way, she felt his deception—and his resentment—in her bones. She should just hang up, but the thought made her feel weak. She was tired of being weak.

She braced herself before answering, struggling to keep her voice level. "You're not supposed to contact me."

"You can't prove this is me. It's your word against mine." He sounded smug but sober, which might be a problem. Drunk Howard was volatile. Sober Howard was calculating. She wasn't sure which was worse.

His voice went low and sleazy. "I know your secret. I know where you went this morning."

Despite the heat blasting through the Uber, Grace went cold to her soul. Was he following her? She glanced through the Uber's rear window but didn't see his BMW. He'd borrowed a phone. Maybe he'd borrowed a vehicle. He could be anywhere. Goose bumps spread up her arms.

"What?" She hated the way her voice trembled.

"I know your secret," Howard repeated, his tone shifting the statement into a threat.

Fear thudded in Grace's chest. He'd heard the tremor in that one-syllable response, and as always, her weakness thrilled him. He fed on it, like a parasite. Scaring her made him happy. No, not happy. Howard was never happy. But he took sick pleasure from manipulating her.

"Want to know how I know?" He didn't wait for a response, and her fear swelled into horror and disgust as he told her.

"You're a monster," she whispered.

He laughed, and his tone went low. "I'll have your child taken away. You can't even support yourself. You're a horrible mother."

Her throat went dry as flour. She wanted to throw him a snarky retort, but she couldn't utter a single word. A wave of helplessness hit her. If she hadn't been sitting, her knees would have buckled. She would never get away from him.

Echoing her terror, he whispered in an aggressive tone, "You are mine. I will never let you go."

CHAPTER
TWENTY-TWO

An hour later, Bree huddled on the wet grass while the ME examined the tarp-wrapped body. A dozen feet away, Matt conferred with two forensic techs.

Circling the SUV, the usually cool and professional Dr. Jones emitted a rare emotional outburst. "What the actual fuck?"

Bree lifted both hands into the air. The gesture felt appropriately helpless.

Like her.

"He went from hiding his victims to flaunting them in your face?" Dr. Jones snapped her gloves on with atypical violence.

"That's exactly what happened." But Bree's head was full of questions. "It doesn't make much sense."

"No." Dr. Jones asked, "The kids didn't see, did they?"

The question redirected Bree's gaze. "No. Thankfully, they're in the house. As soon as the body is removed, Matt's parents are coming to get them." Unfortunately, there was no way to conceal her address from the public. Everyone knew where she lived. "As much as I hate to make them go—they both have the flu—I don't know how they can stay here."

"I'm sorry you're all going through this."

"Thanks."

"What you do is important." Dr. Jones gestured toward the body on the SUV with a blue-gloved hand. "And that is the proof. We need to catch this SOB."

"We do." Bree nodded. Her neck muscles were so tense, the small movement was almost painful. She rubbed at a knot at the base of her neck, but it refused to give.

Dr. Jones lifted the edge of the tarp. "You said you know who she is?"

"Yes. Her name is Jana Rynski." Bree pulled her phone from her pocket and called up a picture of Jana.

The ME agreed with a nod. "We'll confirm." She dropped the tarp. "I'll unwrap her on the table, just like the first three. On first glance, the presentation appears to mimic the others, but I don't want to make assumptions."

"There's always the chance a different killer is copying the disposal method." As hard as Bree tried to contain case details, information always leaked. "But Jana was Ally Swanson's close friend, so the cases are already connected."

"We'll dot the i's and cross the t's." Dr. Jones stepped back. "Nothing more I can do here. We'll get her back to the morgue. I have two ahead of her, but she'll go on the schedule ASAP."

"I'd appreciate it." Bree moved aside to let the ME work.

Matt approached. "I called over to the jail. Chevy is still there. He didn't make bail yet. He didn't do this." He pointed to the tree.

Bree said, "We need a time of death before we know if he's guilty of murder."

Matt continued. "Last night's rainstorm probably washed away any evidence along with the tracks, but forensics will try."

Bree assumed they wouldn't find any evidence. "He didn't use the driveway. The motion sensor would have picked up his vehicle. He couldn't get close to the house either, or the alarm system would have alerted."

Matt's brother had wired the house with enough security to rival a casino. Even the barn had cameras and sensors.

"I'll have Nolan add a security camera to the parking area. We'll get an electrician out to run wire, maybe add another circuit."

Frustration bubbled up in Bree's chest. Her voice emerged as sharp and tight as concertina wire. "Why not an eight-foot fence topped with an electric current? Armed guards and turrets? We can just turn the farm into a prison."

Matt put a hand on her shoulder. "It'll be OK."

"It doesn't feel that way."

Matt squinted toward the street. "He would have parked on the street and carried her over here, just as he probably did for the bodies in the clearing." He turned and stared at the body again. The ME's assistant was positioning a gurney close to the SUV. A black body bag lay open on top, waiting for Jana's body. "If we were already home, he could have stood on the top of the vehicle."

She tried to picture it. "Unless he carried a ladder from the street, that's the only way I see this being set up."

"A ladder would have made noise."

"We were occupied with Kayla last night," Bree said. "By the time I fell asleep, I wouldn't have heard a rocket launch in the yard."

"But Brody would have."

"Yeah. True. I always feel better when he's around," Bree agreed. "But why? Why take this chance? He was so very careful to hide the other three bodies."

"This"—Matt swept out a hand—"was in-your-face bold."

"Yes. I don't like it." The farmhouse pulled Bree's gaze again. Quaint and cozy, it projected wholesomeness, from the wide porch to the cow-shaped mailbox. This was home, and it had been invaded by evil.

"The kids will be fine," Matt said.

"I know. I'm grateful to your parents." If Bree had to handpick people to act as the kids' grandparents, she couldn't do better than George and Anna Flynn. She almost smiled, but the tug of her mouth stopped cold at the sound of the body sliding off the hood of her car onto the gurney. The killer knew where Bree lived. How much more did he know about her? How hard would it be to track the kids to the Flynns' house? "Your parents have an alarm, right?"

"You bet. Nolan set them up. It's solid, and I'll make sure they use it."

"OK. Good." She felt like a frozen statue that could shatter into a million pieces at the slightest tap. *Keep it together, damn it.*

"We're going to catch him."

"We are." Bree mentally drew a cross over her heart, another pledge to her sister, or rather, to her sister's memory.

Movement on the road caught her attention. Two runners stood on the yellow line, gawking.

"Shit," Matt said under his breath.

Bree had been careful to keep communication off the radio to delay the press's arrival until after the body had been removed. More than a dozen people crawled around her property: forensic techs, the ME and her assistant, and a handful of deputies. None of them would break radio silence. They all had families of their own. They understood.

The two joggers turned into looky-loos. One pulled out his cell phone and held it at arm's length, obviously taking pictures or video.

Anger burned like a torch in Bree's chest. She stalked down the driveway toward the road. Houses were spaced wide apart in this area. Her closest neighbor was a half mile away. She didn't recognize either of the joggers, but both had the ultra-lean builds of long-distance runners. They were in their midforties, dressed in black running pants and brightly colored jackets with expensive brand logos.

She took two yoga breaths to clear her voice of the fury gathering in her heart. It wouldn't help her here. She summoned a polite tone. "Excuse me. Would you please stop filming?"

Pointedly not looking at her, the man with the camera scoffed. "You can't do anything about it, Sheriff." His face twisted in a nasty sneer.

"This is a public road, and there is no legal expectation of privacy in public. The First Amendment and all that."

Bree swallowed a sarcastic retort. Another yoga breath. *Be nice. It's the last thing he'll expect.* "Do you live around here?"

His eyes shifted from his phone screen to Bree. Surprise flashed in his eyes. He'd expected—maybe even wanted—a confrontation. Well, she wouldn't give it to him. He'd have to find his fifteen minutes of inflammatory internet fame somewhere else.

He scowled, sizing her up, clearly suspicious. "Couple of miles away."

The other man slunk a few paces away, as if he wanted to distance himself from his running partner.

"Then we're neighbors." Bree held out her hand. "I'm Bree Taggert."

Filming Guy lowered the camera, hesitated, then gave her hand one single shake. He released her as if her palm had burned his. "I know who you are."

"What's your name?" She dropped her hand.

"You can't bully me. My brother is a lawyer," he said in a know-it-all voice. "I haven't committed a crime or an infraction of any kind. I don't have to tell you my name."

Bree suppressed an eye roll and a heavy sigh. This guy was spoiling for an altercation. "No, you don't. But we are neighbors."

He shoved his hands into the side pockets of his jacket but didn't respond.

"I'm asking you, as a *neighbor*, to not put my house on the internet. Children live here." She let that fact sink in for a minute. There were no laws requiring him to do this, except those of common decency. "It would upset them to see their home on the news."

He shifted his weight from foot to foot. Her moral appeal made him acutely uncomfortable, like a full bladder. He nodded toward the house. "What happened?"

It would be on the news soon enough, Bree knew, and she decided to be honest. She had nothing to lose by telling him. If she gave a little, maybe he would too. "Someone left a dead body at my house."

Shock widened his eyes. His gaze flickered to the medical examiner's van. Bree glanced over her shoulder. From this vantage point, the emblem on the side of the van wasn't legible, and a cruiser blocked the view of the gurney. She'd give him the benefit of the doubt. Maybe he hadn't known death was involved. Maybe he would be less of an asshat now that he did. She turned back.

He went still. "The serial killer? He was here?"

"I don't know for sure." She hesitated. "But off the record, one neighbor to another, I think so."

"That's fucked up." He scraped the toe of a running shoe on the asphalt, still contemplating his recording.

"Come on, Phil," his friend said. "Just delete the video. You don't want to give that sicko any attention."

If Phil were a cat, his ear would have flickered just once at his friend's plea. But Phil didn't move for a full minute. Neither did Bree. She'd laid out her request simply. He would either do the right thing or be a dick. From the conflict on his face, his decision could go either way.

"*Phil.*" The friend's tone grew an *I can't believe you* edge.

"*Fine.*" Phil bit off the words like a chunk of exceptionally tough beef jerky. He raised his phone, tapped the screen, and swiped left a few times. "Deleted. Happy?" He seemed angry that he'd been pressured to be decent.

Bree nodded. "Thank you," she said, and added sincerely, "I really appreciate it."

"Sure. Whatever." Huffing, he turned away. He and his friend jogged away. Neither looked back.

Bree pivoted on her heel. Matt stood fifteen feet away. She walked to him.

"I would have punched him." Matt's eyes followed the runners.

"No, you wouldn't," she said. "He wasn't doing anything illegal. But thanks for not interfering."

He exhaled hard through both nostrils, much like his horse, Beast. "How did you get him to cooperate?"

"I was nice."

Matt snorted. "Assholes really hate that."

"They do. But also, thanks for wanting to punch him."

"Anytime," he said. "Though you could have put him on the ground if you'd needed to."

"Still, it's always nice to have backup."

Matt turned as she drew even with him, and they walked back down the driveway, shoulder to shoulder. She almost took his hand like she normally did when they were at home. Then she remembered a dozen cops were crawling all over their side yard. *Oh, the hell with it.* She walked closer, resting her head against his shoulder.

He drew her close for a few seconds, wrapping one arm around her. "It's going to be OK. We're going to get him."

"I know. I just need a minute."

"Same." Matt gave her a squeeze.

"Sheriff!" Dr. Jones called.

With a sigh, Matt dropped his arm. Bree stepped away and they headed toward the medical examiner.

Dr. Jones pointed to the body. The black bag gaped open, revealing the tarp-wrapped body. "When we lifted her, an envelope fell out of the tarp."

Bree and Matt crossed the wet grass and stared down. A clear plastic zip-top baggie lay on the ground next to the gurney. Inside was a plain white envelope, the kind used for business correspondence. Block letters on the front spelled out *SHERIFF TAGGERT*.

Matt made a noise that sounded suspiciously like a growl. He pulled gloves out of his pocket and tugged them on before taking the bag by a corner. Being careful not to disturb any potential prints, he opened the top and slid the envelope clear of the plastic bag. The flap wasn't sealed. He lifted the top and withdrew a single sheet of paper.

His eyes hardened as he unfolded it. "I'm calling my dad. The kids need to leave. Now."

Bree's throat turned sour, the acid from her coffee rising as she read. The message was simple and direct. Her insides knotted themselves, and she pressed one hand to her burning solar plexus.

The message was written in the same block print as her name.

I'M DONE HIDING.

CHAPTER

TWENTY-THREE

On the second trip to Crystal Rynski's home, Matt embraced the gloomy weather. Sunshine and a blue sky would have felt inappropriate. He and Bree stood in silence on the sagging wooden stoop while they waited for Crystal to respond to their knock.

Crystal knew the second she opened her front door. Matt could see the horror—and panic—in her eyes, and his heart split wide open, like a tree hit by lightning.

"No," she muttered, almost to herself.

"I'm so sorry," Bree said. "Can we come inside?"

Crystal didn't respond. She just stood there staring at them and saying "No" over and over. "Not my Jana."

Bree gently nudged the woman back a step. Wrapping an arm around her shoulders, she steered her back to the tiny living area.

Matt followed them through a haze of cigarette smoke. The backs of Crystal's legs hit the recliner and she collapsed onto it. She seemed to shrivel, as if the life force had been leeched out of her body. Her breaths wheezed in and out, too fast, too shallow.

Bree crouched in front of her and took her hands. "Take deeper, slower breaths."

Crystal wheezed. "I don't want . . . to breathe . . . at all."

Matt's heart felt like it had been cleaved into two pieces.

They stayed for a respectful fifteen minutes, but Crystal didn't have any information for them, and they didn't want to share details about her daughter's death with her. In the end, they left her sobbing.

◆ ◆ ◆

They trudged back to the SUV and climbed in. Matt started the engine and turned the heat on full blast. His insides were cold through and through. He steered the vehicle back toward the road.

Bree rested her head on the seat and closed her eyes. "Telling them is bad, but leaving them alone afterward feels even worse." She sighed hard.

Matt shook himself, like a dog shedding water. They couldn't afford to let emotions cripple their investigation.

Bree pressed a palm to the side of her head. "I feel so useless. How do young women protect themselves when we don't even know how the killer is targeting his victims? We think he attacked Jana in her apartment, but how did he get in?" She paused. "Until we have a time of death, let's shift focus back to Ally and head over to the motel where she worked. We still don't know where Ally was staying during her last week. She had to be somewhere." Bree shook her phone. "The new body hit the press."

"Didn't think it would take long," Matt said.

"Unfortunately, no."

Ten minutes later, Matt turned his Suburban into the parking lot of the Shady Acres Motel, a single, two-story strip of rooms hunkering on the side of a rural highway. The next business, a gas station, was a half mile down the road. Gray clouds had crowded out the earlier burst of sunshine, casting a depressing gloom over the depressing building. Drizzle peppered the windshield.

The Suburban bounced through a pothole. Bree's official vehicle had been towed to the county garage. After forensics had picked it clean of evidence, the hood would be repaired and the windshield replaced.

Matt parked in front of the office. "This place has been a problem since back when I was a deputy."

"And it's still a problem." Bree stared at the office. A neon vacancy sign glowed in the dirty window. "Mostly drug dealers, prostitution, and people on the brink of homelessness. They rent rooms by the hour and the week."

People lived in shitty motels when they had no other options.

Matt shut off the engine. "Do we know anything about the manager?"

"Not really. Turnover is high." Bree used her lapel mic to report their location to dispatch. "I doubt there's much career advancement."

They stepped out of the vehicle. Though the rain was light, the wind swept it sideways, right into Matt's face.

They strode into the office. The room smelled of mold, dust, and burned coffee. A skinny dude of about fifty perched on a stool behind the counter, his arms crossed over a NY RANGERS emblem on his hoodie. He shifted his gaze from an ancient TV playing a house-remodeling show with the volume on low. The dude did a double take on Bree's uniform. He stood slowly, unfolding his arms and shoving his hands into the kangaroo pocket of his sweatshirt.

Matt tensed. Hands in pockets put him on guard instantly.

"Is there a problem, Sheriff?" the clerk asked.

Bree walked to the counter. Matt veered right and turned sideways, keeping his back to the wall and trying to watch the entrance, the door that led into the back, and the clerk's hands, which could emerge from those pockets holding weapons.

Bree stopped a few feet away from the counter. As she introduced herself and Matt, she turned slightly sideways, presenting a narrower target. The move was automatic. She rested both hands on her duty belt. The posture looked casual—like hooking your thumbs in your front pockets—but Matt knew the stance also positioned her for quick access to her sidearm and expandable baton. "We need to ask some questions about one of your employees. What's your name?"

"I'm Simon Lewicki." Simon was as stiff as a mannequin. Why was he so on edge?

Matt didn't like the expanse of window any more than Simon's hands in his pocket. Raindrops on the glass, the brightness of the office, and the dimness outside combined to give poor visibility and rendered anyone in the parking lot practically invisible. At the same time, the office had a fishbowl feel. On second thought, fish in a barrel—a clear barrel—would be a better metaphor. Either way, situations like this one gave Matt hives. Things could go sideways before you could blink.

Bree asked, "How long have you worked here, Simon?"

Simon licked his lips. "Five months."

"Then you know Ally Swanson," Bree said.

"Um. Not really." Simon pulled his hands from his pocket and set them on the edge of the counter. "I mean, maids work day shift. I work mostly nights."

"But you sometimes work day shift?" Matt glanced at the window, where daylight shone through the dirty glass. "Like today."

"Not that often," Simon evaded.

"But you've met Ally?" Bree's tone remained polite but persistent.

This wasn't a Hilton. Shady Acres had approximately thirty rooms. They couldn't have so many employees that one would lose track.

Simon shuffled his feet, shifting his weight back and forth as if he couldn't get comfortable. "A few times." He avoided eye contact as he answered, then his gaze settled back on Bree's face.

Clearly, Simon did not want to answer the question. He knew Ally better than he wanted to admit. Why was he being vague? What was he hiding?

Bree's eyes narrowed slightly, watching Simon's reaction. "Did you know she was dead?"

Simon looked away for a second, but he was not shocked. He knew. Sweat broke out on his forehead, shining in the unhealthy fluorescent glare. The office was barely warmer than outside. It wasn't the temperature making him perspire. "I heard something like that."

"What did you hear?" Bree tilted her head.

Simon tugged at the neck of his hoodie. "Just that she was dead."

"Do you know how she died?" Bree asked.

"Not the details." Simon picked up a paper clip and toyed with it.

"It was on the news," Matt pointed out.

Simon shot him a nasty glare. "I don't watch mainstream media. It's all lies and propaganda." He sniffed, like a coke addict. "I heard the other employees talking about it. They said that serial killer got her."

"Yes," Matt said. "She was murdered."

Simon's throat undulated as he swallowed.

"When was the last time Ally was here?" Bree asked.

Simon jerked one shoulder. "I don't know."

"Could you check?" Bree's tone remained polite but firm.

"I don't know." Simon tugged up his shirtsleeve, revealing a botched tattoo of a tiger. The creature's face was distorted, the eyes cartoonishly crooked. Simon absently scratched the tiger's nose.

"I could come back with a warrant to see all your records," Bree said in a cool voice.

Simon paused, then fixed his sleeve. "I guess it wouldn't matter."

A motel that regularly harbored illegal activity didn't invite additional scrutiny.

He took two steps sideways to an ancient desktop computer. The machine was bolted to the counter. Simon tapped on the keyboard for a few minutes. The computer chugged, as if the simple query were about all it could handle. "Looks like her last shift was about two weeks ago."

"Would you print out her schedule for the last two weeks she worked?" Bree softened her face, almost—but not quite—smiling.

"Uh. Sure." But Simon looked the opposite of sure as he clicked the mouse. In the corner, a printer whirred. He snatched two sheets of paper from it and thrust them at Bree. His gaze shot to the glass door. Did he not want anyone to see him cooperating with a cop? Or was there some other reason?

"Thanks." Bree scanned the papers. "Is this Ally's current address?"

Matt glanced over at the paper. The address listed was Ally's father's house.

"That's the only address we have on file for her." Sweat beaded on Simon's upper lip. He was way too nervous.

"Was Ally a good employee?" Matt asked.

Music sounded from Simon's pocket, a tinny version of "Baby Got Back." Simon stuck his hand in his pocket. Matt couldn't breathe until he withdrew a phone. Simon glanced at the screen, then wrapped his fingers around it tightly enough to whiten his knuckles.

Matt repeated the question.

Simon tucked his phone away. "Not really, but it's a shit job, so that's kind of what we expect."

"That makes sense," Matt agreed. "Were you surprised when you heard she was dead?"

"Uh," Simon stammered. "I was surprised about the whole serial-killer thing, you know? You hear about them on *CSI*, but they don't seem real."

He hadn't directly answered the question. Lying was hard for most people. Most would evade or dance around the answer before answering with a straight lie. Why would Ally's death not be a surprise?

Matt tried to make eye contact. "This one is very real."

Simon met his gaze for one breath, then blinked away and shuddered. "Do you need anything else?"

"We need to talk to your other employees," Bree said.

Tires grated outside. Headlights swept across the parking lot and window. A large SUV continued past the office and parked at the end of the building. Matt couldn't see the make or model.

Simon stiffened. "The maid is on the clock right now. You can talk to her after her shift."

"Another body turned up this morning." Bree leveled him with her signature no-bullshit glare. "We're now investigating four murders."

"If you watched mainstream media, you would have heard about it," Matt added.

Bree continued. "We're going to talk to the maid now."

"Did Ally leave any personal possessions here?" Matt asked.

"No. They keep their personal stuff on their cart while they work. Anything left lying around here gets stolen." Simon's voice rose. "I really need to get back to work."

Watching TV?

Matt glanced back at the SUV in the parking lot. He didn't see the door open or the interior light turn on.

Bree raised both hands in front of her body. "Thanks for your help today, Simon."

He gave her a tight-lipped nod.

"We'll be back." Bree turned toward the door.

Outside, Matt stuck close. He didn't like the vibes Simon was giving off. The rain had picked up again.

About twenty feet from the office, Bree stopped. "He's hiding something."

"His behavior is definitely suspicious." Water trickled down the back of Matt's jacket. "Could be anything. He might know something about Ally's murder, or he might take payouts to look the other way while illegal business is conducted."

Bree whipped out her notepad and wrote down the makes, models, and license plate numbers of all the vehicles in the parking lot. "Do you see the maid cart?"

Matt scanned the front of the motel and spotted a door propped open by a wheeled cart. "Second story."

Bree stashed her notepad and started for the exterior steps. They jogged up the metal staircase and peered into the open door. The maid was plugging in an upright vacuum cleaner. She was about sixty years old, dressed in black leggings, a sweatshirt, and rubber gloves. With a bone-thin body and a poof of frizzy white hair, she looked like a cotton swab wearing sneakers.

"Excuse me," Bree called.

The maid jumped, tripped over the vacuum, fell backward, and landed on her butt on the dirty beige carpeting.

Matt rushed forward. "Let me help you up."

"Sorry for startling you," Bree said.

Matt put one hand under the maid's elbow and gently lifted her to her feet. Her skin was thin, loose, and as wrinkled as a brown paper bag. Extensive sun damage blotched her skin with darker brown spots.

Bree introduced herself and Matt.

The maid removed her rubber gloves and hung them on the handle of the vacuum.

"I'm Fiona Carlsbad." The maid winced and rubbed her backside.

"Are you all right, Fiona?" Bree asked.

Matt hoped she hadn't broken anything.

"I'm fine." Fiona brushed herself off. "I'm sturdier than I look. But I don't have the padding I used to." She chuckled.

"We'd like to ask you some questions about Ally Swanson."

The older woman tsked and shook her head. "Nasty piece of business. Those poor girls. I hope whoever killed them gets what's coming to him."

So did Matt. "First, we need to find him."

"I'll help any way I can," Fiona said.

"How well did you know Ally?" Bree asked.

"Not well. Normally, there's only one maid on duty. Occasionally, if the motel is full—which is rare—then they might schedule two. I've been working here for four years, since my daughter overdosed and left me to raise my grandson. My social security doesn't feed a growing boy *and* pay the rent." She sucked in a breath as if it were painful.

"I'm sorry that happened to you," Bree said.

"Thank you." Fiona swiped at an angry tear. "He's ten now. Luckily, he's a good boy. I want to keep him that way. This job lets me work while he's at school. I'm home when he's home. I don't want him unsupervised. It's the only reason I'm still here. They're good about giving me days off when school's closed."

Matt said, "That surprises me. Simon doesn't seem like a proponent of flexible hours."

"Fuck Simon." Fiona rolled her eyes. "He's useless." She chuckled. "I actually show up for work, which is not typical for most of the employees. The owners won't let him fire me. I'll be here long after Simon moves on."

"Did Ally ever talk about anyone following her?" Bree asked. "Stalking her? Anything that scared her?"

Fiona shook her head. "We didn't talk much. I don't have time for chitchat when I'm here. I clean, and I go home."

Bree glanced at the doorway, then brought her attention back to the maid. "My deputies arrest people here now and then. Is there any chance that Ally saw something illegal and someone needed to keep her quiet?"

Fiona shrugged. "I guess anything is possible, but this lot tends toward small-time crime." She circled a bony hand in the air. "A few Oxy, cheap hookers, not enough money for most people to kill over. Then again, with drugs, ya never know." She froze, her brows knitting, the freckled skin on her forehead wrinkling like a shar-pei. "Speaking of drugs, Ally was an addict. She never told me, but I recognized the same behavior in her that I saw in my daughter. She'd come to work high, her hair a mess, slurring her words. Her moods were all over the place. She'd lost weight." She paused, staring down at her work-roughened hands for a second. "In a related note, Ally was turning tricks here. I saw her coming out of rooms when she wasn't working. She'd have cash in her hand. Men would come out soon after her. It happened more than once."

"Did you ever check to see who had rented those rooms?" Matt asked.

"Nope." Fiona gave him a look. "I don't have time for other people's problems. I mind my own." She glanced at the door. "That said, room twenty-eight has a broken heater, so it isn't being rented right now. I'm pretty sure Ally was crashing in it."

"Did you know Ally was gay?" Bree asked.

Fiona jutted out one hip and propped a hand on it. "No. But attraction is irrelevant. She needed money for drugs." She said the last sentence with just the slightest suggestion of *duh*.

"Wouldn't Simon notice if she'd been living in one of the rooms?" Matt asked.

With a sigh, Fiona dropped her hand. "A while ago, I saw her coming out of the back room of the office. Simon came out behind her. He was buttoning up his pants, so she was having sex with him too, which would be one way to convince him to keep his mouth shut about her hooking at the motel and/or living in room twenty-eight."

Bree followed up with a few questions, but Fiona was out of revelations. "We appreciate your candor, but Simon will know you told us about room twenty-eight."

Fiona waved off Bree's concern. "You do what you have to do. I'm not afraid of Simon."

They took her contact information and let her get back to work.

"Get a count on security cameras." Bree said. "I'm going to get a search warrant for room twenty-eight."

Matt walked the length of the second story, counted two cameras, then headed down the steps. He spotted a camera mounted under the eaves on each end of the building.

Bree was on her phone, typing with both thumbs and talking on the speaker. "Thank you." She pressed "End" and looked up. "Warrants come through pretty fast for a high-profile investigation."

"Two cameras on each level." Matt led her toward the office. He pointed to a camera aimed at the office door. "There's another."

Back in the office, Matt spotted another camera in the corner of the ceiling.

Simon was not pleased to see them. "What now? I don't know anything else."

"Don't you?" Bree leaned on the counter. "Did you see Ally doing anything illegal at the motel on her off-hours?"

"I would have reported illegal activity." Simon shoved his hands back into his sweatshirt pocket and avoided her gaze.

Bree could still see the lie in his eyes. "We'd like the key to room twenty-eight."

Simon's jaw went hard. He knew why. "That room is currently out of order."

"We know," Bree said. "That's why we'd like to see it."

"Fucking Fiona," Simon muttered.

"Don't mess with her," Matt warned. "I'll stake out this place every night for the next year."

Simon's frown deepened until marionette lines formed on both sides of his mouth.

"We'd also like the surveillance footage from all your cameras for the week ending last Wednesday." Bree pulled out her phone and read him the dates encompassing the window of Ally Swanson's death.

"The whole week?" Simon protested.

"Yes," Bree confirmed. "All of the cameras. How many are there?"

"Six," Simon grumbled, then turned to the back room. "Give me a couple of minutes." He returned quickly, holding a flash drive. "Two of the cameras are down. Here's the feed for those dates for the other four."

Matt pocketed the flash drive.

Bree's phone vibrated. She glanced at the screen. "We're going to have a look in room twenty-eight."

"Don't you need a warrant for that?" Simon scowled.

Bree raised her phone. "Already have one. I'll see that you get a copy. The room should be empty, right?"

"Right," Simon grumbled.

"Key?" Bree held out a hand.

He fished a key card out of a drawer and handed it over.

Room twenty-eight was on the second floor. Matt and Bree jogged up the steps, then flanked the doorway as Matt inserted the key in the slot. Nothing clicked, but the lock opened when he turned the latch. He pushed the door open a few inches. Something skittered across the floor. A rodent? Matt's skin crawled. A good reminder to always wear boots, even in the summer. You never knew what you'd have to walk into.

Matt pulled a small flashlight from his pocket.

Bree did the same, then led the way into the room. Matt stuck close. The smell of mold and something worse—and unmistakable—invaded his nostrils.

Decomp.

Matt stepped sideways and used the butt of his flashlight to flip the light switch, illuminating the usual furniture: two saggy double beds, a single nightstand between them, one chair, and a battered dresser. Half the dresser drawers hung open. The dim light didn't penetrate the shadowed corners.

Before he could scan the room for dead bodies, a live one charged them.

Chapter Twenty-Four

A floor lamp crashed to the ground, the bulb shattering. A man tackled Bree, his shoulder ramming into her ribs. She flew backward, landing on her ass in the doorway, blocking Matt. Her assailant tried to step over her, but she grabbed his leg and yanked. "Oh, no, you don't."

The move upended him, and he landed flat on his face on the concrete. He scrambled to break free, kicking at her head. She clutched his foot to her chest. "Stop." She tucked her chin, evading a boot to the face by an inch, and yelled, "Sheriff's department!"

He ignored her command, crabbing backward toward the stairwell, still yanking at his boot.

Matt clambered over Bree, but their assailant's boot tread caught her chin. Dots starburst in Bree's vision. Pain launched from her jaw through her neck and head. She lost her grip, and he tore his boot from her hands.

Rubber scraped on concrete as he scrambled to his feet.

"Bree?" Matt's voice penetrated the fog.

She squinted, clearing her vision. He was half-turned toward the fleeing man.

Bree waved him on. "I'm fine."

He left her and sprinted after the man.

Bree struggled into a sitting position. Matt took the stairs two at a time. He leaped over the last step and first-floor walkway. He landed on the asphalt without breaking stride, moving like the athlete he was. She could picture him charging up a beach with a Viking horde, broadsword in hand, ready to pillage a city.

The man who'd charged her was barely ten yards ahead of him, running toward the corner of the building, already struggling to maintain pace. Bree could hear him gasping for air across the parking lot.

Matt shouted, "Stop. Sheriff's department."

But the man kept going. Matt caught him in a half dozen strides. He reached out, grabbed the man's shoulder, and pulled. The man's feet kept moving, and he toppled backward, landing on the blacktop with an audible grunt. Matt pounced, flipping him to his belly and handcuffing his hands behind his back. With the assailant restrained, Matt patted him down, then looked up at Bree and waved.

She returned the wave, her ears ringing with the motion. Adrenaline ebbed, and pain throbbed through her face. She touched her mouth. Her lip was already swelling, and her hand came away wet with blood. Running her tongue around her teeth, she decided they were all still there.

With the help of the railing, Bree heaved herself upright. She pulled her weapon and made sure room twenty-eight was now empty. Then she called for a patrol unit, brushed the dirt off her ass, and joined Matt. He'd moved the man under the roof's overhang, out of the rain.

The man sat with his hands cuffed behind his back, his legs jutting straight out in front of him. Sweat coated his face in a greasy sheen. His lungs were still working like a fireplace bellows to recover from the very short sprint. An oversize jacket swam on him, the fabric too filthy to determine its color. His pants were also too large and equally dirty. Homeless, she'd bet.

Matt hadn't broken a sweat, nor was he breathing hard.

"Backup's on the way." She sized up the man in cuffs.

Six feet tall, an unhealthy one fifty, with pockmarked cheeks and the gray pallor of a man barely shy of dead. His age could have been anywhere from thirty to sixty.

"What's your name?" she asked.

"I don't have to tell you that." His mouth curved in a strange grin.

Matt gestured to the assortment of objects he'd removed from the man's pockets. A small pocketknife, a can of sardines in mustard, a handful of brown M&M's, three small rocks, and a yo-yo. "No ID."

"What were you doing in there?" she asked.

"I was hungry," he said in a disturbing singsong voice. "I know she had food."

Drunk? High? Neither felt quite right.

"Who had food?" Bree didn't want to put her face close enough to his to smell his breath or check his pupils. He didn't seem aggressive now, but he *had* tackled her, though that action could have been driven by fear. Thinking the room would be empty, she hadn't identified herself before entering. But still, a handcuffed man could spit and bite. Human bites could be nasty.

"Her." He shrugged. "I need my stuff."

"Where's your stuff?" Matt asked.

"My bag. I need my bag." Agitated, the cuffed man began to squirm.

"We'll find your bag," Matt said. "We won't let anything happen to it."

The man settled. "OK."

"Back to the woman. How do you know she had food?" Matt asked.

"I saw her take it in." He sounded distracted. "She didn't bring it out."

Bree tried again. "You saw a woman with food. Do you know her name?"

"Nope." He turned his face upward and smiled. "But she had a whole box of food. I saw it. I want it!"

"What did she look like?" Bree asked.

His eyelids drooped. "Don't remember."

"Wake up." Matt gave his shoulder a brief shake. "Do you remember where or when you saw her?"

"Nope. Nope. Nope." With a lift of his shoulders, he began to sing "Bohemian Rhapsody." The quality of his voice and impressive range stunned Bree into silence for a full minute.

Matt finally said, "Didn't expect that."

"Nope," Bree echoed the cuffed man.

Simon crossed the lot and stopped to glare at the man. "What's going on?"

Bree tilted her head toward the cuffed man. "He was in room twenty-eight."

"Then he was trespassing." Simon puffed up like a rooster. "Fucking squatters are a real problem."

"Do you want to file a complaint?" Bree was tired. Her face ached, and Simon was a jerk. She would get Todd to run a background check on him.

"I don't know. I need to see if he damaged the room." He turned toward the staircase.

"Hold on," Bree called after him. "You'll have to wait until we've finished searching it."

Changing course toward the office, he muttered something that sounded like *fucking cops* under his breath and stomped away. "I'll be in the office. Let me know when you're done."

"Will do," Matt said in an annoyingly cheerful tone.

Simon spun around. "Can you make him shut up?"

The cuffed man continued to sing away, seemingly unaware of what was happening around him.

"Hey, buddy." Matt squatted until he was at eye level.

The man ignored him. Matt shrugged.

"Seriously, what are you going to do with him?" Matt asked Bree.

"I don't know." Bree rubbed at her jaw.

"Let me see that." Matt shined his flashlight in her face.

"Hey." Bree held up a hand, blocking the beam from searing her eyeballs.

"Sorry." He stepped closer, squinting. "That's gonna leave a mark. You need ice."

Bree agreed. "Later."

A few feet away, the man in cuffs continued to sing. A patrol unit turned into the lot, Deputy Juarez at the wheel. Bree waved him over. "Watch him while we search a room."

"Yes, ma'am." Juarez stepped out of his vehicle. "What happened to your face?"

Bree sighed and gestured to the cuffed man.

Juarez opened his trunk and rummaged in a first aid kit. He pulled out a cold pack and massaged it before handing it to Bree.

"Thanks." She pressed it to her face. "We shouldn't be long."

Matt jogged up the steps with an irritating bounce to his step. Bree trudged along behind him. Every footstep sent a spike of pain through her jaw and neck.

Matt stepped across the threshold. "Something smells dead in here."

"I swear, I can't find another dead body. Not today." She pulled her flashlight from her duty belt and shined it into the closet. Empty. She moved to the bathroom. A brown water stain on the ceiling was shaped like a bear. Mold dripped down the wall. "There's a leak in the roof and more mold than grout in the bathroom."

Matt shined his light on a plastic bag near the door. With one gloved hand, he opened it. "Very random odds and ends, like someone raided a junkyard."

"Probably the homeless guy's stuff."

Matt lifted one bedspread, then the other. "Nothing."

"Then what is dead?" Bree scanned the room. There wasn't another space big enough to conceal a body. Could the smell be coming from the next room?

Matt bent over and shined his flashlight under the dresser. "Ugh."

"What?"

"Dead rat." Matt straightened, walked back to the door, and propped it all the way open. "Better than a dead person."

"Also better than a live rat."

Matt illuminated a trail of brown pellets that looked like rat droppings. "I wouldn't assume there aren't any live rats in here."

Bree paused midstep. "I love animals, but rats creep me out." She stuffed the cold pack into her pocket, donned gloves, and checked the drawers. "I feel like there should be something here. Ally had to have stuff, right? Even if it wasn't much stuff."

"Everyone has stuff," Matt agreed, pointing to the plastic bag. "Even the homeless guy has stuff."

And yet the room was empty.

Bree's gaze roamed the walls. "He said he saw her bring in a box, and she didn't leave with it."

Matt lifted the mattress with one hand. "Nothing under here. He could be wrong."

"But Fiona also said Ally had been living here," Bree said. "If you were crashing illegally in a motel room, you wouldn't leave your stuff out. Someone might take it. I'm sure Ally knew the other inhabitants of Shady Acres weren't above stealing."

"True."

So where did she hide it?

Bree went into the bathroom, opened the vanity, and shined her flashlight into the hole where the pipes connected to the wall. She returned to the main room and shined her flashlight on every inch of wall. *It must be here somewhere.* The homeless man had been so insistent.

Then she spotted a flash of green in the air vent next to the dresser. "There."

Matt crossed the room. "The screws are loose." He turned them with his fingers and popped off the louvered cover to reveal a backpack stuffed into the vent.

Bree took a picture, then pulled it out. A plastic storage box was jammed behind the backpack. She snapped another pic, then removed the box as well. Lifting the lid, she found a few canned goods, a can opener, chips and crackers, and a stack of candy bars. She unzipped the backpack. The main compartment was filled with clothes. She dug down past some socks and found a wallet. She opened it. Ally Swanson's driver's license stared back at her. "Seems Fiona and the homeless dude were right. This is where Ally was crashing." The wallet also held thirty-six dollars in small bills. Bree set aside the wallet and found a half-empty bottle of cheap vodka shoved between a flannel shirt and a pair of threadbare yoga pants.

She opened the front pocket of the backpack. Prescription bottles filled the space.

"What did you find?" Matt looked over her shoulder.

"Drugs." Bree shined her flashlight inside. "Looks like a few pills in each vial." The labels had been scraped off. Bree opened one bottle. "These look like Vicodin." She tried another. "Hydrocodone."

"How many bottles?"

"Five. Just a few pills in each." Bree zipped the pouch. She opened the last compartment and pulled out a brochure for a pregnancy counseling center. "She knew she was pregnant."

"Not enough money or drugs for her to be dealing," Matt said.

"No. It's more likely she was using the drugs personally, pregnant or not." Bree straightened. "I'll get a crime scene unit out here, in case this is where she was abducted."

"I hope the surveillance camera facing this room is functioning."

"Same." Bree made her call, then they went back down to the patrol vehicle. She crouched in front of the cuffed man. "Do you want to tell me your name now?"

He grinned. "Nope." The rotten breath that accompanied his answer nearly made Bree's eyes water.

She stepped away and faced Juarez again. "I want to hold him for now—at least until we've watched the surveillance vids and forensics has gone over the room." But she didn't want to put him in jail if he'd actually just been looking for food. This man was likely homeless for any number of possible reasons. He clearly had issues. He needed a shower, clean clothes, and a hot meal. She'd much rather get him help than send him to jail.

"Charges?" Juarez asked.

"Trespassing for now," Bree said.

Juarez wrote in his notepad. He looked up. "Assaulting a police officer?"

Bree shook her head. "I hadn't identified myself when he tackled me. Run him by the ER and get him checked out."

"You don't think he's just high?" Juarez asked.

"Who knows?" Bree lifted a shoulder.

Juarez frowned. "He looks like he could use a meal anyway." He opened the rear door and helped the man inside gently but firmly. The man didn't stop singing. He finished "Bohemian Rhapsody" and launched into "Under Pressure."

Juarez slid into the driver's seat. To Bree's surprise, he began to sing along with the man in the back seat. As if by mutual agreement, Juarez took David Bowie's part, letting the homeless guy continue as Freddie Mercury. Juarez closed the vehicle door, muffling the sound of their harmony.

Bree shot Matt a look. They both burst out laughing.

"This feels completely inappropriate." Bree snorted. "And it makes my face hurt."

Matt tipped his head and pinched the bridge of his nose for a few seconds. He held up a hand. "I can stop." But his shoulders still shook.

Bree wheezed. "Welcome to the bizarro world of law enforcement."

Matt blew out a sharp breath. "Right?"

Recovered, Bree strung crime scene tape across the hotel room's doorway. They waited for forensics to arrive, then headed for their vehicle.

Matt drummed his fingertips on the steering wheel. "Simon could be the father of Ally's baby."

"We have no proof he had sex with her. Even if he did, there's no proof the sex wasn't consensual. Also, if she was hooking for drug money, any of her clients could have impregnated her." Bree's seat belt clicked into place. "We'd need a warrant for Simon's DNA, and we don't have enough evidence to establish probable cause."

"Let's circle back with Todd at the station and see if he's turned up anything. We can run a background check on Simon."

"Even if he did get Ally pregnant, it wouldn't mean he killed her—or the other girls." Matt shifted into drive and left the space.

"True, but Simon knows more about Ally's activity than he's saying."

CHAPTER TWENTY-FIVE

With her first shift complete, Grace perched on a stool in the back of the restaurant and waited while her rideshare app searched for an available vehicle. On the other side of the room, the kitchen staff bustled around stainless-steel tables, using the slow period between lunch and dinner to prep for the Friday night crush.

Her feet hurt, and she was exhausted. She hadn't waitressed in a long time. How was she going to manage full days, care for Riley, and help her mother with chores long-term?

She rubbed a knot in her calf. She would suck it up. That's what would happen. A wave of depression crashed over her. She'd thought she'd hit bottom years ago. There was nothing like being homeless with a baby to humble a person. Unless it was being homeless with a four-year-old. The visit with social services had scared the hell out of her. If Grace didn't have housing, they could take Riley away.

Howard would help make that happen. He'd testify against her.

Panic filled her like a swarm of bees, fear buzzing through her veins.

She had to make this work. She couldn't go through that again. She couldn't sweat through every day, begging friends for help, wondering if she and her child would have a roof over their heads or food to eat.

She used to know which food pantries had the best offerings and which days were best to pay them a visit. She had no desire to experience that life again.

"Can I give you a lift?" Isaac asked.

Grace looked away from her phone. Isaac was grabbing his coat from the closet. He worked in the kitchen. A few years older than her, he seemed nice, but Grace was done with trusting anyone. Howard had been nice when they'd first met. When he was sober, he could turn on the charm like a faucet. He'd love bombed her. Flooded her with presents and compliments. He'd even bought Riley a few toys. He'd made Grace feel like she was special, cherished. She'd fallen hard and spent the next few months trying to be the best girlfriend she could be. She'd cooked his favorite meals, kept his house scrupulously clean, kept Riley quiet when he was working. She'd been pleasant and taken care with her appearance. Look where that had gotten her.

This time would be different. She would be independent. Was that even possible for her now? How would she ever make enough money to pay rent and buy food? She didn't have a car. Taking an Uber with a kid was tough. The car seat had to be hauled along. Some cars were harder to get the seat installed. Drivers could be impatient. Once, Riley had puked in an Uber on the way to the pediatrician.

She managed a small smile as she lied. "I have a ride on the way, but thanks for the offer."

With a wave, Isaac left through the back door.

Grace checked her app. Shared rides were cheaper but took longer to arrive. She was on a very tight budget, though. Until she received her first paycheck, she had barely enough money to pay for the Ubers and Lyfts she'd need to get to work. So, she'd wait. Her parents were allowing her to live with them for free for the first three months. After that, she'd have to pay rent.

But everything was different now.

If they found out, would they renege on their arrangement? Would they kick her out? What if child services came calling? What if Howard made accusations? She couldn't win.

If it weren't for Riley, she wouldn't even care. Her daughter was her light—the only reason she got out of bed every morning.

Grace chewed on her straw. When she'd gotten pregnant with Riley, she'd left rather than face her father's wrath and her mother's even more cutting disappointment. She'd been raised to be a "good girl." Sex was never spoken about. Grace hadn't even worn shorts or sleeveless tops until she'd left home. At her parents' request, she'd been excluded from sex ed class. She'd been clueless. Thankfully, Grace's friends had been more than willing to educate her. Of course, some of that information hadn't been correct, and Grace had been rebellious—hence Riley.

Now she was too tired to be defiant. She'd do whatever her parents wanted if they just let her and Riley stay. She'd cook and clean and dress like a freaking nun if it meant security for her little girl.

Water sizzled on the grill. A line cook scraped away. The greasy odor filled Grace's nose, turning her stomach. She rose, slinging her small purse onto her shoulder and heading out the back door before she lost her free lunch. Outside, she welcomed the damp air. She turned her face to the sky and let the drizzle cool her skin. The wind shifted, bringing the odor of the dumpster closer.

Tears gathered in her eyes. What was she going to do? She wanted to curl into a ball, close her eyes, and give up. Her phone buzzed. She looked at her phone screen. Uber had found her a ride, but it was Riley's photo on her lock screen that made her stand up straight. She didn't have the luxury of being able to give up. Riley needed her mother to make a life for them. A wave of nausea hit, and she couldn't afford to be sick. Grace breathed deeply, willing her stomach to stop churning. Tears ran down her already-wet cheeks.

A gray sedan pulled up to the side of the restaurant. Both Uber and Lyft signs glowed on the dashboard. It wasn't unusual for drivers to work for both companies. Wanting nothing more than to get away from the smells, Grace headed for the vehicle.

She was almost there when something made her pause, just a feeling that all wasn't right.

The driver cracked the window. Grace leaned over, trying to see his face. But the window was tinted.

"Grace?" he asked.

He knew her name. That was normal. Yet Grace's feet didn't move. Her body didn't want to get into the car, but a cancellation fee would eat into her budget. She needed to get home. She needed to see Riley. She took one step. Then her brain kicked into gear. She hadn't looked at the vehicle details on the app. She woke her phone. The car coming for her was a black Honda CR-V, and it was still ten minutes away. But what were the odds of someone else named Grace calling for an Uber at this time and place?

Instinct pulled her feet backward. The urge to run came from somewhere deep inside, an instinct Grace couldn't understand or override. She knew with every cell of her being that if she got into that car, she'd die.

She spun, terror hijacking her coordination. Her feet tangled over each other, and she stumbled, falling to one knee. She pressed a palm to the ground and pushed to her feet.

The sedan door flung open. The driver launched himself out of the vehicle. *No!* Grace dug the ball of her foot into the concrete.

Run. Run. *Run.*

Her muscles bunched. She pushed into the ground, propelling her body forward, back toward the restaurant. She tried to scream for help, but panic wrapped around her throat like strong fingers, silencing her voice.

Behind her, boots scraped on the concrete. An arm wrapped around her waist, lifting her feet from the ground.

"No!" She swatted and kicked at him, tried to twist away. One of her sneakers connected with his leg. He grunted. His hold weakened.

Grace's sneakers touched the ground for two seconds. She pulled away. Hope flashed, as bright—and short-lived—as a firecracker.

He hauled her off her feet again. She struggled, twisting and arching, desperation making her movements wild. A fist slammed into the back of her head. Pain exploded in her skull. Her vision dimmed, and her body went limp. Disorientation squashed thoughts of escape. She could do nothing but hang, helpless, as he tossed her into the trunk. The lid slammed down before Grace could fully process what had happened.

She beat her fists on the trunk, but the car rolled into motion. The smells of dirt, rubber, and metal filled her nose, and she gagged.

A minute before she'd thought begging for her parents' forgiveness was the worst thing that could have happened to her.

She'd been wrong.

CHAPTER TWENTY-SIX

"I'm going to check on the kids." Worried, Bree dialed Luke's cell number while Matt drove toward the station.

Luke answered on the second ring. "Hey."

"Hey. How are you?"

"I'm OK." He yawned. "Doing a little homework. It's only been, like, a few hours."

"I know. But I worry. How's Kayla?"

"She's eating a Popsicle and watching that Australian cartoon with the blue dog. George is making soup."

"OK. Good."

"Aunt Bree, we're fine," Luke said. "Being spoiled rotten, actually."

"Also good. Don't push the schoolwork, OK? Get some rest."

"Is that Aunt Bree?" Kayla yelled in the background. "Can I talk?"

"Hold on," Luke said. "Aunt Bree, be careful."

"Always."

Kayla's nasally voice came over the phone. "Grandpa is making soup, and Grandma got puzzles down from the attic." The little girl sounded better than when she'd been at home.

"That's nice."

"I like having a sleepover here. Grandpa says I can stay here whenever I want, even when I'm not sick." Kayla sounded very happy for a child with the flu.

"That's really nice." Bree choked up and cleared her throat.

"Here's Grandma." Fabric rustled over the connection.

"Bree?" Anna asked.

"Just checking in on them," Bree said.

"They're fine, but you call whenever you need to." Anna always knew what to say. "Kayla's fever is down, but we expect it will come back later this evening. They usually do. Don't you worry, though. George is on top of it."

"I know he is." Gratefulness swamped Bree. "Thanks so much for taking care of them."

"We love having them here, and you know George is never happier than when he gets to doctor people," Anna said. "Now, you and Matt look after each other. Stop by if you have time tonight, anytime."

"Yes, ma'am." Bree ended the call. "Your parents are the best."

"Now that I'm an adult, I have to agree with you."

"You didn't always think so?"

"Well, I was a teenager." Matt chuckled. "Dad always wanted to talk about *everything*."

"The horror."

"To a teen, it was." Matt grinned.

Bree called Dana next to check on things at the farm. The horses were fine. Nolan had just checked on them, and he was going to stay overnight and help Dana keep watch. Bree hung up and lowered her phone.

At the station, she went into her office. Marge appeared in three seconds, setting a cup of coffee in front of Bree. "You have messages, but first, breathe. They'll keep."

Bree lifted the coffee and drank deeply. There wasn't enough caffeine to make her brain feel fully functional today. Her phone vibrated, and Madeline Jager's name appeared on the screen.

"Let it go to voice mail." Adjusting her cardigan, Marge turned toward the door.

"No point. She'll just keep calling." Bree pressed "Answer." "Sheriff Taggert."

"Sheriff," Jager said. "I heard about what happened to you this morning. Was it him? Did the serial killer leave that body at your house?"

"Of course we don't have information from Dr. Jones yet, but I believe so."

"Is your family safe?"

"Yes." Bree waited for the catch. Jager was never this nice.

"I'm glad." Jager cleared her throat. "We had an emergency meeting of the board of supervisors. We'll approve extra funding for overtime."

"That will be helpful."

"Are you going to call the FBI?" Jager asked.

Bree decided on the spot, surprising herself with her quick answer. "Yes. They have resources we can't access, and we could use all the help we can get."

"We agree, and we'll leave that decision to you."

"Seriously?" Bree would have stopped the outburst, but exhaustion had lowered her guard.

"Yes." Jager sighed. "The fourth body makes it impossible to deny that you were right. We have a serial killer in Randolph County." Jager produced *serial killer* with some difficulty. Her voice sounded strained, as if the call were using all her available energy. "He must be stopped at all costs."

"I'm glad we're on the same page." Bree was going all out anyway, but not having to simultaneously fight the board was a nice change.

"That was all. I just wanted to say be careful. This killer seems to have targeted you."

"I will. Thank you for your concern."

Jager ended the call without a single criticism. Bree lowered the phone and stared at it. Then she made the call to the FBI field office in Albany.

Matt appeared in the doorway as she set down her phone. "What's wrong?"

"I had the strangest call." Bree summarized her conversation with Jager.

"Weird."

"Honestly, it's a bit disconcerting. We had a rhythm, you know? She'd be hostile. I'd grind my molars. Animosity worked for us. I don't know what to do now. Cooperation just doesn't feel right." Jager's acquiescence was so out of character, it made the hairs on the backs of Bree's forearms stand straight up.

Matt frowned. "Don't drop your guard. The board is calculating. They can't deny the serial killer, so they've shifted into *back the blue* mode. It'll pass, probably when overtime starts adding up. Also, consider that giving you full authority fully absolves them of any responsibility. If shit goes even more sideways, it's your neck on the line."

"I knew it was too good to be true." Bree was almost relieved to know that Jager probably had an ulterior motive, like the ground was solid beneath her feet again.

"I just requested help from the FBI." Bree lifted both hands in a *giving up* gesture. "While we are capable of running this investigation, we are short-staffed and overextended due to this flu. We've been lucky so far this week in that usual local criminals have been quiet."

"They probably all have the flu too," Matt said.

"We can hope that continues until we've recovered, but our killer is escalating quickly. We can't keep up." Bree shuffled through her messages. None were related to the case. She tossed them aside.

"What's the ETA for the FBI?"

"Don't know yet. They're also short-staffed due to the flu and a missing-child case utilizing local resources, but I was promised a callback ASAP." She set her palms on the desk and pushed to her feet. "Now, let's get to the conference room and try to make some sense of this case."

"Todd is already there." Matt withdrew.

Bree gathered her notes, grabbed her laptop, and headed for the conference room. Matt was hanging a photo of Jana Rynski on the board next to the pictures of Ally Swanson and Trish Bitten. Todd concentrated on his laptop screen.

Bree settled at the table with her notepad, files, and computer. "Todd, did you run the ViCAP query?"

"I did." Todd tapped on his keyboard. "Our lack of information made for broad search parameters. We don't even have a cause of death for two of the victims. Wrapping remains in tarps isn't a unique concept, but the camouflage print *is* unusual. I only found one set of remains where the killer also used that type of tarp to wrap his victims. But that crime was solved, and the killer convicted three years ago. He's currently serving a life sentence in Nebraska. I ran a second query using tarps of any kind, thinking maybe this killer changed that aspect of his pattern. The second query returned a few dozen unsolved cases, but only two that fit the other identifiers. One of those cases is a body dump site in South Carolina. Two sets of female remains were found in the woods near I-95 in 2015. In the second case, a woman was found in a state park in Delaware in 2018. I have calls in to the detectives in charge of both of those cases. We'll see if I turn anything up when I speak to them."

"Good work. Keep at it." Bree referred to her checklist. "Let's move on to individual cases, starting with Jana. Her mother spoke to her at eight thirty-five Tuesday evening. The neighbor also saw Jana at her mailbox between five or six p.m., confirming she was still alive at that time. Do we have Jana's phone records?"

Todd scrolled on his computer. "We do. I see the phone call with her mother Tuesday evening. The call wrapped up at 9:02. That's the last time she used her phone. Her typical pattern was to use her phone every day for at least a text or two."

"Who did she typically text with?" Bree asked.

"Her mother, her neighbor, her boss." Todd dragged two fingers along his laptop trackpad. "Also a bunch of random numbers that aren't regular contacts." He typed a note. "Scarlet Hair Salon, Randolph Dental Care, Speedy Lube, Vital Care Network, the community college, Sal's Pizza." He looked up.

"No red flags," Bree said.

"None," Todd said. "Her phone service provider doesn't retain text message content. Unless we find Jana's phone, we won't have details of her texts."

Bree checked her notes. "She didn't show up to work on Thursday, which is not typical behavior, and she was dead this morning." She pictured the blood stains in Jana's apartment. "She was likely taken either Tuesday after nine p.m. or Wednesday evening after dark. I can't imagine anyone attempting to haul a bleeding woman out of her apartment in broad daylight."

Matt tapped a knuckle on the whiteboard. "Chevy was stalking Jana at her apartment and at her place of employment."

"We haven't linked him to any other victims," Bree said.

"Is it possible he killed Jana and then tried to make it look like the serial killer took her?" Todd asked.

"He pissed in her bed and set it on fire." Matt underlined a bullet point. "I'd say anything is possible with Chevy."

"But," Bree said, "we didn't publicize the detail about the camouflage tarps."

Todd drummed his fingers on the table. "There were no media photos of the bodies?"

"I don't think so." Bree rubbed the back of her neck. "The bodies were bagged before they were removed from the clearing."

"Let's check social media." Todd scrolled for all of forty-five seconds. "There's a photo." He turned his laptop to face Bree and Matt. On the screen, a tarp-wrapped body lay half-buried under dead leaves.

"Who posted it?" Matt asked.

Todd tapped on his keyboard. "Nick West from WSNY News."

Bree's skin heated. "Where did he get the photo?"

Todd checked his screen. "Doesn't say."

Matt leaned closer. "That looks like one of the original bodies in the clearing. The photo has been cropped in close, so I can't tell which one."

Bree jabbed a finger at Todd's laptop. "We will find out who took that picture. We've had no luck finding the department leaker up until now, but the number of people who were in that clearing is limited."

"I'll review the crime scene log and refine the list according to who arrived before the bodies were removed," Todd said.

Matt blew air through his nostrils. "People suck."

"Hardly matters now," Todd added. "Once a photo is on the internet, there's no way to erase it. The information about the tarps is out there."

Matt leaned on the wall, intentionally tapping the back of his head on the whiteboard three times.

"I'll call Nick West and ask him to take it down." Bree and the young reporter had an on-and-off rapport of sorts. This post seemed beneath him, but he occasionally dipped a toe on the wrong side of the moral tightrope. "But you're right, Todd. The damage is done."

That wouldn't stop Bree from making her point with the reporter. If she let this inch go, other reporters and news stations would take a mile next time.

Bree checked the time. A typical autopsy would take about four hours. "Dr. Jones will do the autopsy ASAP. Hopefully, we'll have an approximate time of death soon and can then inquire as to Chevy's whereabouts. Until then, let's move on to Ally."

"We learned that Ally was likely prostituting herself for drug money. She was crashing in an empty room at the motel as well. The manager, Simon, denies knowing her well, but the other maid thinks Ally was having sex with Simon, probably so he'd ignore her extracurricular activities at the motel. Simon claims to barely know her, which is clearly a lie. We need a full background check on Simon."

"Already ran him." Todd clicked his trackpad. "Because he was Ally's boss. He doesn't have a criminal record. I'll dig deeper and see if I can link him to the other victims."

"You interviewed Trish Bitten's boyfriend and sister?" Bree asked Todd.

"Yes. Earlier today, after I talked with Detective Dane about the original missing person case filed with the Scarlet Falls PD." Todd opened a new window on his computer. "Dane made a copy of the surveillance video from the college parking lot." Todd played the video, fast-forwarding through a few minutes of no activity. "Here comes Trish now."

They watched a young woman stride through the snow, a dark-blue backpack slung over one shoulder. She wore a pale-blue puffy jacket, skinny jeans, and ankle boots. Her white hat matched a thick scarf wound around her neck. Heavy black gloves covered her hands. She dropped the backpack into the back seat, then started the engine. While the car warmed up, she scraped frost off the windows. Then she drove away.

Bree wondered how long she'd lived after this moment. "I don't see anyone following her."

Todd fast-forwarded again. "Ten minutes pass before we see another student." A dark-haired girl walked through the parking lot, cleared her windows, and left the campus. "The winter term is limited, with less activity on campus than during the regular semester." He played the video again, making a circle around Trish's car with his finger. "The

SFPD identified the surrounding cars. All were students who had legitimate business on campus."

Matt leaned in to get a better view of the screen. "He could have been waiting for her near the entrance to the college, then followed her vehicle."

Todd stopped the video. "We have no way of knowing. The road leading to the college is rural. No cameras. Trish's vehicle hasn't been located. The SFPD worked the case for months, but eventually, they had to back-burner it."

The longer a case dragged on without a resolution, the less likely it was to be solved. Detectives had to work fresher cases.

"I'm still going through the case file," Todd said. "We still don't have an ID on the last body?"

"Correct," Bree verified.

"We've received initial forensics reports from the clearing and Jana's apartment," Todd said. "I only had a chance to skim them so far, but I haven't seen anything interesting. The clearing contained very little. No water bottles. No cigarette butts. No litter. Reports on soil sample, entomology, et cetera, will take time."

"Copy us, and we'll all go through them." Bree believed in fresh eyes on reports. You never knew what detail might stand out to different people. "Have you made any progress obtaining Jana's and Trish's transcripts?"

"The college hasn't complied yet, but Trish's transcript is in the SFPD file, and forensics found a copy of Jana's in her car. I'm not sure what to think about what I've found." Todd turned to his file. He removed two pages and set them side by side. "As we know, the two girls didn't attend school at the same time. But they did have a few of the same general education classes. For one of those—Statistics 101—they had the same professor."

"How popular is this statistics class?" Matt asked.

Todd laid a palm flat on the page. "The class fulfills a specific graduation requirement. About a hundred and fifty students take it each semester. I know we don't love coincidences, but they happen."

"Over the past two years, at least six hundred kids took that class?" Matt asked.

"That's right," Todd said.

"Who is the professor?" Bree asked.

Todd rested a finger on a name. "Howard Killian."

Shock glued Bree to her chair. She didn't move for two heartbeats. "I arrested him the other night. You were still out sick." She summarized the domestic violence call.

"Maybe it's not a coincidence," Todd said.

"Where is Howard Killian now?" Matt asked.

"Out on bail." Propping her elbows on the table, Bree rubbed her temples with two hands. "Let's go see him." She'd locked the key Grace had given her in her bottom desk drawer. "We can return his key."

"Killian knew two of the victims." Matt stretched both arms over his head. "That makes him a prime suspect."

CHAPTER
TWENTY-SEVEN

Matt helped Bree load her gear into a patrol vehicle. There was nothing wrong with his Suburban, but it didn't have law enforcement bells and whistles, like a mobile data terminal. While she adjusted her seat and steering wheel, he donned his Kevlar vest. He'd been shot in the past and wasn't anxious to repeat the experience. Anytime they embarked on a risky call, he suited up. Domestic violence perpetrators were dangerous enough. Howard Killian had been promoted to serial killer suspect.

Bree gave him an approving side-eye and nod. "Plan on wearing that until this is over."

"I do." He secured the Velcro strap and shrugged back into his sheriff's department jacket.

Bree drove out of the lot. Matt checked on the kids and the farm.

Bree's phone buzzed. "FBI." She answered the call and uttered a few monosyllabic responses before ending the call. "An agent will be here first thing tomorrow. I'll have Todd forward her as much information as possible so she can begin to review the case tonight." She made a quick call to Todd.

Ten minutes later, Bree cruised to a stop in front of Killian's house. Matt scanned the property. Despite a dark-gray sky and zero sun, no lights glowed inside the house.

Bree unfastened her seat belt. "His vehicle isn't here. Doesn't look like anyone is home."

"When was he released?" Matt asked.

"Wednesday afternoon." Bree slid out of the vehicle.

Matt joined her on the sidewalk. Music blared from a house nearby, and the neighborhood smelled of barbecue. "He's had a chance to catch up on his missed sleep from a night in jail then."

"He never made it to jail. He spent his single night in custody in the station holding cell. Alone." Bree led the way to the front door. They flanked the entrance and knocked. Nothing moved in the house. No lights turned on. No footsteps approached the door.

"It's happy hour on a Friday. You said he was drunk when you arrested him. Maybe he's out at a bar, telling his sad story to his pals."

"That's plausible." Bree knocked again. The house remained still and quiet.

Matt pressed his ear to the door for a few seconds. "All I can hear is the music from down the street. Do you want to check the back of the house?"

"No. We don't have a warrant, and we're not going to get one based on two of the victims taking Killian's very popular class, along with six hundred other local kids. One piece of circumstantial evidence won't establish probable cause." Bree turned and surveyed the street. "I don't see his vehicle. He must have gone somewhere."

Matt cupped his hand over his eyes and peered through the narrow window next to the front door, but the interior was too dim to see much. He stood back. "We could park down the street and watch the place for a while. There's a spot behind that massive pickup."

Bree nodded. "Good idea. If he doesn't show up soon, we can talk to the neighbors. Maybe someone has seen him in the past couple of days."

They returned to the patrol unit, and Bree moved the vehicle down the street. If Howard drove by them, he'd see the sheriff's vehicle, but he was most likely to approach from the other direction, and the monster truck provided decent concealment.

Bree slouched down in the seat. Matt did the same, settling in to do nothing. Stakeouts were mind-numbing. The hardest element was the boredom. The rain picked up, drumming on the roof of the car and sluicing down the windows.

"This rain will never end," Bree said. "I'm tired of mud."

Their breath fogged the windshield. Matt wiped it with a leftover restaurant napkin he found in the door pocket.

A mud-splattered pickup truck turned onto Killian's street. The truck slowed as it passed Killian's house, then continued.

"Can you see the plate number?" Bree asked.

"No." Matt pulled his binoculars from the glove compartment. "It's covered in mud, like the rest of the vehicle."

"Like the whole freaking town. We're going to need to change the town name from Grey's Hollow to Grey's Wallow."

The pickup turned around in Killian's driveway and went back the way it had come. It turned the corner and disappeared from view.

"Wrong house?" Bree asked.

"Felt like they were casing the place." Matt rolled his shoulders and concentrated on the house.

"What's that?" Bree pointed through the windshield. A beam of light flashed in one of Killian's front windows. The light arced and disappeared.

"A flashlight," Matt said.

"In the daytime? That's suspicious."

"Killian could have spotted us and is trying to pretend he's not home." Matt reached for the door handle. "Let's go see who it is."

Bree grabbed her uniform hat from the back seat. They slipped out of the vehicle and walked back to Killian's house. Rain plastered Matt's hair to his head. From the sidewalk, Matt scanned the windows but saw nothing. They walked to the front door. He shielded his eyes with a hand and peered through the window. A light bobbed in the back of the house.

Something squeaked behind the house. Matt froze. He lowered his voice. "Did you hear that?"

Bree nodded. They both remained motionless, listening.

A scraping sound emanated from the backyard.

Matt mouthed, "Whoever is inside used the back door."

Bree lifted a palm to the sky. She whispered, "Killian could be inside, avoiding us. The only conditions of his bail set by the judge were to not leave the state without permission, to not possess a firearm, and to stay away from Grace. I'm sure his attorney advised him not to talk to us."

A metallic bang inside the house drew them up short. Bree's hand went to the gun on her hip. "On second thought, let's check around back." She pressed her lapel mic and reported a possible break-in to dispatch, who promised backup would be en route when available. Bree drew her weapon and led the way around the house. Matt's boots squished in the saturated grass.

Matt eased an eyeball around the corner, searching the shadows for shapes or movement. "Don't see anyone," he whispered. They passed a window, the blinds drawn tightly.

Bree stepped around, creeping through a few feet of wet grass onto a square concrete patio. Shoulder to shoulder, they skirted a rusty table and two worn wicker chairs. The sliding glass door stood open a few inches. Matt's instincts went on full alert. His pulse quickened, echoing in his ears. He drew in a deep breath and held it for a few seconds, then slowly emptied his lungs, lowering his heart rate and heading off the adrenaline dump that threatened to tunnel his vision.

He gestured toward the opening. Wind stirred the air, disturbing a pile of leaf debris accumulated against the foundation. A sheer curtain blew back and forth through the door opening, as if the house were breathing.

Bree moved to one side of the door. Matt stood at her shoulder. She eased over the threshold. Matt followed her in, the curtain curling around his body, holding him back. He disentangled the fabric, freeing his legs. A thud sounded from the next room. Whoever was inside was attempting—but failing—to be quiet.

Pale gray light shone from the hallway that led to the front of the house, but the back of the house was dim.

Matt and Bree crept through the family room. Matt spotted a large shadow moving around the kitchen, using a flashlight to search the room. Matt gestured, but Bree had already seen it.

Something banged. The figure grunted. His flashlight brightened the ceiling as he rubbed his forehead.

Matt swept a hand across the wall. The lights came on. The figure spun to face them, leaving Matt and Bree blinking at Grace Abbott's father.

"Sheriff's department!" Bree leveled her gun at him. "Let me see your hands."

Mr. Abbott raised his bowling ball–size fists into the air. His hands held only the flashlight. "I'm not armed."

"Turn around," Bree instructed. "Put your hands on the back of your head."

Mr. Abbott complied. Matt moved forward to cuff him. After he was restrained, Matt turned him around and patted down his pockets. He found keys and a wallet.

"What are you doing here?" Bree asked.

Mr. Abbott frowned. "Looking for Grace."

Matt asked, "Isn't she at your house?"

"She was." Mr. Abbott rattled the cuffs behind his back. "She got her old waitressing job back. She worked her first shift this morning. She was supposed to be done by two o'clock. She never came home." He glanced around the kitchen. "We thought maybe she was with *him*."

"Did she say she wanted to return to Killian?" Bree asked.

Mr. Abbott's jaw clenched tightly enough to crack a molar. "No."

"Then why would you think she would?" Matt pressed. "She's only a couple of hours late." But Matt didn't like it.

Mr. Abbott turned his head to meet Matt's gaze. The anger in Abbott's eyes alarmed Matt. "Because she is who she is. She has a history of making bad decisions when it comes to men." He inhaled and blew the air out in a short snort. "Look, I don't think she'll go back to him. But if he called her begging to talk, she might give in. She's easily swayed. Just basic female weakness."

Bree's eyebrow shot up, but Mr. Abbott didn't seem to catch the irony of calling females weak when one was currently holding him in custody.

Heat blasted up Matt's spine. He opened his mouth to respond, but Bree tapped his forearm.

"Mr. Abbott," she began in an admirably neutral voice. "Where is Grace working?"

"Weekends," he said. "On Route 40."

"We know it." Bree pulled out her phone, pressed a button, and raised the phone to her ear. Weekends was a sports bar famous for its triple-decker burgers and bottomless french fry baskets. "How did Grace get to work?"

Mr. Abbott said, "Uber. She was supposed to be home around two thirty."

"Did you call Weekends?" Matt asked.

Mr. Abbott cocked his head. "What do you think? Of course I did. They said she left at the end of her shift. She's not answering her phone.

If he convinced her to meet with him"—he circled his head to indicate their current location—"this would be the logical place."

Bree lowered her phone. "Grace's calls are going right to voice mail."

Which meant the phone was either turned off or the battery was dead.

Bree tapped the phone on her thigh. "Has Killian been in touch with her?"

Mr. Abbott's head jerked in a tight shake. "I told her if she talked to him, she had to find somewhere else to live."

Thereby ensuring that Grace would not tell her father if she had talked to Killian.

Lights swirled through a window that overlooked the street. "Backup is here." Bree took Mr. Abbott by the arm and led him toward the sliding glass door.

"You can't arrest me!" Mr. Abbott protested. "I was just looking for my daughter."

Bree steered him through the opening. "Breaking and entering is illegal."

"The door wasn't locked." Abbott jerked his arm away. "I didn't break anything."

"You still can't enter someone else's home without permission," Bree said.

Matt scanned the house. Everything looked normal, except a trash can that had been knocked over.

"That was an accident," Mr. Abbott grumbled. "It was dark. I bumped into it. I just want to find Grace." His voice crackled, the first sign of emotion breaking through his tough-guy facade.

Matt wondered if Mr. Abbott regretted the hard-ass stance he'd taken with his daughter.

Bree took his arm firmly. "We're going outside."

"If you arrest me, I can't find her." A note of panic lifted his tone.

"We're going to look for Grace," Bree assured him as she chicken-winged his arm, using the leverage to propel him out of the house.

"He searched my pockets." Mr. Abbott jerked his chin toward Matt. "I didn't take anything."

Bree sighed. "Do you promise to go home and stay there?"

Being arrested on Friday night would mean spending the weekend in jail. She clearly didn't want to arrest Grace's father.

Mr. Abbott stopped resisting, but Matt stuck close anyway. Abbott was mountain-size. Even in handcuffs, a man with his sheer mass could do some damage. Bree could handle herself just fine, but she didn't need another physical confrontation, not after the boot she'd taken to the face at the motel. If Abbott resisted, it would be like trying to manhandle a mule.

Abbott bowed his head for a minute, then raised his chin and looked Bree, then Matt in the eye. "I do."

"You're giving me your word?" Bree asked.

"Yes." Abbott nodded.

"Then I won't arrest you at the moment." Bree spun him around and removed the handcuffs. They left through the open slider. After closing the door, Bree marched Abbott around to the front yard. She gently propelled him toward his truck. "Go home. Stay there."

"Thank you," he said over his shoulder. "Please find my daughter."

A sheriff's department patrol vehicle pulled up to the curb. While Bree spoke with her deputy, Matt walked to the next-door neighbor's house and rang the bell. Matt noted the doorbell was a camera model. Digital chimes sounded inside, and a dog burst into a frenzy of yapping.

A sturdy middle-age woman in yoga pants and an oversize hoodie answered, concern creasing her brow. A skinny Chihuahua mix charged down the hall with a *Flintstones* Dino-like chorus of barking. She blocked him with a foot, but he darted around the woman's ankles and lunged at Matt, growling. Barely ten pounds, the dog's age showed in the solid white of its face and muzzle.

The woman crouched and tried to catch the dog, but it slunk out of her reach. "Damn you, Ripper." The admonition came out with no heat, merely resignation and a little humor.

Ripper lunged at Matt's foot. Matt didn't react, which seemed to confuse the dog.

The woman blew a chunk of sandy-blonde hair from her eyes. "I got him from the shelter a couple of months ago. I thought adopting a senior dog would be easier, but Ripper here is quite feisty for his age. He scared the bejesus out of the mailman yesterday." The woman stood back, watching as Ripper stopped barking and sniffed Matt's boots. "You don't seem afraid."

"I was a K-9 handler for the sheriff's department." Handlers took turns playing the suspect in training exercises. A full-grown German shepherd delivered a hell of a hit, even through a bite sleeve. Matt looked down at the dog circling his feet. He doubted Ripper's teeth could even pierce his boot. If the old dog did manage to bite, he'd probably leave most of his teeth stuck in the thick leather. "He's fine, ma'am."

She sighed. "He's not fine. He's a jerk. But he's my jerk, and I love him."

Matt snorted. "I understand."

"You're here about him?" She inclined her head toward Killian's house.

"Yes, ma'am."

The woman crossed her arms. "Did he hit her again?"

"Mr. Killian's house was broken into," Matt said. "Have you seen him?"

The woman huffed. "I'm not sorry someone broke into his house. He's an awful person."

Matt didn't disagree. "I still need to talk to him."

"I haven't seen him since he was arrested a few days ago. Can't say that I'm sorry about that either. This is a nice neighborhood, except for him. If I see him outside, I avoid him."

"Has he been hostile to you?"

"He's just miserable, always complaining about ridiculous things, like kids running across the lawn or someone walking too close to his stupid Beemer." She rolled her eyes. "Even the Girl Scouts skip his house during cookie season."

"Have you seen his vehicle in his driveway?" Matt asked. "Any other signs he's been home?"

She tilted her head and tapped a finger to the corner of her mouth. "I think his car was there yesterday when I left for work around seven a.m., but I can't be a hundred percent sure."

Matt glanced at the doorbell camera. "Does your doorbell camera show Mr. Killian's driveway?"

"It does." She pulled her phone from a pocket on the leg of her yoga pants and opened an app. "I had a package delivered yesterday at 9:07 in the morning." She turned the phone so Matt could see the screen. The bottom of Killian's driveway—and the rear of his BMW—was visible in the background.

"Any other recent videos?" Matt asked.

"There's activity on Sunday, but that's it, sorry." She lowered her phone. "I don't get many visitors."

"Have you seen his vehicle today?" Matt asked.

She shook her head. "I was off today. The only time I've set foot outside is to take Ripper out back to do his business. Neither of us loves this wet weather."

"Could I have a copy of that video from Thursday morning?" Matt asked.

"Can I download it?" She opened her phone again. Matt walked her through the download-and-send process before returning to

Killian's front yard, where Bree was waiting. He relayed the neighbor's information.

"I've put out a BOLO on Killian and his vehicle," Bree said. "Grace, as well."

"Now what?"

"Let's go to Weekends and see if they have surveillance video showing Grace leaving. Killian's brother bailed him out. We'll pay him a visit and see if he knows where Killian is." Bree looked away. "We need to find Grace. I know she's only been missing for a few hours, but I don't like this situation at all. I'd like to find her."

Matt finished her thought. *Before she ends up dead.*

CHAPTER TWENTY-EIGHT

Weekends was hopping early on a Friday evening. Music blared, and people crowded the vestibule. Bree badged and elbowed her way past the crowd of waiting patrons to the hostess podium. "I need to see the manager."

The young woman remained bent over her computer screen. A wall of glossy, dark hair blocked her face. "I'm sorry. We're very busy. How many in your party?"

"None." Bree lowered her badge in between the girl's eyes and her screen.

"Oh." She jerked upright. Her eyes, heavily lined in black, snapped open wide. Light glinted on a gold stud in the side of her nose. "I'll get her." She scurried toward the back of the restaurant.

Someone dropped a metal pan, the sound reverberating over the general chaos. Bree rubbed her temple. Her head still ached from her encounter at the motel. The cacophony of noises in the sports bar echoed in her brain like a jackhammer in a gymnasium. The crowd at the bar burst into cheers and hoots. Bree assumed their team had scored.

The manager hurried to the lobby a minute later. She was about thirty-five, in standard black pants and a black button-down blouse. A name tag read MANAGER in large letters, with TAMARA spelled out in smaller ones beneath her titles. Her brown hair was pulled back into a neat bun. She gestured Bree and Matt to follow her. They passed the restroom and entered an office the size of an elevator.

Tamara blew a hair off her face. "Would you please close the door?" Matt did.

"Sorry about the cramped space, but the noise level on Friday nights is earsplitting." Tamara had to turn sideways and sidle past her desk to get to her chair. "Is this about Grace? Her father called earlier. He seemed upset. I'll tell you the same thing I told him: I didn't come on until after Grace had left for the day. The assistant manager was on schedule this morning. But I know that Grace started her shift at ten and clocked out around two."

Bree perched on the edge of a plastic chair. "We'd like the exterior security camera footage."

"Of course." Tamara swiveled her chair to face a desktop computer. She tapped on the keyboard until a grid of tiny windows appeared. "We have cameras on the front and rear doors, and two in the back parking lot." She clicked away. "Here's Grace standing just outside the back door a few minutes after two." Tamara turned the screen to face them. The camera faced the rear of the restaurant. Grace huddled under the eave, leaning on the building, rubbing her biceps, a rain jacket zipped to her chin. At 2:10, she pushed off the wall and walked away from the building.

"That's not very useful," the manager said. "Let me look for another angle."

She minimized the window and enlarged a different one. "This camera is mounted on the parking lot streetlamp." The view showed half of the lot. Raindrops on the lens made the video slightly blurry. The rear corner of the building was visible in the periphery.

The manager rewound to 2:09 and let the video play. A man and child walked across the lot. They climbed into an SUV and drove away.

Grace entered the screen at 2:11, just as the shadow of a vehicle appeared in the corner. The bumper and front one-third of a light-colored sedan inched into view, but the corner of the building concealed the rest of the vehicle. Glowing signs on the dashboard read UBER and LYFT.

Grace walked to the side of the vehicle. She stopped next to it and said something, presumably to the driver. She looked down at the phone in her hand, then took one step backward. Her hands rose and she shook her head. The shadow of the driver's-side door moved across the pavement. A shape rushed toward Grace. She turned, tried to run, and stumbled to one knee. The figure grabbed her around the waist, hauled her off her feet, and swung her over one shoulder. Grace kicked and flailed, but he never wavered. He disappeared behind the building. A minute later, he returned to the driver's side of the vehicle. The door closed. The vehicle backed out of sight.

No one spoke for two heartbeats.

"She was kidnapped." Tamara stared at the screen. "In broad daylight. Right out back."

Matt stroked his beard. "Looks like he pretended to be her Uber. Did he know she was calling one? Or did he get lucky?"

"If he was intentionally targeting Grace, how did he know where she was or that she would call for a ride?" Bree asked.

"Killian might know where she'd worked in the past," Matt suggested. "Maybe he even had something of hers bugged. He could have been keeping tabs on her movements long before this."

Bree scooted closer to the desk. "Can you rewind and advance frame by frame?"

"Yes." Tamara worked her mouse.

Grace appeared. Tamara stopped the video, then clicked each frame one by one until the vehicle appeared.

"Stop." Bree leaned closer.

Matt moved from his position leaning on the wall to crouch next to the desk. "Can't see the license plate because of the angle of the vehicle."

"Can you tell the make and model?" Bree asked.

"No," Matt said. "All I see is a medium-size gray, silver, or tan sedan."

"Killian drives a silver BMW 328i." Bree gestured.

Matt pulled out his phone. "Here's the same model." He compared the images. "Can't see the vehicle very well, but BMWs have distinctive headlights. I don't think that's a Beemer. Maybe Rory in forensics can make the video clearer."

Bree had no doubt Rory would match the make and model of the car. "Doesn't matter. If Killian wanted to snatch Grace, he would borrow a vehicle, not use his own." She pointed to the computer. "Keep going."

Tamara clicked through more frames. She stopped when the figure rushed Grace. "I assume you want to see her attacker?"

"Yes," Bree said.

He slowly came into view.

Bree watched the slow-motion progression of frames.

Tamara moved forward and back through the video until she stopped. "I think this is the clearest image."

The attacker was in profile to the camera. His face was in shadow, but his clothing was clear. He wore jeans, black athletic shoes, and a black baseball cap with the brim pulled low. The hood of his jacket was also pulled over his head. His shoulders were broad, and he was quick on his feet, like an athlete.

"Definitely male," Bree said. "But can't see his face at all. Can you zoom in on his hands?"

Tamara enlarged the area.

"He's white," Bree said. "No visible tattoos."

"The wide-angle lens creates some distortion at the edges of the video, making it hard to determine his size," Matt said. "He towers over Grace, but she's petite, so that doesn't mean he's unusually tall."

"Not a small man, though," Bree said. "He just tossed her over his shoulder like it was easy."

The serial killer had carried dead bodies to the clearing and had hoisted one into a tree at Bree's house. She shared a look with Matt. He was thinking the same. The serial killer had taken Grace.

Bree turned back to Tamara. "I need a copy of those videos."

"Already on it." Tamara inserted a thumb drive into the computer. "I've copied it. I can also send it via email."

Bree handed her a business card with her email. Underneath the official sheriff's department phone number, she wrote her personal cell number. "I want you to call or text if you learn anything else."

"I will." Tamara traded the thumb drive for the card. Then she opened an email portal, started a new message, and attached the video clips. She pressed "Send."

"We'd like to see the employees' exit," Bree said.

"Of course." Tamara led them through the kitchen to a metal door. A row of jackets on hooks lined the wall. Tamara grabbed one and pushed open the door. They all stepped out onto the concrete walkway behind the building. Tamara slid into her coat and flipped up the hood. Drizzle dampened Bree's face.

She recognized the spot where Grace had waited. They retraced her steps toward the side of the building. On the other side of the narrow street, a dumpster sat in a U-shaped screen of white PVC fencing. "You can drive all the way around the building, but the kidnapper chose to back up."

Matt jerked his chin toward the camera mounted on the nearest light pole in the center of the lot. "He probably saw the camera."

Bree scanned the area, replaying the video in her mind. "He could have been here before, or even scouted the premises earlier today."

"Bree!" Matt pointed to the ground.

Bree followed his direction with her gaze. Near the curb, a cell phone lay on the dirty asphalt. The screen was cracked. She took a picture of the phone, then tugged on a glove and picked it up. Bree tapped the screen. "Passcode protected." They'd take it to Rory. He'd be able to access the data.

She slid the phone into an evidence bag.

Tamara huddled and shifted her weight between her feet. "I hope you find her. This is horrible. I can't believe she was kidnapped right behind the building. How can I keep my employees safe?"

"Make sure everyone has an escort to their car. I'll need the names and contact numbers for employees who were here at two o'clock this afternoon." Bree would have a deputy speak to each one of them.

"I can email you a list." Tamara whipped out her phone. "I need five minutes in my office."

Bree's phone buzzed. She glanced at the screen. The ME was calling. "Excuse me."

She stepped away to answer the call. "Sheriff Taggert."

"I stayed late to finish the autopsy. You want an emailed preliminary or do you want to come here?"

Bree needed to talk to Rory, and forensics was in the same municipal complex. "We'll be there in ten minutes."

CHAPTER TWENTY-NINE

Matt tried to look at the body on the table with detachment, but he found it impossible. He'd met Jana's mother. He'd been inside Jana's apartment. He'd seen her painting. A couple of days ago, she'd been a living, breathing young woman. She'd hoped and dreamed. She'd worked hard to fulfill those goals. She'd been tough too. She'd struggled with roadblocks, like her lack of money, a disabled mother, and a lazy, abusive boyfriend.

And now she was dead.

Matt shuffled a bootie-covered shoe on the tile as he stared down at Jana Rynski. She'd been a slight girl, barely bigger than a child. Did she even weigh a hundred pounds? The stapled Y-incision looked obscene on her narrow body, like something out of a horror flick. Although not visible, her organs, which had been removed one by one to be weighed and examined, were currently in a plastic bag, stuffed into the body cavity under the staples. Thankfully, Dr. Jones or her assistant had replaced the skullcap and scalp. Dr. Jones cared for her charges with the utmost respect, but the autopsy was by its very nature an insult to a body that had already been desecrated. Intellectually, he knew that Jana was no longer present in that shell. The flesh and blood that had once housed her were already beginning to decompose. But viewing the damage inflicted by her killer—and the necessary further violation of her body to catch him—gave Matt a nauseated ache in the center of his chest.

The ME gestured to the side of Jana's head. "This is officially a homicide. She died of blunt force trauma, a hard blow to the head." Dr. Jones motioned to a skull X-ray on the light board. "Her skull was cracked. Whatever was used had a sharp edge." She returned to the body, parting the hair to show a long gash.

"The wound would have bled heavily?" Matt asked.

"Yes. Head wounds produce copious amounts of blood," Dr. Jones confirmed.

"Time of death?" Bree asked.

"We had to break rigor to perform the autopsy," Dr. Jones said. "I'm estimating she's been dead eighteen to twenty-four hours."

At ambient temperature, rigor mortis loosely followed a twelve-twelve-twelve pattern. Muscles contracted for the first twelve hours after death, remained stiff for the next twelve, then softened over the last twelve.

Bree glanced at the time on her phone. Six p.m. "She died between six o'clock last evening and midnight."

"Correct," Dr. Jones confirmed.

"Did she have any other injuries that could have bled heavily?" Bree asked.

"I saw no other life-threatening injuries," Dr. Jones said. "But there's significant swelling and bruising around the head injury."

"She didn't die right away," Bree said.

"No, she didn't. Bruises, swelling, and bleeding only occur while the heart is still beating. So she was alive for at least a day after sustaining the head injury."

"So he broke into her apartment and tried to kidnap her. She resisted. Can you tell if he struck her in the head or if she fell and hit her head? Forensics didn't find any sign that she hit her head while falling. No blood on the kitchen counter edges or furniture."

"Considering the injury is on the left side of her head and the downward angle of the blow, being struck by a right-handed person taller than her seems likely."

"Lividity seems . . . random?" Bree gestured to a purple discoloration on the side of the body. "I don't see a pattern."

"I agree," said Dr. Jones. "She was moved after death, likely a few times. She clearly spent some time on her back after death, but then she was moved."

"She would have been transported to the farm, probably in the trunk of a vehicle, in a different position," Matt said.

"And she spent some hours in the tree as well." Dr. Jones sounded weary.

Matt scanned the body, his gaze stopping on Jana's forearms, which were bruised. Her fingernails were also torn. "Defensive injuries."

"Yes. She fought him." The ME's voice turned sad. "He killed her anyway."

"Tissue under her nails?" Bree asked.

"We swabbed, but it doesn't look promising." Dr. Jones shook her head. "Her fingernails were freshly trimmed, and her body was washed, like the others."

"Any evidence on the tarp?" Bree asked.

"Forensics took swabs, et cetera." Dr. Jones's mouth mashed into a straight line. "He's not leaving much behind for us to work with." She sighed hard. "There is one thing that stands out. She was pregnant."

Matt froze. "Pregnant?"

Dr. Jones nodded.

"Like Ally." Bree shifted back on her heels, as if the news had rocked her. "How far along?"

Dr. Jones frowned. "About seven or eight weeks."

"She probably knew, but barely." Bree crossed her arms over her waist. "Any sign of sexual assault?"

"No." Dr. Jones lifted a hand in a *stop* gesture. "No vaginal tearing or bruising, and no semen. In fact, no sign that she had recent sexual intercourse at all."

"Anything else?" Bree asked.

Dr. Jones shook her head. "I wish. Lab reports on swabs and tox screens are pending."

"Thanks." Bree led the way out of the autopsy suite.

Matt stripped off his PPE. Though neither of them had touched anything, they both thoroughly washed their hands before leaving. If he could have taken a decontamination shower, he would have. "Chevy didn't kill her."

"No. He was in custody last night." Bree dried her hands on a paper towel and tossed it into a trash can. "Let's see Rory and track down Howard Killian."

The county forensics lab was in the same building as the medical examiner's office. They made their way down the maze of corridors to the lab. Rory MacIniss worked on a laptop at a stainless-steel table. In his thirties, he was tall and thin, with a slightly adolescent face that belied his age.

Bree rapped her knuckles on the door, and Rory motioned for them to enter.

Like most municipal employees in rural departments, Rory wore multiple hats, but computer forensics was his first love. Bree handed him Grace's phone in the evidence bag and explained the circumstances. "Of course check for prints, but we think she dropped the phone while fighting with her kidnapper."

Rory nodded. "What specific information are you looking for?"

Bree's shoulders rose and dropped. Frustration—and potentially a little desperation—edged her voice. "Recent texts and calls. Activity on her Uber account. Anything else that might help us find her. We also have this." She handed over the thumb drive. "See if you can clean up an image of the man who kidnapped her. We have a partial picture of his vehicle. See if you can match the make and model."

Rory examined the phone and drive. "You think the serial killer has her?"

"We do," Bree said.

"Then this is my priority. I'll get busy immediately." He turned toward the laptop. "You'll be available later tonight?"

"We'll be available all night," Matt said.

"Same." Rory's chin jerked down in a solemn nod. "I won't leave until I have what you need."

"Thank you," Bree said. "Anything notable from the other crime scenes?"

"The black fibers embedded in Ally's skin came from 4mm black Paracord," Rory said. "Unfortunately, it's very common. Sold online and in hardware stores all across the US. So, that's not going to be much help. We found residue of dish soap on her skin, assuming that's what he used to wash her. We're working on determining the brand, but again, I doubt that will prove useful in locating him."

"But if we find him," Bree said, "every bit of evidence that ties him to the crimes will help put him in prison forever."

"Let's hope." Rory's gloved hand closed into a fist. "We've finally caught up with processing evidence. I'll email the reports."

"Thanks." Bree turned toward the door.

Matt followed. There would be no sleep for any of them until they found Grace.

Bree practically jogged back to the vehicle. Matt drove to Walt Killian's house. Howard's brother lived in a new town house development near the interstate.

"It's the end unit." Matt motioned toward a faux stone–fronted unit with a glossy black door.

Bree kept her hand near her weapon as they flanked the door and knocked.

A man of about forty opened the door. He scanned Bree's uniform and frowned. "Yes?"

Bree introduced them. "Are you Howard Killian's brother?"

"I am. I'm Walt." He leaned back, puffed out his chest, and folded his arms, his posture stiff.

"We're looking for Howard," she said.

"Haven't seen him since I bailed him out." He took a step backward.

"Do you know where he might have gone?" she asked.

"Nope. I bailed him out because he's my brother, but we're nothing alike. We don't hang out together. That said, I won't work against him." He pushed the door.

Matt slapped a hand on the cold steel. "Grace is missing."

Walt's lips rolled in, as if he wanted to say something but was holding back.

"Did Howard say anything about wanting to talk to her or see her?" Bree asked.

"I already said I can't help you." He shut the door in their faces.

"Fuck." Matt stepped back, the back of his neck heating. "What now?"

They turned back to the narrow driveway. A tall woman appeared from around the side of the building. She was about the same age as Walt. She wore jeans and a light sweater. "You're looking for Howard?"

"We are," Bree said, her hand moving to rest on her duty belt.

"I'm Bethany Killian, Walt's wife." She rubbed her biceps. "I heard you talking to my husband. Is Grace OK?"

"We don't know," Bree said. "We just want to find her."

She rubbed one sock-clad foot on the opposite ankle. "My husband would like to give you information, but he has a strange sense of loyalty toward a brother who has never shown any back." She propped her foot against her shin like a stork. "Howard hangs out at a bar on Tenth Street in Scarlet Falls. It's called the Filling Station. The bartender there has called Walt a few times to collect Howard."

"Do you know if Howard has any friends?"

"I have no idea. I actively avoid him as much as possible. But I met Grace once. I told her she could do better. I hope you find her." She turned and disappeared around the side of the house, where Matt assumed there was a door.

"I feel like we're chasing our tails," he said. "That bar is a half hour from here."

"I agree. I'll send two deputies to the bar to ask about Howard." She used her radio to issue the order while Matt started the engine. "We can't waste time driving all over the county. I doubt Grace is at any public place."

"We need to eat." Matt put the vehicle into gear and turned toward his parents' house. "We can stop at my parents' house, check on the kids, and grab food. If I call ahead, it'll be faster than going to a deli."

"I can't get Grace out of my head." Bree rubbed her eyes. "I don't want to find her dead body tomorrow."

"I know. We're doing everything we can. Every cop on duty in the region is looking for her and Killian. But we still need fuel."

"OK." Bree dropped her hands. "Assuming she was taken by the same predator that killed Jana and the other three women, we'll continue to work their cases. If we find the killer, we should find Grace."

"Best we can do."

A few minutes later, Matt parked at his parents' house. They climbed out of the SUV. Bree rushed to the back door as if she hadn't seen the kids in a month. Matt opened the kitchen door and held it for Bree. She shoved her phone into the holder on her duty belt.

The room smelled of freshly baked bread. Matt's mother stirred something in a pot on the stove, which was weird. His dad usually did the cooking.

"Where's Dad?" Matt shed his jacket.

His mom frowned. "He went to see Cady. He didn't like the way she sounded on the phone, and Todd is working. You know how he is."

"I do." Matt slung his jacket over the back of a chair. His dad might have retired from his family practice, but he still volunteered at clinics, covered for other physicians, and maintained his continuing education requirements to keep his license current. He would always be a doctor in his heart.

From under her no-nonsense cap of short gray hair, his mom appraised them with shrewd blue eyes. Her gaze landed on Bree. "You look pale. I'll make you some tea to go. I imagine you've had more than enough coffee for one day."

"Is that possible?" Matt asked.

His mother shook her spoon at him. "It is if you like your stomach lining."

Matt shot Bree a look. The corner of her mouth twitched.

"Tea sounds nice." Bree shed her own jacket. "Can I help?"

"No." Anna waved her wooden spoon at the doorway that led to the den. "Go see the kids. I'll pack this up for you. It'll be ready in a few. I can tell you want to get back to work."

Bree deposited her jacket on an empty chair. She and Matt stopped to wash their hands before stepping through the doorway. A short hall led to the tidy den, where Kayla and Luke, clad in a mix of pajamas and sweats, sat on a sectional couch watching TV.

"Aunt Bree!" Kayla emerged from under a fuzzy blanket like Godzilla and threw out her arms.

Bree sat next to her, hugged her close, and pressed a palm to her forehead. "No fever. How do you feel?"

"My nose is stuffy, and my head hurts a little, but I'm OK." Except for chapped lips and a red nose, she looked and sounded fine.

"Luke?" Bree asked.

"Tired, but OK." Luke patted his belly. "George has been cooking all day. I don't like missing school, but I'll admit, having a day off to veg out is kinda nice."

Luke maintained top grades, held a part-time job, and played sports, in addition to pitching in with horse care. Most adults couldn't handle his workload.

Kayla settled back into the cushions. "You hafta eat some, Aunt Bree. It's soooo good."

Matt inhaled deeply. The smells reminded him of being home sick when he was a kid. He felt too young for nostalgia, but there it was, a spongy feeling in the middle of his chest. He grabbed a leftover piece of bread from someone's plate and pointed to Kayla with it. "My dad has been making the same soup and bread since I was your age."

"That long?" Kayla's eyes bulged. Her incredulous tone suggested Matt was a hundred years old.

He grinned. "Practically forever."

"You're so lucky," she said in a wistful tone.

"I am." Matt ate the bread. "Are you ready?" he asked Bree.

"Yes. Sorry, kids. We can't stay. Just wanted to check on you." She met Matt's gaze, stress creasing the outer corners of her eyes.

Matt stood. He offered Bree a hand. She took it, and he hauled her off the couch. While she ducked into the bathroom, Matt headed for the kitchen.

His mom was loading cookies into a container. She nodded toward an insulated picnic bag. "There are roasted chicken sandwiches, along with two travel mugs of black tea and a couple of apples. Do you need anything else?"

"No. That's perfect. Thanks, Mom." Matt gave her a hug. "I know you weren't thrilled when I returned to law enforcement, but I appreciate your support."

"Well, you *were* shot in the line of duty, but it's who you are. I respect that, even if it worries me." She loaded the container of cookies into an insulated bag, then rested her head on his shoulder for a few seconds. She gave him a pointed look. "Drink the tea instead of coffee."

"No promises. We might need high octane."

She huffed. "Love you."

"Love you too."

The door opened, and Matt's dad led his sister, Cady, into the house.

"Is everything OK?" Matt's mom asked.

"Just adding another patient to the infirmary," Dad said in a cheerful voice. "Todd isn't home, and Cady is a bit dehydrated. I gave her the choice of here or the ER."

"I'll be fine. I wanted to stay home, but you know Dad." Cady sank into a kitchen chair. Protests aside, she looked sicker than either Kayla or Luke. Cady's face was dead white beneath her freckles, and her skin looked papery.

Matt's mom's mouth pursed with concern. "What can you drink?"

"I don't know if I can keep anything down." Cady spied cookies cooling on the rack and covered her mouth.

"She'll have some electrolyte solution with plenty of ice." Dad lifted a black duffel bag. "I'll take your things upstairs and grab some meds for that nausea."

After watching their dad practically skip from the room, Cady dropped her head to rest on her folded arms. "He's never happier than when he has a bunch of sick people to take care of."

"You are so right." Mom laughed, but her eyes were worried as she poured blue liquid into an insulated cup of ice.

"You do look terrible," Matt said.

Cady turned her head, so her cheek was pressing on her arms. She gave Matt a miserable look and shot him a middle finger when their mother's back was turned.

"Very mature." But Matt felt better knowing his sister was well enough to snipe with him.

Mom set the cup next to Cady's face. "Small sips."

"What are the kids doing?" Cady asked without lifting her head.

"Watching a Marvel movie," Matt said. "Not sure which one."

"Sounds good to me." Cady shuffled out of the room, cup in hand, her steps weak and slow, a study in misery. Matt empathized. Nausea was the worst.

"I'll bring you some crackers." Mom frowned at Cady's back after she disappeared.

"She doesn't look good." Matt stared at the doorway. He could hear the action-movie sounds wafting from the sickroom.

Mom patted his arm. "Your dad will keep a close eye on her. She'll be OK."

A minute later, Bree walked into the kitchen. "This flu is taking out the whole town." She turned to Matt. "Ready?"

He picked up his jacket. Bree tugged hers on. Matt grabbed the bag of food, and they headed back outside, leaving the warmth of the house behind. A steady cold rain slid down the back of his neck and dripped down his spine.

"Where do you want to go first?" he asked.

Bree rubbed the bridge of her nose. "Let's go out to the Abbott farm. Maybe Grace confided more in her mother than her father." She had her phone in hand before they reached the patrol unit.

"We'll eat on the way." Matt dug into the bag and pulled out a sandwich. After peeling the plastic wrap halfway down the sandwich, he handed it to Bree.

She ate with one hand and drove with the other. They had no time to waste.

Grace Abbott was in the hands of a killer.

CHAPTER THIRTY

Bree ate half the sandwich and handed the leftover piece to Matt. "I'll eat the rest later."

While she agreed with Matt that they needed fuel to work, the trip to the morgue had ruined her appetite. Instead, she headed for the drive-through at Starbucks. "I'm sorry. Tea is not going to cut it tonight."

Matt stuffed her leftovers into the insulated bag. He sniffed the tea his mother had packed and closed the spout. "Make that two."

While she drove and they guzzled coffee, her deputy called to report that Howard Killian had been at the bar in Scarlet Falls at lunchtime but had left around one o'clock.

"We just can't catch a break." Bree drained her cup.

"He can't hide forever," Matt said.

The GPS announced they'd reached their destination. The Abbotts lived in a sprawling one-story home on an oversize lot near the outskirts of town. Bree scanned the dark yard as she and Matt walked to the front door. Chickens clucked somewhere.

She knocked. The woman who opened the door was small like Grace. Similarities between mother and daughter extended beyond physical characteristics. Mrs. Abbott's driver's license said she was only forty-two. She could have passed for a decade older, at least. She wore baggy jeans, a sweatshirt, and beat-up sneakers. Her blonde hair was streaked with gray and bound in a tight ponytail. Lines bracketed her eyes, and the circles under them were dark enough to be bruises.

Bree introduced herself and Matt.

"Are you here about Grace or my husband?" Mrs. Abbott wiped her hands on the hem of her apron.

"We're focused on finding your daughter," Bree said.

"You best come in then." Mrs. Abbott stepped aside, turned, and led them back to a kitchen organized with military precision. Plates, mugs, and glasses lined open shelves. The rectangular table was long enough to seat a dozen on the matching benches. Two teenage girls washed and dried dishes on autopilot.

"Girls," she said. "Go to your rooms. I'll finish the dishes later." With a mumbled "Yes, ma'am," they fled, leaving it eerily silent for a house with eight—nine—children in it.

"Riley and my younger children are in bed," Mrs. Abbott said.

"How is Riley?" Bree asked.

"Getting acquainted with her family. The twins are only six, so Riley has built-in playmates," Mrs. Abbott said.

"Where is your husband?" Bree would be very angry if Mr. Abbott hadn't kept his word about staying home.

"In the garage, fixing something." Mrs. Abbott nodded toward a door. "He can't be still."

"May I?" Matt gestured toward the garage door.

Mrs. Abbott consented with a gesture of surrender, and he disappeared through the door. Mrs. Abbott leaned both hands on the table. "Are you any closer to finding Grace?"

"Not yet." Bree leaned a hip on the counter. "What did Grace do since she moved home?"

Mrs. Abbott's fingers clutched the edge of the butcher block like claws. "She's been helping with chores, taking care of Riley, making the necessary calls about a job . . ."

"Did she go anywhere?" Bree asked.

"Just to work this morning."

"Did she seem normal?"

"I don't even know what normal is for her anymore. She slinks around the house like a stray cat." Mrs. Abbott pushed away from the counter, picked up a huge chef's knife, and positioned it over a red onion. The knife sliced with mechanical precision, each slice identical to the last, the knife moving fast enough to make Bree curl her own fingers into her palms.

"Tell me about this morning," Bree said.

The knife paused, halfway through an onion. "She was up at five, pitched in with breakfast and cleanup. She booked a ride with Uber and left for work around seven thirty."

"Seven thirty?"

"Yes." Mrs. Abbott gave Bree a quizzical look. "Why?"

Because Grace didn't start work until ten.

Bree pulled her notepad and pen from her pocket. "I'm constructing a timeline of her day. She didn't say she needed to run an errand after work?"

"No. She specifically said she was coming straight home."

Bree sent Rory a quick text, asking him to check Grace's Uber and Lyft apps for activity from the morning. Grace could have needed to stop at a store or the post office or any number of routine errands, but the fact that she'd chosen not to tell her mother put Bree on alert. "We'd like to see Grace's room in case there's something that might indicate where she's gone."

"Of course." Tight-lipped, Mrs. Abbott led the way out of the kitchen and down a hall. They passed two bedrooms, each crowded with two sets of bunk beds, like dormitories. In the third room, Riley sat on an opened sofa bed, flipping through a picture book on her lap. Grace's clothes were folded on a nearby table. The two had been sharing the room.

"What book is that?" Mrs. Abbott went into the room and held out a hand.

Riley handed over the book automatically. "It's about unicorns." She wore a threadbare nightgown several sizes too large, clearly a hand-me-down. Instead of her usual explosion of color, the gown was a drab beige. Bree wondered if Riley had chosen the nightie or if it had been chosen for her.

Bree crouched to Riley's eye level. "Do you remember me?"

Riley nodded.

"Are you OK?" Bree asked.

Riley's gaze darted to her grandmother, then back to Bree before the child nodded again. She looked fed and clean and as comfortable as to be expected, considering she was living with virtual strangers.

"Where's my mommy?" Riley asked. "She promised she'd come back right after her work, but she didn't."

Bree kept her voice neutral. She wouldn't lie to the child, but there was no reason to give her nightmares either. "I'm not sure. I'm hoping to find her soon."

To her surprise, Riley wrapped her arms around Bree and gave her a quick squeeze. "Thank you," she said in a small voice.

The child is safe.

The thought wasn't as comforting as Bree wanted. An image of Grace, dead-faced and wrapped in a tarp, popped into her mind. She banished it. Cops usually planned for the worst-case scenario, but at this moment, dwelling on it wasn't helpful.

"Let's get you a glass of water." Mrs. Abbott extended a hand. Riley took it and left the room with her grandmother.

Bree opened each drawer. Grace didn't have many possessions other than basic clothes and a few books. Bree checked between the pages, looking for receipts or notes. She found a small toilet kit hanging on the back of the door. She opened it. Grace was very low maintenance in the beauty department. Bree unzipped a side pouch and pulled out a bag of candied ginger. She stared at it for a minute, then zipped the pouch just as Riley skipped back into the room. The mattress springs creaked as she clambered onto the bed.

"I'll tuck you in in a minute," Mrs. Abbott said to Riley, then turned toward Bree.

"We'll see ourselves out," Bree assured her and left the room. She found Matt and Mr. Abbott in the kitchen.

Mr. Abbott stood at the kitchen sink, scrubbing under his nails with a brush. "You haven't found my daughter." His voice was full of accusation and resentment.

"No, sir, not yet," Bree said. "We'll keep you updated."

Mr. Abbott's head bowed, and his broad shoulders caved in. He said nothing as Bree and Matt left the house.

In the vehicle, Bree told Matt about finding candied ginger in Grace's toilet kit.

"Isn't that a natural nausea remedy?" he asked.

"Yes."

"Maybe she's coming down with the flu."

"Or she's pregnant."

Matt froze. "Fuck. Ally and Jana were both pregnant. Two could be a coincidence, but three? No way."

Bree's phone buzzed as she fastened her seat belt. "It's Rory." She punched "Answer." "You're on speaker, Rory. Matt is here also."

"I'm in Grace's phone," he began. "I went right to her Uber app. She called for a ride a little after two o'clock this afternoon, but when the driver arrived at Weekends, she wasn't there."

Which confirmed the kidnapper most likely had pretended to be her ride.

"Also," Rory continued, "you were right about her using Uber early this morning. She booked a ride at 7:31 and arrived at 7:58 this morning." He gave them an address.

"One more thing," Rory said. "The vehicle in the surveillance video at Weekends is a Honda Accord. Of the available colors, champagne, white, and silver are the best possibilities. I'm also trying to clean up the video for more details."

"Thanks, Rory!" Bree ended the call. "I'll have Marge pull motor vehicle records, see how many light-colored Accords are registered in our area."

"Going to be a long list," Matt said. "There are a few hundred thousand Accords registered in the state."

She lowered her phone. "Let's go check out that address."

"Already on it." Matt worked the dashboard computer, a.k.a. the mobile data terminal. "Tax records say the property is owned by a nonprofit, Vital Care Network." He tapped on the keyboard. "Reverse search on the address shows the property is currently occupied by Choices for Women. It's a pregnancy counseling center."

"That sounds familiar." Bree repeated the name in her head. "I know! There was a brochure for a pregnancy counseling center in Ally's backpack." She called Todd using voice commands. When he answered, she asked him to check the file. "There should be photos of the brochure in the file."

Papers shuffled on the line.

"Got it," Todd said. "You are correct. The brochure says, 'Choices for Women: Sexual Health Resource Center. Free and confidential.'"

"Vital Care Network also sounds familiar," Matt said.

"Yes!" On Todd's end of the call, keys clacked. "Jana's phone records! She called Vital Care Network two weeks ago."

"So, we've linked Jana, Ally, and Grace to this center. That can't be a coincidence." Bree tapped her forehead. "Todd, I want you to call Trish's sister, Diane, and point-blank ask her if Trish had been to the center."

"Dr. Jones didn't find any sign of a fetus in Trish's autopsy," Matt pointed out.

"True, but Trish could have thought she was pregnant," Bree said.

"I'll call her sister now." Todd ended the call.

Matt checked the website, then looked at his phone. "The center just closed."

"Let's drive by." Bree entered the address in the GPS. "Maybe someone is still in the office."

They headed for the address. The center was located in the end position of a small shopping center. A Laundromat was the opposite anchor. Bree parked in front and stared at the building. The windows were obscured by posters listing services: pregnancy testing, counseling, and STD screening. Huge capital letters spelled out FREE & CONFIDENTIAL in red.

"The lights are still on," Bree said. "Let's knock on the door."

Matt pointed. "I see someone moving around inside."

They stepped out into the rain. Bree hurried to get under the awning, which felt ridiculous. She was already soaked. She knocked on the door and waited. A woman dressed in scrubs came to the door. She pointed to the CLOSED sign.

Bree pointed to her badge.

The woman unlocked and opened the door with an annoyed, "Can I help you?"

"Yes." Bree waited.

The woman stepped back and admitted them into a small lobby. She was about fifty, with a thick, frizzy, salt-and-pepper bob. A name tag proclaimed her to be Darla. "We're closed."

"We know." Matt took up a lot of space in the small vestibule.

Bree had no time or patience for sweet-talking anyone. "You probably know we're working on a murder case."

That got Darla's attention. Her eyes widened. "Is this about the serial killer?"

"Yes," Bree said. "So far, two of our victims have been to your center. I'd like to give you two additional names for you to check your records."

Darla's chin snapped up. "I'm sorry. You'll need a warrant."

"You're not a licensed medical facility," Matt said. "HIPAA doesn't apply."

"We pride ourselves on our confidentiality." She tucked some hair behind her ear, but her hair was too thick, and it immediately sprang out again.

Bree tried again. "We don't need their records. I just want to know if they came here."

"No." Darla gestured toward the door.

"They're dead," Matt snapped. "They aren't going to object."

Darla pointed to the door in a *don't let it hit you in the ass* way. "We could be sued by their families. The dead have the same rights to privacy as the living. Get a warrant or get their next of kin to request their records."

Frustrated but not surprised, Bree tried to think of another argument. With two identified victims and her missing woman linked to the center, she would be able to get a warrant, but that would take time. She also didn't think Grace was being held captive in the center. Places open to the public weren't good stashing spots for kidnapping victims. The center wasn't big. She looked through the doorway into a waiting room. Maybe there was room for three or four consultation rooms and a small amount of office space. The walls appeared cheap and thin, not substantial enough to cover the sound of a woman banging or screaming.

Bree's phone buzzed. She glanced at the screen. Todd. "Excuse me. I need to take this call." She stepped into the waiting room and answered the call.

Todd blurted out, "Diane confirmed that she drove Trish to the center for a pregnancy test a week or two before she went missing, and that the test was positive."

Four out of four. Trish, Ally, Jana, and Grace were all tied to Choices for Women.

Bree wanted to scream. "And she withheld this information from the police?"

"She didn't think it would matter. No one else knew, not even the boyfriend, and she thought the information would devastate their parents."

"OK. Thanks, Todd. I need you to get a search warrant for the center. I want staff records, everyone who works there. We need to know who was there when the victims visited the center." Darla was never going to part with those records until a judge made her.

"I'm on it," Todd said.

Bree punched "End" and slid the phone back into its holder on her belt. A row of framed photographs caught her attention. Most showed volunteers raising money for the center. Bree stepped forward and squinted at each photo until she recognized a face at what appeared to be a community Bowl-a-Thon. Her gaze locked on the woman sitting behind a stack of brochures, her hands folded on the table, smiling for the camera.

She turned to Darla and tapped on the photo. "Who is this?"

Darla stepped into the waiting room and leaned over the chairs to look at the photo more closely. "That's Sandy. She's been a volunteer here forever."

Bree had been right. It was Sandy Zolek, Jana's boss at the Sunrise Café. "Thanks for your help." She made eye contact with Matt. "Let's go."

They hurried out to the vehicle.

Bree slammed her door closed. "It can't be a coincidence that Sandy Zolek volunteers here. She's involved in this. I know it." She pounded a fist on the steering wheel. "That lead she gave us about the black car? I'll bet she was trying to throw off the investigation."

"I agree," Matt said. "When are we storming the castle?"

"As soon as we can scrounge up a piece of hard evidence to support the link between the victims."

They drove back to the station and went into the conference room. Todd was at the table, the case reports spread out on its surface.

Matt paced the conference room. He wanted to move on the information, and he was less concerned about potentially breaking a law or two.

But Bree had to care. It was her responsibility to ensure they followed the law. She held up a hand in a *halt* gesture. "We need something else. We have no proof Sandy knew the other women or that she was there at the same time as Jana."

"We don't have time." Todd banged a fist on the table. "Jana was killed quickly. We need to rescue Grace."

"I know." Bree popped another antacid into her mouth. "Trust me. I'm ready to breach doors at the Zolek farm, but we need something else. One connection to the victims isn't enough to justify a raid."

Marge entered the room, a few sheets of paper in her hand. "I dug into those motor vehicle records. I have a list of all the light-colored Honda Accords registered in the region. There are thousands." She handed Bree a stack of papers.

Bree's phone buzzed. Rory. She handed the papers to Matt and answered.

"I got it!" Rory said. "I sharpened the video, and you can see the license plate of Grace's kidnapper reflected in a puddle. I'll email the photo now."

"You're a genius." Bree reached for her laptop.

"I know." Rory signed off.

Bree opened the email and downloaded the photo. "Todd, run this plate." She read off the numbers and letters.

A minute later, Todd smacked the table with a palm. "The vehicle used by the kidnapper to grab Grace is registered to Eric Zolek."

"Now we can get a warrant." Bree's blood hummed as the pieces of the case snapped into place. "Let's move. I want to go after Grace ASAP."

CHAPTER THIRTY-ONE

Matt crept up the driveway of the Zolek farm. Rain started up again, pouring down in a steady sheet, filling the ruts in the dirt lane immediately, the ground already saturated. He tried to avoid the deepest puddles, but mud sucked at his boots. Rain dripped off the brim of his sheriff's department baseball-style cap.

Just ahead of him, Bree skirted a puddle and turned toward the front of the house. Matt took up a position on her left flank. Bree's deputies split up to cover the front door, plus the house's rear and side entrances. Todd, Juarez, and the K-9 unit followed a dozen feet behind Matt and Bree. Considering the size of the property, Bree had requested assistance from state police, including a K-9 team or two, but they were currently busy searching for a lost dementia patient.

Since the Zoleks had already killed four women, Bree had argued that they might harm Grace or use her as a hostage if they were warned prior to entry. She'd pushed for a no-knock warrant. Thankfully, the judge had agreed.

Bree motioned for the deputy carrying the breaching ram. He moved forward and slammed the black metal into the door just above the dead bolt. The lock was old and gave immediately. The door sprang open. Matt followed Bree inside, the light attached to his rifle sweeping across a wood-floored hallway.

A second bang signaled the breach of the rear door. Deputies surged into the house, turning right and left, illuminating corners, synchronizing their movements like the well-trained team they were.

Where are the Zoleks?

They'd made enough noise that most homeowners would have been startled awake. They would have leaped out of bed, jumped into pants, and/or grabbed weapons.

But all Matt saw and heard were deputies.

Bree was reading his mind, as usual. They headed up toward the second floor. Narrow spaces like doorways, corridors, and stairwells were fatal funnels, choke points you had to go through with limited ability to see threats. Fatal funnels were where fatalities most often occurred. Stairwells and long corridors were the worst. At least a doorway could be moved through quickly.

Matt's pulse thrummed, and all his senses turned on high alert. He took a deep breath, held it for a few seconds, then eased the air out of his lungs. He forced his gaze to keep moving, to encompass the entire stairwell and the landing above. Working the angles for maximum visual penetration while concealing himself as much as possible with each tread, Matt went up the stairs. On the second-floor landing, he moved down the hall, stopping beside the first doorway. Bree took the opposite side. The door was open. Matt took a quick peek around the frame. He spotted a bed and a dresser. The visible corners of the room were clear.

Two more deputies passed them and proceeded down the hall to the next doorway. Matt focused on his. He went through first, staying high, sweeping right. Bree went low and left. Matt cleared his blind corner, trusting Bree to do the same. Then he dropped to one knee and looked under the bed. "Clear."

He heard Bree open a closet door. "Clear."

They left the room. The two deputies were clearing the next room. Matt passed their doorway and ducked briefly into a bathroom. He swept aside the shower curtain, aiming his rifle into the tub. Empty.

Backing out, he moved to the last door in the hall. It was closed. He and Bree assumed their usual positions. Matt reached for the doorknob. If anyone was inside, they had to know their house was being raided. No one could sleep through the noise of the battering rams, boot steps, and voices.

The sound of claws on hardwood caught Matt's attention. Greta and Collins appeared at the top of the stairs and moved toward them. The shepherd was a black shadow in the dimness. Collins let Greta sniff the bottom of the doorway. The dog inhaled but showed no real interest. Collins moved her back.

Matt opened the door, and he and Bree cleared it quickly. Clothing and personal items indicated this was the primary bedroom. The bed was unmade, the sheets dragged down onto the oak planked floor. One pillow sat askew in the middle of the mattress. The comforter was tangled at the foot of the bed.

Bree reached toward and touched the bed. "Still warm. They heard us somehow before we got to the house."

Either they'd been watching, or they had set up some kind of surveillance.

"So where are they?" Matt asked.

"They can't have gotten far." Bree led the way back downstairs.

Todd greeted them in the kitchen. "House is clear."

"Moving on." Matt left the house. His gaze roamed over the shapes of outbuildings in the dark yard. So many places to hide.

And plan an ambush.

Clouds and rain obscured the moon and stars. Deputies were moving into a large storage shed. In the open doorway, Matt could see tractors and other large equipment. He nodded toward the large barn. Bree and Todd followed him. The double doors were tightly closed. Matt took hold of one of the door handles and pulled. The big wooden door slid on overhead tracks. Bree and Todd swept into the space, rifles lifted.

Cows occupied pens along the sides of the barn. Some dozed knee-deep in straw. Others lay curled on the ground. A few animals chewed on hay. Heads rose as Matt, Bree, and Todd walked down the aisle, peering into each pen, making sure no humans were buried in the bedding. A cow lowed as Matt shifted some deep straw. They reached the end of the barn and turned into a large space filled with milking equipment.

They quickly cleared the space and moved forward to another room, which housed milk tanks. The huge metal cylinders were raised off the ground. Matt dropped to the floor and shined his light under them. No feet. No people. They checked around the tanks but found no one.

Leaving through a back door, they approached the second, smaller barn. Matt used the same procedure to open the door. The smaller barn contained three large stalls. Only one was filled with bedding. The door stood open. With partitions six feet tall and constructed of cinder block, the stalls were made to hold something bigger than the average cow. A ripple of unease tracked up Matt's spine.

Back in the barnyard, Greta barked.

Matt spun, hoping the dog had picked up a scent, but he immediately saw the dog wasn't alerting. Her bark was a warning. Greta had moved into a protective position in front of Collins, who was shifting backward slowly, tugging the dog with her. Collins's eyes were locked on something in the dark barnyard.

Matt stepped out of the small barn and squinted through the rain. Todd followed, stopping just behind him.

Bree joined them. "What's going on?"

"I'm not sure—" An angry snort cut off Matt's words. A shape moved in the shadow between the two barns.

A deputy clearly found the switches because exterior lights turned on, illuminating the barnyard—and a huge animal standing less than fifty feet away from them. Black and white like the other cattle, this was no cow. Clearly a bull, he was the size of a cow and a half, with massive shoulders, a thick neck, and a chest as broad as a barrel.

He snorted and pawed the ground, his power and aggression on full display.

"I'm pretty sure he's not supposed to be loose," Todd said from the barn doorway.

Remembering the heavy metal bar securing the barn door when he'd been to the farm, Matt was sure the animal had been let out intentionally to slow them down—or kill them.

With a furious bellow, the bull charged.

CHAPTER
THIRTY-TWO

Bree's heart catapulted into her throat.

Mud shot from under the giant animal's hooves as it rushed across the barnyard. Bree raised her AR-15, putting the huge beast in her crosshairs. Where did one aim to take down an animal of that size? The head? The heart? Where was the heart exactly? How many bullets would it take to bring him down?

Deputies scattered, diving behind cover and jumping over fences. Collins hauled Greta back into the dairy barn and slid the door almost closed. The only cover for Bree, Matt, and Todd was the barn they'd just exited—the same barn Bree assumed the bull should be in.

If they locked themselves in the barn, they'd be stuck there—with the bull outside—and Grace still being held somewhere on the property.

That couldn't happen. They had to find her before the Zoleks decided it was too much effort to drag her along with them. She could testify against them. They wouldn't leave her behind alive.

Her finger curled around the trigger as she aimed at the beast's head. But the bull came to an impressive sliding stop in the middle of the yard. Pawing at the ground, he sent puddle water and chunks of mud flying. His wet hide glistened in the barnyard light. He rushed another couple of feet, then slammed his front hooves into the ground.

Bree swore the earth shook. Rain blurred her vision. Blinking, she adjusted her grip on her rifle. "How do we get him back in his stall?"

"Carefully?" Matt asked.

The bull dropped his head and hunched his shoulders. His neck craned and swayed as he side-eyed them.

"We need him contained so we can find Grace," Matt said. "You and Todd cover me from both sides."

Bree sidled toward the fence that met the corner of the barn. Todd slow-walked behind a few empty barrels. Bree stepped behind a partition. The bull seemed confused, torn between which one of them he wanted to rush. He turned in a circle and bobbed his head.

Matt moved away from Bree, then took off his hat and waved it. "Hey, bull. Here, boy."

"What are you doing?" she hissed.

"Getting him to chase me." Matt stepped squarely into the opening to the barn.

"You are not a bullfighter."

"Do you have a better idea?"

"I do not," she admitted. "But I don't have to like yours." But he was right. They didn't have time to waste—not if they were going to save Grace.

Matt whistled. The bull spotted him and pawed the mud. Bree's lungs locked down.

If that animal trampled Matt . . .

Pushing aside the thought, Bree slid her finger inside the trigger guard and aimed at the animal's head. A three-round burst through its skull should stop it.

She didn't like to operate in *shoulds*.

Matt walked backward, still waving the hat. "Here, boy. Come on."

The bull bellowed, dropped its head, and hunched, muscles bunching, preparing to launch. It shot forward, its agility and speed impressive—almost incredulous—considering its sheer bulk. Matt spun and took off like a sprinter. He raced into the stall and waited for one heartbeat, until the bull was nearly on top of him. Then he vaulted the cinder block sidewall. The bull charged into the space and stopped. His hooves slid on the bedding. He spun, bellowing and shaking his head.

Matt circled around to the stall door, then closed and locked it. Inside, the bull slammed against the door. The entire barn rattled.

Bree breathed and lowered the rifle. The adrenaline dump left her shaky and a little nauseated. But there was no time to recover. "Let's get out of here." She led the way out of the barn. "I'm not sure that stall is going to hold."

Matt followed, closing the big rolling barn door behind him. He doubled over, hands on his thighs, and took two deep breaths.

"You all right?" She rested a hand on his shoulder.

"Yep, but that was hairy."

"No shit." Bree was still queasy, and she hadn't been the one in danger. She'd come to depend on him—and not just for the physical help with the animals, kids, and work. She depended on him in a way she'd never allowed herself to depend on anyone before. Her heart needed him. He was her sanity when life went sideways, her solace when times were hard, and he amplified her happiness when times were good. Everything was better and easier with him in her life. Just the thought of losing him made her chest ache with an unbearable emptiness.

Matt straightened. "Let's find Grace."

Collins and Greta emerged from the dairy barn, and everyone got back to work. Greta raised her head, her nose working, sniffing the air.

"Has she caught any scent yet?" Bree asked.

"No." Collins shook her head. "But it's a big property. We've only begun."

Todd jogged over. "Both barns, the two sheds, and the garage are clear. We found fresh tire tracks behind the garage."

"Where did they go?" Bree scanned the farm.

Todd pointed. On the other side of the open field, the black shape of the old barn and silo jutted into the night sky.

"Which vehicles were in the garage?" Matt asked.

"A Honda Accord and a pickup truck," Todd said. "There's one empty bay."

"Find out what Sandy Zolek drives and put a BOLO out on the vehicle and on Sandy and Eric. We're going to follow the tracks."

Todd stepped aside to use his radio.

Matt fell in beside Bree. "That old barn has plenty of room."

"In the middle of nowhere too," Bree said. "You could scream until your voice gave out. No one would hear you."

Todd waved a few deputies to remain behind. The rest of them loaded into vehicles and started across the field. They parked a hundred feet shy of the old barn and got out. The silo stood another fifty feet behind the barn.

As soon as Collins unloaded Greta from the rear of the K-9 unit, the dog's head snapped to and she began to lean into her harness. She'd caught a scent. Following the dog's lead, the deputies moved faster, as if the dog's energy were contagious.

Bree slipped on a patch of mud and went down on one knee. Pain zinged through her leg. She held her rifle out of the muck and lurched to her feet again. Half the team headed toward the old barn, but the dog beelined to the silo. She sniffed the weeds at its base, stopped at the door, sat, and whined.

"Good girl," Collins crooned. She yanked a stuffed hedgehog out of the cargo pocket of her pants and tossed it to the dog. Greta caught it in the air, sank her teeth into the toy, and gave its neck a sharp shake. Wagging her tail, she made it squeak over and over, like a small animal in distress.

Glancing at the dilapidated barn, Bree gestured for Todd to clear the broken-down building. He and two deputies veered off. Bree approached the silo's door. The wooden door looked to be thick and was secured with a heavy-duty padlock. "We're going to need bolt cutters."

"Bree!" Matt lunged forward and grabbed her elbow. "Stop!"

She froze. "What's wrong?"

He pointed, his face grim. She followed his gaze upward. In the beam of his flashlight, a clump of brownish-red sticks was affixed over the door, just under a small eave, about two feet above her head.

A booby trap.

She barely breathed out the word. "Dynamite."

CHAPTER THIRTY-THREE

The hairs on Matt's arms stood at attention. His intestines curled into the fetal position, and his body went so still he could feel his own heartbeat. Every cell in his being was waiting for a giant *kaboom*, every instinct telling him to get the fuck away from the explosives.

Bree called out to her deputies, "We have an explosive device here. Everyone move back."

Matt studied the booby trap. "I see a wire running along the door-frame." Was that a— His heart fumbled a beat. "The wire is connected to a hand grenade."

"Assuming if we open the door, the pin is pulled and the whole thing blows up?" Bree hadn't moved.

"That's my assumption as well." Matt used his flashlight to scan the ground around them and the front of the building. He didn't see any additional dynamite or grenades.

"Moving back now." Bree took one very slow step back, stepping into her own footprints.

Matt did the same, moving just as carefully.

When they were fifty feet away, Bree lifted her phone. "I'm calling the BDU." The closest state police bomb disposal unit was in Albany, roughly an hour away.

Todd emerged from the barn. "The old barn is empty. The tire tracks continue. It looks like they drove right across this field and into the woods."

Matt brought him up to speed on the silo and its booby trap.

"We dealt with old dynamite found in a mine a few years ago," Todd said. "Dynamite usually needs a blasting cap to detonate, but old dynamite can be volatile. The sticks can sweat nitroglycerin, which crystallizes on the outside and makes it extremely sensitive. Just a touch could set it off, even without the grenade."

Something dark and glossy on the silo roof caught Matt's attention. "What is that?"

Todd cocked his head. "I think they're solar panels."

"They're powering a generator," Matt said. "That's where they're keeping the women. We need to get in there."

Bree lowered her phone. "BDU's ETA is ninety minutes."

"We can't wait that long," Matt said. "We have no idea what condition Grace is in. I'm going to get a better look."

Bree shook her head. "All personnel need to remain a safe distance from an explosive."

"Good thing I'm a civilian." Matt walked toward the silo. Stopping twenty feet away, he walked a circle around it, using his flashlight to slowly examine as much of the exterior as he could.

"Everyone else stand back." Bree followed him.

Matt stopped on the side opposite the door. The old concrete structure had a column of square holes stacked one on top of another, running all the way up the side. Each square measured about two feet across. Wooden panels were affixed over each square, like boarded-up windows. A horizontal metal bar spanned each panel. "Any idea what those windows are for?"

"We didn't have a silo, but the neighbors did." Bree had been raised on a farm for her early childhood. "The hatches are closed as the silo is filled up with grain."

He studied the setup. It was a simple mechanism.

"The horizontal bar is a mechanical lock," she said. "If you turn it to the vertical position, you should be able to remove the panel. It takes some muscles, though."

He put a hand on one of the bars and tried to turn it. But it wouldn't budge. He shined his flashlight around the edge of the panel. "Someone fixed the panel in place with masonry screws." He moved his flashlight up the squares. "Wait. Only the bottom five are fastened shut." He stuffed his flashlight into the cargo pocket of his pants. "I'm going to climb up there. If she's inside, we'll figure out a Plan B to get her out. If the silo is empty, then we move on and leave this to the BDU."

"Can't jostle the dynamite."

The silo was built of cement block. Matt didn't think it was going to budge when he climbed it. But if it did, it could potentially spew chunks of concrete. "I want you to move back."

He and Bree exchanged a look, communicating with no words.

Putting themselves at risk was part of the job, but in this instance, there was no need for more than one person to risk their life. Matt didn't want the person who had guardianship of two children to be the one in danger. He could see the understanding—and the conflict—in her eyes. But even though she clearly didn't like his decision, she reluctantly agreed.

"I love you," she said.

"I have no intention of dying tonight, but I love you too."

"Be careful." She stood her flashlight in the dirt, pointing up, then went back to the rest of the team.

Matt pocketed his light and began to climb. Standing on the fourth bar, he reached up to the sixth and turned the bar. It was rusty and stiff, but he was able to muscle off the panel. "Look out below." He tossed it onto the weeds. Then he pulled out his flashlight and shined it into the silo.

The interior had been converted from silage container to a room with two cots. A young woman lay on one of the cots, her arms and legs secured with Paracord. Duct tape covered her mouth. She stared up at him, her eyes white-rimmed, wild, and terrified.

Two things simultaneously shocked Matt. The woman was heavily pregnant.

And she was not Grace.

As he digested this information, her body curled tighter, her muscles tensing, her eyes closing. A muffled groan of pain sounded from behind the duct tape.

CHAPTER THIRTY-FOUR

Impatient, Bree called out to Matt, "What did you find?"

But he wasn't focused on her. He was calling into the silo, "It's going to be all right. You're safe now. We're going to get you out of there. I'll be right back. Just hold on."

Had he found Grace?

Instead of senseless fretting, Bree worked the radio and a satellite map on her cell phone, checking on the BDU's ETA and coordinating with state troopers patrolling the roads that surrounded the farm.

Matt came down twice as fast as he'd gone up and jogged back to her. "There's a woman inside. Not Grace. The silo is outfitted like a prison cell." He described a concrete cage worthy of a horror movie. "The solar panels are powering a portable heater."

"But where's Grace?" Bree asked.

"Maybe the woman inside knows."

"We still need to find Grace."

"But we can't leave this woman here." Matt pulled at his beard. "Pretty sure she's in labor."

Fuuuuuuck.

"Then how are we going to get her out?" she asked.

"We can't wait for the bomb squad." Matt gestured toward the silo. "That's no place to have a baby. Bree, she's tied up and gagged. *In labor.*"

Bree had never been in labor, but she couldn't imagine delivering under these circumstances.

Todd joined them. "The BDU isn't going to want to move the dynamite. It's too unstable. Last time they soaked it in diesel fuel and burned it on the spot."

Bree studied the concrete wall of the silo. "Can we get one of these lower hatches open?"

"I don't see why not." Matt gestured to the edge of the lowest one. "Screws can be unscrewed, right?"

"I have a tool kit in my vehicle. I worked construction in college. I'll figure it out." Todd returned to the back of his patrol unit to grab the kit.

"Worst-case scenario, we haul her out of that hatch." Matt pointed to the open hatch ten or twelve feet up the side of the silo.

Another feat Bree could not imagine. That would take some serious muscle.

"I'm going inside to untie her, get that gag off so she can breathe, and see what kind of condition she's in." Matt retrieved his backpack from the rear of Bree's vehicle and slung the bag over one shoulder.

Bree brushed water off her forehead. Her hat and hair were saturated. Rain dripped into her eyes. She turned to Matt. "OK. You go in after her. I'll leave Todd and three deputies with you." She turned to her chief deputy. "Juarez and Collins are with me. We're going after Grace."

"I don't—" Matt started to protest.

Bree raised a hand. "You are the strongest one here, and Todd knows his way around tools. If anyone can get that poor woman out of there, it's the two of you." The task would require patience, skill, and sheer strength. Despite her *no PDA in uniform* rule, she kissed Matt on the lips and repeated, "I love you."

He returned the kiss and the sentiment. "Be careful."

"No worries. We're taking Greta with us." Bree had come to appreciate and rely on the dog. Greta was the most useful of all of them. If Grace managed to get away from the Zoleks, Greta would track her. She could potentially sense a person hiding in the woods, lying in wait. There was no suspect who could outrun her.

"She's a rock star." Matt nodded. "I can't count the number of times Brody saved my ass."

Bree updated dispatch, called for an ambulance, and requested any additional backup she could get from anywhere: state police, local PDs, surrounding county sheriffs. At this point, she'd welcome a few hall monitors.

As she turned toward the tire tracks and the dark woods, she heard Matt calling out reassurances to the captive woman. Collins loaded Greta into the K-9 unit. Juarez rode with Bree.

"Why didn't the dog alert on the explosive?" Juarez asked.

Bree steered her vehicle in a path parallel to the tire tracks. "K-9s are usually trained either to find explosives or drugs, because of the extreme risk when dealing with explosives. To find drugs, the dog has to get close to people and places. Explosives require a different, more cautious approach. Since we encounter more drugs than explosives, Greta was trained as a drug dog."

"We need another dog," Juarez said. "You could have been blown to bits."

He wasn't wrong.

Bree eased off the gas pedal and followed the tire tracks onto a game trail that bisected the woods. Between the darkness and the rain, she could barely see fifteen feet ahead. The path was maybe a foot wider than her vehicle. Her tires skidded, the rear end of the unit sliding sideways. She steered into the skid until the car lurched to a stop.

Juarez opened the door and looked back at the rear tires. "Hold on. Someone else skidded out here too." He shined his flashlight on a deep tire rut perilously close to a fat tree. "I think they got stuck here. There are footprints. Someone got out and pushed."

Bree crossed her fingers that getting mired had cost the Zoleks time. Ahead, water covered the path. Something red flashed.

Taillights? Were they that close to catching the Zoleks?

Juarez closed the door, and Bree pressed the gas pedal. The car swerved and slid. The rear of the vehicle dropped off the trail into a shallow gully. She looked in the rearview mirror, but all she could see behind them were the headlights from Collins's K-9 unit. Juarez grabbed for the chicken strap. Bree's breath locked down. The car stopped sliding.

She and Juarez exhaled in unison.

Bree shifted into reverse. The tires spun. She rocked the car forward and back until the tires gained traction, then let the vehicle ease back onto the trail. The car rolled forward. The trail climbed, then opened to a small clearing.

Collins pulled the K-9 unit alongside and lowered the window. "The trail is washed out ahead."

Bree tapped her thumb on the steering wheel. Through the open window, she could hear the patter of rain on leaves and the rush of water over rocks. She used the dashboard computer to pull up a map of the area. A creek wound around the small, wooded hill they were currently parked on.

She didn't want to give up. Their taillights hadn't been far ahead. A crash reverberated through the darkness.

"Did you hear that?" Collins asked.

"Yes."

"It sounded close," said Juarez.

Bree shifted into park and called out the window to Collins, "Can we get through on foot?"

Collins nodded. "I think so."

"Let's do it." Bree updated dispatch and stepped out of the unit. She went to the trunk and hefted her backpack.

Bree, Juarez, and Collins trudged through the woods in silence. The trail narrowed, where half of it had been washed downslope. The dog remained calm, raising her nose now and then to smell the air, but she clearly wasn't picking up anything. Water had infiltrated Bree's boots, and her backpack felt like it weighed a hundred pounds. Her adrenaline spike had ebbed, leaving her bone-weary.

They rounded a bend in the trail. Greta pulled Collins to the side of the trail. The dog leaned into the harness, her nose up.

"She's picked up a scent."

CHAPTER
THIRTY-FIVE

Matt hated splitting up from Bree, but she was right. They had to do the jobs that best suited their skill sets. She could take care of herself. She'd built a good team of loyal deputies, and he needed to have faith in all their abilities. Juarez and Collins—and Greta—would have her back.

On the bright side, she was far away from the unstable dynamite, which made him feel much better. The kids needed her.

He climbed the hatches and dropped his backpack into the silo. The two-by-two hatch was a tight squeeze, and his entry wasn't pretty. Holding a rope tied to a vehicle bumper, he turned, intending to put his feet on the wall and lower himself slowly, but his foot slipped. He smacked face-first into the concrete wall. He dropped the remaining distance, landing on soft knees.

The smell of a camp toilet nearly gagged him. Grabbing his pack, he skirted the solar-powered space heater to reach the woman on the cot. She cried silently as he peeled the tape from her mouth and cut the ropes binding her. "It's OK. I'm going to get you out of here."

She sobbed into his shoulder, then her body bowed with tension. "I thought they were going to kill me. I think the only reason they didn't is they didn't want to take the time."

Matt held her hand as she panted for a minute and tried to remember the childbirth section of his first aid class. "How far apart are the contractions?"

Her body relaxed, the contraction over. "I don't know."

Matt checked the time. "What's your name?"

"Sabrina. Sabrina Hopkins."

Matt pictured the desperate man crying in Bree's office just a few days ago. "Is your father's name Joel?"

She nodded.

"He never gave up looking for you."

Sabrina cried harder.

"Do you know what happened to Grace?" Matt asked.

Sabrina shook her head. "They took her a little while ago."

"Have you been in this silo since August?"

She nodded. "They took me outside to exercise once a day."

Just like prison.

She pushed off the cot and sat up. "They tied the ropes so tight, my hands and feet are asleep." She wore a pair of large sweatpants and a warm sweater, but her feet were bare.

With no idea what kind of trauma she'd experienced, he didn't want to touch her without permission. "Is it OK if I massage your feet?"

She nodded and rubbed her hands together. Her feet were swollen and cold. Matt massaged them to get the blood flowing. He felt something odd on her soles and lifted her foot to see crisscrossed scars.

She flushed. "They beat my feet with a horse whip in the beginning to keep me from running away."

Matt wanted to find Eric and beat him with a whip. He could think of only one reason to kidnap multiple pregnant women and hold them prisoner. Eric and Sandy had been selling babies. So many questions rolled through him: How many times had they gotten away with it? What had happened to the mothers?

Sabrina doubled over, holding her swollen belly with both hands.

Matt checked his watch. Six minutes had passed between contractions. "Can you stand?"

He held her arm as she slowly straightened her legs, wobbling only a little. She was tiny, slight of build, maybe an inch or two over five feet tall. Her basketball-size belly didn't seem big enough to hold a full-term baby.

"We can't use the door. It's booby-trapped." Matt didn't use the word *explosive*. "My buddy, Chief Deputy Harvey, is working on opening one of those hatches. Our only other option is to hoist you up through the one I used." He watched her face for any sign that she thought that would be impossible.

"If that is the fastest way out, I will get through it." She wiped her eyes and sniffed. "I don't want to have my baby in here." A long, involuntary groan sounded from her lips.

Matt looked at his watch. Five minutes since the last one. No time to waste. "I'm going to check with the deputies outside about their progress."

Because that hatch seemed ridiculously small and high. The whir of a drill sounded. Matt went to the wall and called up, "Todd? How's it going out there?"

"The screws are coming loose," Todd yelled back. "I'll have the hatch open in a few."

As if reading his mind, Sabrina said, "I'll do anything to get out of here."

"OK, then we will get you out." The sound of wood scraping came from outside. A minute later, the second-to-lowest hatch opened, and Todd stuck his head inside. He held a rechargeable drill in one hand. "There's an EMT and an ambulance here waiting."

Matt almost sang "Hallelujah." He squeezed Sabrina's hand. "Your parents will be so glad to see you."

He helped her to her feet. She waddled toward the opening, both hands cradling her belly. Halfway to the hatch, she stopped and doubled over. Her groan sounded primal.

Matt waited until the contraction passed. He helped her to the hatch. "Can you put your feet through?"

"I don't think I can bend that way." She was sobbing. "I just want out."

Matt leaned out the hole and called to the EMT, "Get the backboard."

They passed it through. Todd came with it. Matt strapped her onto it. Then he and Todd lifted the board and passed her through the hatch to the EMTs.

As soon as the medics had her, Matt exhaled. His relief was short-lived as he remembered Bree was chasing a pair of killers.

"Have you heard from the sheriff?" he asked Todd as they squeezed through the narrow hatch one by one.

Todd's expression went grim. "The trail washed out. They're continuing pursuit on foot."

CHAPTER THIRTY-SIX

Grace held her breath in the back of the SUV. Her cheek ground into the cargo mat. The duct tape over her mouth forced her to control her breathing. She was trussed like a hog, ankles bound, wrists tied behind her back. Her hands and feet were then tied together, pulling her into a slight backbend. The rope was fastened to an anchor in the bed of the cargo area. She could barely move.

The SUV slid, bounced, and bucked. They'd gotten stuck twice and hit several trees. They could have moved faster on foot. Nausea rolled through her belly. She swallowed and breathed through her nose. With her mouth taped, if she puked, she'd choke.

Tears welled in her eyes. The bottoms of her feet still hurt from where Eric had beaten her with his belt. Punishment for resisting, he'd said. Also, bruised feet would discourage running away.

"Give us a hard time, and you'll learn the meaning of pain," Sandy had warned.

All Grace wanted was to get home to her daughter. She would do whatever was necessary to return to her little girl.

The SUV slid, then lurched sideways, tossing Grace against the side of the vehicle. Her temple slammed into the plastic. Pain shot through her skull, and her vision swam. Helpless, she squeezed her eyelids shut and focused on her breathing.

"Fuck!" Eric yelled from the driver's seat.

Grace opened her eyes. Through the rear window, she could see trees all around.

"The edge is right there!" Sandy shouted, fear lifting her voice to near panic. "Get away from it."

"What do you think I'm doing?" Eric yelled back.

The engine raced. Tires spun. The vehicle shimmied and slid. Another sound carried under the spinning of the tires. Water rushing.

A fresh burst of panic sliced through Grace. The vehicle lurched again. One side dipped lower than the rest. The pull of gravity felt inevitable.

"We need to get out," Sandy cried. Grace heard something being jimmied. "The door won't open. The trees . . ."

The SUV skidded sideways again. Sandy screamed.

Underneath Grace, the world shifted. The vehicle bucked. The cargo area lurched. Grace slid, her momentum stopped by the back of the rear seats. She couldn't do anything to save herself. Tears streamed down her cheeks.

Riley, I'm sorry.

The SUV bounced and bucked. Eric's screams joined Sandy's. Grace's throat closed with terror. Even if she hadn't been gagged, she would have been incapable of yelling. The world halted with a sudden impact. She heard the airbags deploy. Dust poofed through the vehicle.

Grace panted through her nostrils. The SUV had stopped nose-down. She'd been tossed onto the back of the rear seats. Pain rocked through her whole body, then numbness. She moved her hands and feet.

She was alive, and her limbs worked. She didn't feel any broken bones.

Something moved in the front of the vehicle. The SUV dipped. Grace lifted her head. She could see the front seats. Sandy was slumped forward, unmoving. *Where's Eric?* Blood and dust from the airbags covered the dashboard.

The sound of water sent a blast of horror straight into Grace's soul. They'd slid into a creek or river. Grace could barely move, and the vehicle was sinking. She gasped as a wave lapped against the passenger-seat window.

CHAPTER THIRTY-SEVEN

Bree heard branches snap and metal groan as something huge crashed through the trees. Then the woods went silent.

"Did you hear that?" Bree strained to listen, but she heard nothing except rain falling on foliage. Her eyes had adjusted to the dark, though the rain and cloud cover conspired to keep visibility to a minimum.

"Yes," Juarez said.

She broke into a jog, then a run. She'd always been fast, but keeping up with the much-taller Matt on their morning runs had made her even faster. Tonight, however, her energy flagged. Ten years her junior, Juarez drew ahead. Bree pushed her toes into the mud, willing her legs to go faster.

Greta barked and strained into her harness. Collins could barely control the dog.

They followed the vehicle tracks, which suddenly seemed to be moving sideways.

Greta slammed on the brakes but continued to bark.

"Stop!" Juarez skidded to a halt, grabbing a tree and nearly clotheslining Bree with an arm. It slammed across her collarbones just as the wet ground gave way beneath her feet. For a fraction of a second, she felt nothing but emptiness under her feet. Her boots slid a few feet down the nearly vertical embankment. Her heart vaulted into her throat as she grabbed for a handhold. Her fingers closed on a nearby branch. Her body weight hung suspended, the muscles in her shoulders straining, her heels scrambling for purchase. She looked down and saw swirling, roiling dark water.

She flipped to face the earth and pulled herself toward solid ground. The toe of one boot hooked on a tree root protruding from the soil. She blew out through pursed lips as she pushed upward, reaching for a new handhold. Her back muscles strained. Her fingers closed around another branch. She hauled her body upward. *Almost there.* Her other toe found a notch. The branch snapped. Bree plunged downward again. Her boots were suspended in midair for what felt like a full second, then she was hauled upward and dragged over the edge, landing on her face in the mud. Juarez was beside her, his fingers still gripping her backpack.

"Thanks," she wheezed. Her lungs, arms, and legs were on fire.

Nodding, he released her backpack, pressed his hand to the center of his chest, and heaved a deep breath of relief. "Thought I'd lost you."

They climbed to their feet. Bree anchored herself on a sturdy tree branch and looked over the edge. About thirty feet below, the ass-end of an SUV stuck out of the muddy creek.

Was Grace inside?

Bree pushed backward. She dropped her backpack, yanked open the zipper, and pulled out a rope and a couple of carabiners. She lowered her duty belt to the ground, then fashioned a quick makeshift rappelling harness around her thighs and waist. She took an extra length of rope and wore it cross-body. She loaded her pockets with her weapon, multi-tool, and flashlight.

"I should go down," Juarez protested. "No offense, but I have more upper-body strength."

Bree shook her head, then handed him the end of the rope and a couple of carabiners. "I can handle my own weight, but I'm not strong enough to haul you back up here."

Juarez conceded her point with silence, but his face hardened into an unhappy mask. He anchored the rope around a tree and took up the slack.

Bree stepped off the edge backward and repelled down the nearly vertical slope, following the trail of broken foliage plowed by the SUV. Her boot slipped in the mud, but she slid only a couple of feet before the rope—and Juarez—caught her.

At the bottom, she braced a foot on a rock and shined her light on the vehicle. The creek was swollen well above its normal depth, the bank footing as slick as ice. The SUV sat at a forty-five-degree angle, engine down. The driver's window was open, the seat empty. Sandy slumped in the passenger seat, her body held in place by the seat belt. The water had reached her ribs and was level with the creek outside the vehicle. If the vehicle stayed where it was, no one would drown.

But that was a big *if* because the current was wicked.

Metal groaned as the SUV shifted. Pulled by the current and the weight of the engine, it slid farther into the creek. Inside the vehicle, the water rose a few more inches, reaching Sandy's chest.

Goodbye, *if*. Hello, *when*. The SUV was going under. Physics would win. It was just a matter of time.

Bree untied her makeshift harness and left the rope dangling. She tied one end of the second rope to a tree and the other around her waist. After taking up the slack, she shuffled into the water up to her knees. Even in the shallows, the current nearly swept her feet out from under her. She braced herself with a hand on the vehicle and shined her flashlight inside the cargo area. Grace was tied up in the back. Her eyes opened and met Bree's.

The air rushed out of Bree's lungs.

Grace was alive.

But Bree had to get her out of the vehicle before it was swept into deeper water. Grace was tied too securely to escape on her own. Bree would have to go in after her.

She motioned for Grace to turn her face away. After Grace obeyed, Bree swung the butt end of her flashlight at the rear window. The first blow cracked the window. She swung harder. The tempered glass shattered. She cleared remaining pieces by sweeping her flashlight around the frame. Then she returned the light to her pocket.

A scraping sound sent a flash of panic straight into Bree's soul. If the SUV was swept away, Grace was helpless. She'd drown.

The SUV shifted again, sliding another foot into the creek. Bree held her breath and waded deeper, the cold, muddy water swirling at her legs, pushing her sideways, numbing her feet. Heart rate skyrocketing, Bree took hold of the window frame. She let the current lift her legs, then eased herself through the opening. With the vehicle angled down, the water had not reached the cargo area. She knelt, one knee on the back of the rear seats, the other on the cargo bed, and paused for a second. But the vehicle didn't move any farther into the creek.

She inched forward and peeled the tape off Grace's mouth. The young woman gasped and sucked in air.

"No sudden movements, OK?" Bree pulled out her multi-tool and selected the knife.

"OK." Grace's voice was raspy.

Bree sliced through the ropes binding Grace. Slowly, Grace moved her hands around to the front of her body. She flexed her fingers, rotated her wrists, and moved her feet. She was barefoot and wore only her waitressing uniform of slacks and a Weekends T-shirt.

"Are you ready?" Bree asked.

Grace swallowed, then nodded.

Bree untied the rope from her waist and tied it around Grace's. "Use this to pull yourself to shore."

"OK," Grace said, her voice stronger.

"You go first. Take it steady and slow. The water's cold. Brace yourself."

Grace's hands shook as she pushed off the rear seat and semicrawled toward the broken rear window. With a metallic groan, the vehicle seemed to float. The SUV pivoted, the ass-end creeping toward the center of the creek. Grace froze, but they didn't have much time.

"Go!" Bree gave her a nudge. "I'm right behind you."

Grace slid through the open window. The current immediately carried her sideways a yard or so until she got her feet underneath her. Taking up the slack in the rope, she began to pull herself up the bank, hands and feet scrambling.

The vehicle spun a little more. Bree had her feet halfway out the broken window when Sandy screamed.

Fuck.

Bree turned. Sandy had come to. She thrashed, her movements weak.

Bree paused. Part of her said, *The hell with her.* Either Sandy'd killed four young women and kidnapped Grace or she'd helped Eric do it. Bree should leave her and let karma work its magic.

"Help me!" Sandy screamed, her voice high-pitched with desperation.

And Bree couldn't leave her to die. "I'm going to get you out." She climbed over the back seat into water up to her waist. She brought out the multi-tool knife again. "Hold still."

But Sandy was going into full panic mode, thrashing and yelling, "I'm going to die."

Did she think about those young women dying? She'd left a pregnant woman in labor hog-tied in an old silo. If they hadn't found the woman, she and her baby likely would have died. Bree put her resentment aside and did her job.

Cold numbed her fingers, and it took several tries to cut the seat belt. She tugged Sandy toward the driver's side. "Go out the window."

Before they could exit, the SUV lifted, floated, and spun in the current. Sandy climbed out and teetered on the frame for a second before sliding into the water. Bree dived over the back seat and went out the broken rear window. Her body armor caught on the frame. Panic zinged like lightning. Her numb, clumsy fingers snatched at the fabric for a few seconds, until she freed herself and slid all the way out. She didn't have time to take a breath. The water grabbed her and pulled her under like icy hands. Freezing, it closed over her head.

The shocking cold froze her eyeballs and ears.

Her boots landed on the rocky creek bed and she pushed upward. She was sputtering when her head broke the surface. Her eyes and throat burned. Swimming in boots and body armor was a bitch. She paddled like a lame dog but didn't seem to get any closer to shore. A small wave crashed over her head. A floating branch smacked into her back, and Bree inhaled water.

"Sheriff!" Grace called and threw the end of the rope.

Bree grabbed it. Her fingers felt like blocks of ice three times their normal thickness. She could barely feel the rope as she struggled to thrust an arm through the loop Grace had tied at the end. She felt herself being towed to safety. Rocks scraped her legs as she drew closer to shore. On her hands and knees, Bree crawled up the slimy bank. Her stomach roiled, and she vomited creek water until her insides felt like a well-squeezed lemon.

Heavy breathing caught Bree's attention. Sandy scrambled in the mud a few feet away, trying to climb the slippery bank. She glanced over her shoulder, saw Bree, and tried to go faster. But her feet slid, and she went down on her knees.

"Oh, no. You're not going anywhere." Shivering hard, Bree pushed to her feet, lunged forward, and grabbed Sandy's jacket. Then she dragged her farther onto shore.

Bree panted and leaned on her thighs. "Where's Eric?"

Sandy groaned. "I don't know."

Bree spotted footsteps deep in the bank about fifteen feet away. They moved parallel to the creek, then turned to climb the slope on an angle. He'd run away.

"Sheriff!" Juarez yelled from above.

Bree looked up. Matt, Juarez, and Collins stared down at them, smiling.

"You're alive!" Collins beamed.

A dozen feet away, more faces peered over the edge. Todd and two state troopers. Ropes came down. Grace was hauled up. Sandy had been unconscious for a short time. She was unsteady and probably had a concussion. A trooper rappelled down and brought her up. Bree got back into her makeshift harness. Todd and Matt pulled her up. The first thing she did was crawl over and handcuff Sandy.

Bree sat on the soaked ground. Her body felt like a Jell-O mold, quivering and insubstantial. Matt brought her a space blanket. He crouched, then wrapped it and his arms around her. He was warm and dry, and she leaned into him. They said nothing for a full minute.

When Bree pulled away, Todd had wrapped a space blanket around Grace. Matt stood, but stayed close to Bree.

"Thanks," she said. "What happened with the other girl?"

Matt said, "Her name is Sabrina Hopkins, and she's on the way to the hospital now."

"Sabrina?" Bree couldn't believe it. All those months . . . "Tell me someone let her call her parents."

"Before she even got in the ambulance," Matt said.

Sandy moaned on the ground.

"I'll get a stretcher." A trooper jogged into the rain. "Do you need one, Sheriff?"

Bree lifted a hand in a *halt* gesture. "I can walk."

"Me too," said Grace. "I can walk."

Bree gave her a nod of respect. "Are you sure?"

Grace tilted her chin up. "I'm stronger than I look."

"Yes, you are," Bree agreed. She sent Juarez back to the car for her extra boots, socks, and jacket. He took off at a run.

Juarez returned in a few minutes and offered Bree her clothes. But Bree pointed to Grace. She was barefoot and not wearing a coat. Juarez helped Grace into the socks, boots, and sheriff's department jacket. Then he crouched next to Bree and opened a first aid kit. "You could have used the dry boots and coat."

"She needs them more." Bree's teeth chattered.

He shined a flashlight on her. "Let me see your hands. And your face. You're a mess, Sheriff."

Bree turned her hands over in the light. Her palms and fingers were covered with rope burns and small cuts. Apparently, so was her face. She let her deputy clean and bandage her wounds, which were just beginning to hurt.

"You're going to need a couple of stitches." Juarez wrapped her hand in rolled gauze.

"Where's Eric?" Matt asked, checking Bree's pulse.

"He got away." Bree pointed in the direction his footprints traveled.

"He fucking left me to die!" Sandy sobbed.

Collins's head snapped around. "Did he now? Come on, Greta. We have work to do."

Matt touched Bree's shoulder. "I'm going with Collins."

"Me too," she said.

He raised a doubtful brow but stood and offered her a hand. She took it, and he hoisted her to her feet. Small aches nagged at her as she set off in the dog's direction. She wanted to go home more than anything, but she wouldn't be able to relax until they'd caught Eric Zolek.

A state trooper walked over with a heavy NYSP jacket. He handed it to Bree. "Nice work tonight, Sheriff."

She took the coat and shed the shiny blanket. Then she and Matt walked about fifty feet, to where Todd was studying the ground. Collins was unclipping the leash from Greta's harness.

"Here's where he came up the bank." Todd pointed to a trail of footprints. "Uneven stride. Looks like he's injured."

Good. Bree hoped she hadn't said that out loud. "Maybe that will slow him down."

"Greta will find him. He won't outrun her." Collins led the dog to his prints and shouted a command in German. The black dog shot off into the darkness, tearing through the woods like a wolf. Matt, Todd, and Collins followed at a run. Bree stumbled along in their wake. Juarez stayed at her side. He was probably afraid she'd fall flat on her face. But she kept going, running on sheer stubbornness.

Only a few minutes passed before they heard a sharp, high-pitched, human cry.

"She must have him," Collins yelled, and increased her speed.

CHAPTER
THIRTY-EIGHT

Matt rushed into a clearing. Greta had her front paws on the trunk of a tree. He squinted into the rain and spotted a man in the tree.

Good dog!

"Get away!" Sitting on a branch seven feet off the ground, Eric Zolek shook a branch at the barking dog.

Breathing hard, Collins stopped next to Matt. "Ha! She treed him." She snapped the leash onto Greta's collar and shouted a command in German. The dog sat, but her focus never left Eric. Her quarry was right there. She really wanted to bring him down. Part of Matt wanted to see her do it.

"Good girl." Collins fished out Greta's hedgehog reward toy, but she barely glanced at it. "She doesn't think she's done."

Matt didn't think they were done either, not till Eric was in cuffs and behind bars forever.

Todd had his weapon on Eric. "Come down. Now. Keep your hands visible."

Eric climbed down. As soon as his feet hit the ground, the idiot bolted into the trees. Matt was not chasing this asshole through the dark in the rain. He would not take the chance that Eric could get away or that a deputy could get hurt. He waved to Greta, and Collins let the dog loose. Greta took five long strides and leaped. Her jaws clamped around Eric's leg, and he went down screaming.

Matt cuffed him, and Collins dragged the dog off Eric's leg. Greta snatched her hedgehog off the ground and squeaked it over and over, tail wagging, clearly very pleased with herself. Matt was also pleased with her performance.

"My ankle's sprained, and that dog bit me," Eric complained. He looked fine, except for minor cuts and bruises and one mangled thigh. "I'm going to sue."

Matt had nothing to say to the killer, but Greta growled around the hedgehog in her mouth.

Collins patted the dog. "Good girl."

Indeed.

CHAPTER THIRTY-NINE

Matt held Bree's hand while she received three stitches and a tetanus shot in the ER. She wore borrowed hospital scrubs and rubber clogs. She had no significant injuries, and Matt tried not to think about her climbing into a sinking vehicle to save two people. The mental image would be his personal nightmare for some time.

Possibly forever.

Bree climbed off the gurney as if every inch of her body ached. She shoved her wound care instructions into her pocket and led the way out of the curtained bay.

Matt walked beside her in the hallway. "Are you OK?"

"Fine."

"You don't look fine," he said. "You look gray."

"All that creek water didn't go down well." Bree ran her tongue around her teeth. "My whole mouth is gritty. I think I swallowed more mud than water."

He grimaced. "We'll get some of my dad's homemade soup."

"It's too late—too early—to disturb the kids and your parents. What I really want is a hot shower, my pajamas, and my dog."

"Did you ever think you'd want a dog for comfort?"

"Nope." Bree crossed the hallway to a bank of vending machines.

There had been a time when the presence of any dog would have given her an anxiety attack, but she'd mostly overcome her fear. He was proud to have helped, but the credit went to her. She was the bravest person he knew.

He bought her a ginger ale and a pack of peanut butter crackers. "Eric Zolek was treated for a sprained ankle and the dog bite. He's on his way to the jail now."

"Did you question him?"

"He lawyered up before I could say 'Hi.'"

"Ugh." Bree ate one cracker.

"Yes," Matt agreed. "Sandy has a concussion. The hospital is keeping her overnight."

"I assume she lawyered up as well?" Bree closed her eyes against the bright light.

"Nope."

Her eyes snapped open.

Matt's lips pulled back in a fierce grin. "She is so mad that Eric left her behind." He gave a low whistle. "I think she'll blab."

"Sounds promising."

"It'll have to wait until morning." Matt shook his head. "She's getting X-rays and a CAT scan tonight."

"Where is Sabrina Hopkins?"

"Upstairs. I assume you want to see her."

"Grace too." Bree sipped her ginger ale.

"Grace is right down the hall." Matt spotted Mr. Abbott standing at a cubicle entrance. He held a small duffel bag in both hands, worrying the handle with his fingers. He looked relieved when Bree and Matt approached. His discomfort was as palpable as the chill of the hospital and the smell of antiseptic.

"I'd like to speak with Grace," she said.

"I'll go check on discharge paperwork." Mr. Abbott leaned into the cubicle and set the duffel bag on the foot of the gurney. "I'll leave your clothes here." He backed out, and his footsteps faded.

Bree and Matt walked into the cubicle. Grace reclined on the gurney, draped in white thermal blankets.

She smiled. "I told them I'm fine. I just want to go home to Riley."

"Can you give me a statement?" Bree pulled a plastic chair to the bedside.

"Yes. I want to get it done so I can forget about it."

But Matt knew Grace would never forget.

Grace picked the edge of the blanket. "I thought he was my Uber. I was really distracted between the news that I was pregnant—again—and a threatening call from Howard. He said he got me pregnant on purpose. He put holes in his condoms."

"I'm sorry that happened to you," Bree said.

Matt seethed silently. Sabotaging birth control, a.k.a. "stealthing," wasn't a criminal offense in New York, but it should be. He made a mental note to find the scumbag.

"I know that's a whole different subject." Grace stilled her hands by interlacing her fingers. "So, back to the kidnapping. Eric put me in the trunk. I didn't know who he was then, though." She took a breath. Her knuckles whitened. "When we got to the farm, he put me in the silo with that other girl—Sabrina. Sandy came in with food and whole milk for both of us. Told us if we didn't finish everything, they'd beat us. They wanted the babies to grow strong and healthy. They were going to sell Sabrina's baby—and mine." She sobbed once, then pressed a hand over her mouth to compose herself.

Having been in the silo with Sabrina, Matt had already figured out the Zoleks' appalling enterprise.

Grace sniffed, then sighed. "Later—I don't know what time, but it was dark—they barged into the silo, dragged me out, and tied me up in the back of the SUV. Sandy said Sabrina wouldn't be able to move fast enough, so they left her." She tilted her head. "I think they had an emergency plan in place because Eric locked everything up in a minute or so. Then we took off for the woods." She paused for a breath. "The rain and mud were awful. We got stuck a couple of times. Eric had to get out one time and push. They were both really angry." She paused, focusing inward. "We crashed into the creek, and you saved us."

Footsteps sounded in the doorway. Mr. Abbott leaned into the room. "They said you can go now."

"I have to get dressed," Grace said.

Bree stood. "We're going to need more details, but that's a good start."

The nurse came in with a clipboard, and the cubicle was far too crowded. Matt stepped into the hall. Mr. Abbott did too.

They walked about ten feet and leaned on the wall, shoulder to shoulder.

"We're going to do things different this time," Mr. Abbott said without any prompting. "She's going to stay at home, where she belongs—if she wants to, that is. I haven't been the best father. I drew lines, and she felt like she had no choice but to cross them. I should have put her first. Now that I've had her back and met Riley . . ." His words cut off with a choking sound, as if his emotions rendered him unable to speak.

"You'll need to tell her that."

"I will. We all made mistakes. I wish I could go back and change everything." Mr. Abbott's sigh sounded like it came from his huge work boots.

"Can't change the past," Matt said. "The best we can do is try to be better going forward."

Mr. Abbott nodded once.

Bree emerged from the cubicle, and she and Matt left the ER. In the main corridor, they found the elevator. Matt pressed the "Up" button. Upstairs, they headed for the maternity department.

"I'll flag down a nurse," Matt said.

"No need. I see Mr. Hopkins." Bree nodded toward a small waiting area.

He sat in a vinyl chair, his head bowed, his elbows on his knees. His clasped hands dangled between his thighs. Gray hair flopped over his forehead, hiding his face. He looked up as they approached. His eyes were bloodshot and red-rimmed.

"Sheriff!" He jumped to his feet.

Bree extended a hand, and he took it in both of his.

"Thank you. I can't begin to thank you enough. You found her." He wiped his eyes with his hand.

"How is she?" Bree asked.

Mr. Hopkins released her hand and swept back his gray bangs. "She's in labor. My wife is with her." He looked lost. "We didn't know she was pregnant. She didn't tell us." He shook himself. "But as long as she and the baby are OK, we don't care."

Rubber squeaked on tile as a nurse approached. "Mr. Hopkins? You have a grandson. Would you like to see him?"

Tears streamed down his face. "Sabrina is all right?"

"She's perfect," the nurse said. "They're both just fine."

He moved to follow the nurse, then looked back at Bree. "Did you need something from us, Sheriff?"

"Not tonight." Bree smiled. "Go see your family."

Her heart warmed. They had a long road ahead of them, but Bree had a feeling they would be all right. Sabrina had been through hell, but she had people who loved her and were clearly willing to support her. And her parents? They'd just received a miracle.

Matt steered Bree toward the elevator. "Ready to go home?"

"More than ready."

CHAPTER FORTY

Bree woke late the next morning, still nauseated and exhausted. Matt snored beside her. She eased out of bed, extracting her leg from under Ladybug's head. In the bathroom, she splashed cold water on her face.

She opened the closet in search of a towel. She was behind on laundry and down to the last one. She spied a pregnancy test in the back. Must have belonged to her sister. She pulled it out. Not expired.

Nausea rolled through her. Could she be pregnant? Seemed unlikely, but the nausea . . .

There was one way to find out for sure.

A few minutes later, she stared at the little window. Not pregnant.

Matt knocked on the door. "Everything all right in there?"

She opened the door.

His eyes widened at the sight of the pregnancy test. "Is that what I think it is?"

"Yes. Don't worry. It's negative."

"I wasn't worried." His head tilted. "And I wouldn't be upset. Surprised, but not upset. Are you relieved?"

"Yes. Maybe?" Bree wasn't sure. "I feel like I'm already stretched so thin, between work and taking care of Luke and Kayla." If she did get pregnant, work would have to go. She knew that deep in her soul. There wasn't enough inside her to split off another piece. She wouldn't half-ass raising a newborn or her job. Both were too important.

But . . . the thought of a little Viking running around made her smile.

She tossed the test in the trash can. The timing wasn't right. Would it ever be? She glanced at Matt. Someday, she'd marry him. They hadn't discussed it, but she knew anyway. When the time was right.

Matt slung an arm around her shoulder. "Come back to bed. You might feel significantly better if you got more than three hours of sleep."

"This is true, but I really want to see the kids."

Matt reached into the shower and turned on the spray. "Breakfast at my parents' house it is."

They showered, dressed, and went down to the kitchen. Dana had left a note. She and Nolan were out running errands. Bree wrote a note back. Adam had taken care of the horses early. So, Matt and Bree loaded both dogs into the Suburban and drove to his parents' house.

Matt's mom greeted them with coffee and pancakes. "The kids are feeling great this morning. They went with George to get doughnuts."

Matt scarfed down a plate of pancakes. Ladybug barked to go out. Matt stood. "I'll take her."

Bree picked at her food. For the first time—probably ever—she couldn't stomach coffee.

"Is something bothering you?" Anna lifted one hand. "I'm sorry. I don't mean to pry, but I'm always here if you want to talk."

Emotions bubbled out of Bree's mouth with zero control. "I feel like the worst parent this week, leaving them when they were sick. I don't know what I'm doing. I want to be available for the kids whenever they need me, but my job demands a lot of time."

Anna patted her hand. "Bree, the kids don't expect you to be here 24/7. That's not realistic, and frankly, that wouldn't be healthy for them or you. George and I both worked a lot of hours when the kids were young. They got juggled, but they still knew they were loved. They also learned to be independent. That's a good thing."

Bree looked up. "I don't understand."

"Before their mother's death, the kids relied on her to meet almost all their needs, right?"

"Yes, Erin was a great mom."

"I'm sure she was. It shows in the great kids she raised." Anna smiled. "But when she died, they were left alone, with no one else to whom they were close enough to immediately rely on."

"Some of that is my fault." Guilt smothered Bree. "I should have spent more time with them. I avoided Grey's Hollow. I should have been that person. I should have been close to them for their entire lives. I was selfish."

Anna squeezed Bree's forearm. "You were *not* selfish. You were eight when your parents died?"

Bree nodded. "Adam and Erin went to my grandparents. They were old, and I was too difficult to handle." Bitterness rose in her mouth, a sour mixture of regret and anger. "My cousin in Philly took over. She wasn't a warm or social person, but she did her best. She made sure I had counseling and a great education." Now Bree felt guilty for being ungrateful. "I'm not complaining. She had no experience with kids, and she stepped up. I don't know what would have happened to me if she hadn't."

Anna's eyes went fierce. "First of all, you were not difficult. You were traumatized."

"That's exactly what Matt said."

"It takes more than counseling to heal. A child needs to feel secure and loved to express themselves to work through the pain. Children are amazingly resilient, though, and you found a way through. You survived." Her mouth turned up at one corner. "But now you're learning to thrive. There's a difference."

"That's what I want for Kayla and Luke. They need to do more than survive."

"They are."

"Since I moved back here, I feel like the Grinch when his heart grew three times."

Anna laughed. "You're going to be all right, and so will Luke and Kayla. They have you, Adam, and Dana. Now they also have Matt and all of the Flynns."

"I can't thank you enough for accepting us all into your family." Bree had never imagined having so many people in her life. Their generosity was almost overwhelming at times.

"And I can't thank you enough for loving my son. For a long time, we worried he'd never be happy. You never stop worrying, you know, no matter how old they get. Matt lost more than a career when he was shot. He lost his community. He lost his support system. You've helped him build a new one."

To make matters worse, Matt had been betrayed by some of those in his support system, but Bree wasn't sure Anna knew all the details, so she said nothing.

Anna got up and refilled her coffee cup. "I believe it's best for kids to have a community of support. Not everyone has a big family, but they can make friends, establish connections in other ways. Blood is *not* always thicker. Family is more about who you can depend on, rather than who shares your DNA."

Bree thought of the kids' useless, selfish biological father, and her own violent one. "That is very true."

"With the cliché village theory, kids have multiple sources of comfort and advice. Many places to turn for help. People who have varying expertise to contribute."

"I never thought of it that way."

"Do you think it's more reassuring to have one person meeting their needs or a half dozen?"

"You're right," Bree said. "And thank you."

"You're more than welcome. I am always here for any of my kids." Anna patted her hand.

My kids. Anna had virtually adopted Bree too.

Bree's eyes went hot with unshed tears, and she wondered how different her life would have been if she'd had someone like Anna in her childhood. But there was no use in looking back. Her job was to make sure that Luke's and Kayla's lives were better than hers had been. Having the Flynns around eased Bree's mind considerably. She didn't want to be the only person in their world. Anna was right. That measure of dependence wasn't healthy.

Also, Bree could appreciate Anna's presence in her own life now. Bree still had plenty of growing and learning to do. Clearly.

The door opened. Matt came in with the dogs. They were followed by George and the kids.

Kayla ran to Bree and hugged her hard. The little girl wore pajamas, a coat, and rain boots. Luke hugged Bree next. Both kids looked recovered. Both dug into the bag of doughnuts.

Matt plucked out a Boston cream.

Cady walked into the kitchen. She sat down at the table. Her mother brought her a cup of tea and smiled a little too broadly. The door opened again, this time admitting Todd. He sat next to Cady at the big table.

"We have some news." Cady took his hand. "I'm pregnant."

Surprised, Bree felt the pressure of happy tears. She'd never been around this many pregnant women. It felt a bit strange, almost like she was a different species. Until she'd taken that pregnancy test, she'd never thought about being pregnant. But now . . . She put it out of her mind. This was not the time.

George and Anna shared a look.

"We knew," Anna said.

That didn't surprise Bree at all.

Cady sighed. "Of course you did."

"Congratulations to both of you." George beamed. "We'll have a proper celebration when everyone is well." He took Bree's hand and examined her bandage. "I'll change this for you before you leave."

Bree didn't argue.

He frowned and placed a palm on her forehead. "You have a fever."

Bree almost smacked herself on the head. She had the stupid flu. That's why she was nauseated.

She let George herd her to the couch. Someone turned on the TV. Someone else brought her tea and a blanket. She rested her head on the sofa and let everyone else take care of her for a change.

CHAPTER FORTY-ONE

Matt stopped outside the interview room at the county jail. "You're in charge."

Todd said, "Is the sheriff OK with that?"

"It was her idea. She has complete faith in you."

The flu had knocked Bree flat. She wasn't up to questioning Sandy.

A deputy admitted them to the interview room. Matt sat across from Sandy's lawyer, letting Todd face Sandy.

Sandy claimed Eric had been in charge of the operation. She'd offered to turn on him in exchange for a lighter sentence. The DA was working out a deal with her attorney, the details of which would depend on the value of the information provided. No matter what, she would still serve significant time.

Todd began with Miranda rights and introductions for the audio recording. Then he settled into his questions. "How many women did you take?"

Sandy began ticking off names on her fingers. "Grace, Sabrina, Jana, Ally, Trish, Nadia, and Jen. Seven."

"We found Grace and Sabrina. What happened to the others?" Todd asked.

Matt quelled the horror unfurling in his gut.

Sandy studied the dirt under her nails. "Jen was the first. I don't remember her last name. Stoltz, maybe? Something like that. She was so desperate that her parents didn't find out she was pregnant that she was easy to lure. She came to the center inquiring about abortions. When she found out it wasn't that kind of center, she left. Eric found her and brought her to the silo."

Todd didn't rush her.

She continued on her own. "All of this was Eric's idea. He didn't want to lose the farm, and we weren't going to be able to keep it on farming or the restaurant profits alone. Small-time farming is a money suck, and the restaurant's profit margins are too thin. I'd been volunteering at the center for ages, seeing so many women who didn't want their babies, and we knew several couples who paid tens of thousands in legal fees to adopt. Eric saw a supply-and-demand situation."

"Did Jen have her baby?" Todd asked.

Sandy nodded. "A little girl. She went to a couple of lawyers in Florida. Eric thought it was best to put some miles between us and the babies."

"Did the couples know where the babies came from?"

"No." Sandy scoffed. "All they were told is that they were adopting a teenager's unwanted baby."

"Who handled the adoptions?"

Sandy sighed. "Eric's cousin. He's a lawyer."

"You have his name?"

"Dave McGraw." Sandy nodded. "His number is on Eric's phone."

"What about Jen? What happened to her?"

Sandy slid one nail under another to dislodge the dirt. "Eric sold her too. There's a market for girls, you know. Jen was young—just sixteen—and pretty."

"Who bought her?"

"I'm not sure. Dave arranged that too. Some guy came for her in a van. Supposedly, he was taking her to Vegas, but I have no confirmation of that."

Matt wished he had a notepad, but since the interview was being recorded, he hadn't bothered. It would have been helpful to keep his hands busy. It was hard to sit and listen.

"Do you remember anything about him?" Todd asked.

"Not really." Sandy jerked a shoulder. She clearly didn't care.

Matt wondered if Jen was still alive. The human-trafficking business was as nasty as the fake-adoption industry.

"What about Nadia?" Todd asked. "Do you know her last name?"

"No. She was homeless." Sandy touched her temple. "There was something wrong with her. She couldn't even talk in full sentences."

They'd preyed on a mentally ill homeless woman. Matt couldn't wait for Eric to be sentenced, and he hoped Sandy went to prison for a long time, despite her cooperation. The DA felt the families of the missing had a right to know what had happened to their loved ones. The legal system wasn't perfect. Compromises had to be made.

Sandy's hands dropped to the table, the fingers curling into fists. "She had her baby. Eric was getting ready to make arrangements for her." She said this as if he were a travel agent. "But she came down with a fever a week or two after the birth. She went downhill for another week. Then she died."

Matt had no words for a solid minute. Finally, he spit out a question. "When did this happen?"

"Last summer."

The partial skeleton must belong to Nadia.

Sandy went back to studying her nails. "Trish had a miscarriage. She wasn't that far along, maybe four months? But she bled and bled. It wouldn't stop."

"Did you ever consider getting her medical attention?"

Sandy turned her palms to the ceiling. "Under the circumstances, that wasn't possible. Eric's helped a ton of cows give birth. He thought he could handle it. Guess it's more complicated with people."

Matt wanted to scream at her, but that wouldn't get them the information he needed for the victims' next of kin.

Todd kept his cool with an impressively neutral expression. "What about Ally? How did she die?"

Sandy's mouth puckered into a frown. "Ally wouldn't give up. Every time we brought her food and water, or tried to make her exercise—we wanted those babies nice and healthy—she attacked us. The last time, well, Eric went too far with the discipline."

"He strangled her?"

"Yeah." Sandy nodded. "Jana fought too. Eric lost his temper and hit her hard in the head with his flashlight. He was worried someone in her apartment building would hear. She never woke up."

"Why did he dump her on Sheriff Taggert's vehicle?"

Anger snapped in Sandy's eyes, the first sign of emotion she'd exhibited. "I told him that was stupid. He thought he'd throw you all off track, make you think the killer was a psychopath. We weren't serial killers."

But you are.

Todd spent the next two hours gleaning every possible detail from Sandy. They'd burned the girls' clothing. Vehicles were pushed into Grey Lake, the license plates removed and buried separately. The bodies were hidden in the woods.

Sandy had copied the files from the counseling center. She'd listened in on the sessions too. Grace had talked about her job at the bar, so they'd known she was headed right to work. They'd purposely chosen blonde women because Eric thought blonde babies would bring in the highest fees. "It was all Eric. I didn't kill anyone."

Todd leveled a cool look at her. "But you didn't stop him. You didn't help them. You didn't get them medical attention. In fact, you helped identify potential victims and kidnap them."

Darkness lurked in Sandy's eyes. "I tried to have children, but it didn't happen. We didn't have money for treatment." She paused, looking away. "All these girls got pregnant without even trying, and they weren't happy about it." Something vicious bloomed in her expression. "I hated them for that."

By the time they left the jail, Matt felt sick. Not flu sick, but sick to his soul. Had he ever encountered people this evil?

He and Todd walked across the parking lot.

"That went well," Matt said. "You got Sandy to spill everything. I don't care how much she cooperated. The DA and judge aren't going to shave much off her sentence. She and Eric are both going to prison for fucking ever."

"I hope so."

"Seriously, nice work on the interview. It's not easy to keep your emotions in check."

"Thanks, but it doesn't feel great," Todd said.

"I understand," Matt said. They continued in silence for a few steps.

"We got a hit on that motel vagrant, remember him?" Todd asked. "His fingerprints were in the system. He's been missing for months. We called his sister, and she came down to the station. Her brother has a mix of mental illnesses. About six months ago, he decided he didn't need his medication. It was all downhill from there."

"I hope she gets him back on track."

Todd shrugged. "She didn't seem too hopeful, but at least she knows he's alive. She cares about him and will try to get him help. Can't force him, though."

"No, you can't." Matt climbed into his Suburban. "But someone cares about him. I'm going to take that as a win."

Todd agreed with a nod. "On days like this, you have to take what you can." He studied his boots for a few seconds. "I hope you're not mad about Cady."

"Why would I be mad?"

"Because she's pregnant."

"It happens." Matt thought about Bree's test. He wouldn't have minded if it had been positive. But she was right that they were already stretched as thin as cobwebs, and he'd prefer to get married first. Still . . . "But you know about Cady's experience."

She'd had a late miscarriage, and her ex had blamed her for it. Matt still wanted to kill him for that. Maybe not kill him. But definitely beat him up a few more times.

"Yeah." Todd propped his hands on his duty belt. "I want you to know that I intend to marry her."

Matt held up a hand. "This is a discussion for you and Cady, not me. She's my sister, and I'll always be protective of her. But she's also a very smart woman. She is capable of making her own decisions. This is between you and her." Todd was a good man. Matt wasn't worried about that.

Todd exhaled. "Just let me say this, OK?"

Matt shut his mouth.

"I don't want her to think the only reason I would ask her to marry me is because she's pregnant. I want her to know that it's because I love her, and I want to spend the rest of my life with her."

Matt waited, but it seemed Todd had gotten it all out. "Then tell her what you just told me."

Todd smiled. "You think that's enough?"

"I think it's perfect." Matt grinned and said what all protective big brothers said: "And you already know if you ever do hurt her, you will have to deal with me."

CHAPTER FORTY-TWO

Five days later, Bree sat on the back porch and sipped tea. The flu had kicked her butt, but today she was feeling more normal. The rain had finally stopped.

Her phone rang with a call from Todd. He'd been running the department since Bree had been too sick to function.

"I have some news," he said. "They found Howard Killian's car in a ravine not far from his favorite bar."

"Was he inside?"

"Yep. The ME says he's been dead for about five days."

"So, since the night we found Grace." Bree tried to summon some empathy for Howard but failed. He had been nothing short of cruel to Grace, and he'd enjoyed it.

Todd added, "It's too late to determine blood alcohol levels, but other patrons at the bar said he was hammered when he left. Do you want me to tell Grace?"

Blood alcohol levels were only accurate for approximately forty-eight hours after death.

"No. I'll call her. Not sure how she'll respond, and we have a rapport."

"You're better then?" Todd asked.

"Much."

"I'll tell you the same thing you told me. Don't rush into the office. Get well first."

"You've come a long way, young Padawan."

Todd snorted. "I thought you'd want to know."

"Thanks. Matt said you did a great job questioning Sandy."

"Still felt slimy, like I needed to shower afterward. But I appreciate all you've taught me. Get some more rest. We do need you back. Madeline Jager has been here twice. I'd almost rather chase a killer through a dark forest than deal with her."

"You and me both." Bree signed off and lowered the phone.

Across the yard, Matt was helping Kayla give Pumpkin a bath. The pony stood placidly while they scrubbed a winter's worth of dirt from his shaggy coat. The dogs watched from a patch of dry grass.

"Walk him until he's dry." Matt turned off the hose and handed Kayla the lead rope. "You don't want him to roll."

"OK." She led the pony across the grass.

Matt approached the porch, climbed the steps, and perched on the railing next to her chair. The dogs followed at his heels.

"It looks like all the dirt that was on Pumpkin is now on you."

He brushed mud from his jeans. "It's a dirty job. I'm going to get cleaned up. What do you want for dinner?"

"You don't have to cook."

He gave her an assessing side-eye. "I think you need another day or two of rest. Your face is still the color of skim milk."

"You sweet talker." Bree rose. "Go shower. I'll rummage in the pantry. Better yet, I'll look through the take-out menus."

"I like that idea."

They went into the kitchen, where the dogs took turns at the water bowl. Matt carried his boots to the laundry room and carefully placed them on a shelf. He sniffed, then picked up his spare pair. "I can't believe it. There's a hairball in my boot. How did he even get up there?"

Bree spotted Vader on top of the refrigerator. "He's agile?"

"And vindictive." Matt shot the cat a look.

Vader lifted a back leg and began to wash his privates. Bree stifled a laugh.

"I know what he thinks of me." Matt carried the soiled boot to the door and tossed it outside.

"Maybe you should try tuna instead of glares."

Matt eyed the cat. "Nah. This is our thing. If I grovel, he won't respect me."

Bree didn't have the heart to tell him the cat didn't respect him anyway. Instead, she lied. "He'll come around."

He wouldn't. He was a cat.

Grumbling, Matt crossed the room and kissed her on the lips. "She's mine, cat. Get used to it."

Bree kissed him back. But after he'd left the kitchen, she reached up and scratched Vader's head. "It wouldn't hurt you to be nice."

The cat purred.

"I know we've been together longer, but you should give him a chance. He's a good guy."

Vader ran down the front of the fridge like Spidercat and headed toward the laundry room. Bree crossed the room and firmly closed the door. "Now you're just being an ass."

Vader turned and sauntered away, and because she loved them both, Bree went online to order Matt a few new pairs of boots. They were going to need a reserve.

Matt came down just as the pizza guy brought their delivery to the kitchen door. Bree took the warm boxes, her appetite stirring for the first time in a week.

He lifted the lid and sniffed. "Roasted red peppers and mushrooms?"

"Don't worry. The other is sausage."

"Whew." He took the boxes from her and carried them to the counter.

"I'll call the kids."

Matt grabbed her around the waist. "In a minute." He kissed her, then gave her a serious look. "Where do you see us in five years?"

Bree laughed. "Did that pregnancy test freak you out?"

"No." He kissed her again. "But it did make me think."

"Yeah. Me too."

"So? Where do you see us in five years?" He wrapped his hands around her and settled them at the small of her back.

"Oh, you're going to marry me eventually."

He snorted, a grin spreading across his face. "I am?"

"Yep."

"When do you think this is going to happen?"

She rose on her toes and kissed him back. "When the time is right."

"Wanna know a secret? I would marry you today." He pulled her closer. "When do you think it'll be right?"

She flattened her hands on his chest. "I think we'll know."

The back door burst open, and a very dirty little girl screamed, "Pizza!"

"Boots off!" Matt countered.

Kayla began shedding muddy boots and outerwear like a tornado.

Bree smiled as Matt disentangled their bodies and jumped into the mess to gather the muddy gear. She'd marry him today too, but she suspected that was no secret either.

ACKNOWLEDGMENTS

Special thanks to the writer friends who helped me develop this concept: Rayna Vause, Kendra Elliot, Leanne Sparks, Toni Anderson, Amy Gamet, and Loreth Anne White. Cheers, ladies! As always, credit goes to my agent, Jill Marsal, for her continued unwavering support and solid career advice. I'm also grateful for the entire team at Montlake, especially my acquiring editor, Anh Schluep, and my developmental editor, Charlotte Herscher. As far as teams go, I am lucky to have the best.

ABOUT THE AUTHOR

Photo © 2016 Jared Gruenwald Photography

Melinda Leigh is the #1 Amazon Charts and #1 *Wall Street Journal* bestselling author of *She Can Run*, an International Thriller Award nominee for Best First Novel, *She Can Tell*, *She Can Scream*, *She Can Hide*, and *She Can Kill* in the She Can series; *Midnight Exposure*, *Midnight Sacrifice*, *Midnight Betrayal*, and *Midnight Obsession* in the Midnight Novels; *Hour of Need*, *Minutes to Kill*, and *Seconds to Live* in the Scarlet Falls series; *Say You're Sorry*, *Her Last Goodbye*, *Bones Don't Lie*, *What I've Done*, *Secrets Never Die*, and *Save Your Breath* in the Morgan Dane series; and *Cross Her Heart*, *See Her Die*, *Drown Her Sorrows*, *Right Behind Her*, *Dead Against Her*, *Lie to Her*, *Catch Her Death*, and the short story "Her Second Death" in the Bree Taggert series. Melinda has garnered numerous writing awards, including two RITA nominations; holds a second-degree black belt in Kenpo karate and has taught women's self-defense; and lives in a messy house with her family and a small herd of rescue pets. For more information, visit www.melindaleigh.com.